Violet

Leslie Tate

This is a First Edition of the paperback
Violet, Book 3 of the series Lavender Blues: Three Shades of Love
Copyright © March 2018 Leslie Tate
ISBN: 978-1-910094-47-1
eBook ISBN: 978-1-910094-54-9

Published March 2018
By Magic Oxygen
www.MagicOxygen.co.uk

Leslie Tate has asserted his right under the Copyright, Designs and Patents
Act 1988 to be identified as the author of this work.

Edited by Sue Hampton

A catalogue record for this book is available from
the British Library.

Requests for permission should be addressed to:-
The Editor, Magic Oxygen
editor@MagicOxygen.co.uk

Printed by Lightning Source UK Ltd; committed to improving
environmental performance by driving down emissions and reducing,
reusing and recycling waste.

View their eco-policy at www.LightningSource.com

Set in 11.5pt Times New Roman
Titles set in Tangerine

Contents

Dedication

To Sue

Part One

The Girl Who Began Again June 22nd 1960

Once there was a girl who thought there should be more sunshine in her world so she decided to start again with more smiling and plenty of fresh air. But her new life didn't have enough rain to feed the trees so the next day she started a whole new story. Every day she made a new beginning. But even when the sun shone and the rain joined in to make a rainbow, the girl wasn't happy with the day because she wasn't a proper heroine, and stories have to have one of those. Otherwise a mirror and a spell are not enough.

Every time the girl started a new life she tried to be bigger in her own story. She was a princess but the king wouldn't let her climb trees. So she became captain of the ship but she could never find the island. One day she was born a singer and the whole world was her audience with candles in their hands but the trouble was the birds sang a better song. In her next life she was a clever artist but nothing she painted was as lovely as the flowers. Then she started again as a doctor but she didn't know how to fix all the fighting, just the wounds.

By now the girl was a lady, but her knight rode off to battle leaving her asleep. Then she escaped flying on a swan and went up into nowhere. When she began a day as an angel by the end of it she'd forgotten how to be *good. Every new day of each new life she had to throw her story away because the ending wouldn't come and you only know it's a wonderful story when it's over.*

The End. *By Elizabeth Jarvis*

If Beth Jarvis had been watching herself on camera, or observing her actions in a book, she might well have wondered what could have brought her, a woman of fifty with a job and children, to wait for an hour in a busy city restaurant facing the door on a cold February evening. To sit there alone shivering slightly, a figure on the lookout, taken perhaps from one of her half-written stories and positioned there quietly, one hand on some papers while observing the tablecloth.

She'd come as promised, arrived on her own and far too early, made herself do it. A woman holding still, trying not to show.

Because really, considered carefully or looked at as fiction, it was what her friends would call – remembering the advert, the letters crossing, the in-deep expressions and pauses on the phone – crazy or silly, certainly eccentric, a rom-com or sitcom, something she herself wouldn't credit if she read it in a book.

And yet she was here.

To anyone who noticed she might have seemed strange. Sitting in shadow, she was easy to read but not so easy to pin down. They might, like her, have wondered why she'd come here or what she was involved in. They'd have registered her red-lipped look and noted her top – low-cut with sequins – but sensed something underneath, a feel for difference, for questions unanswered, the whats and what-nexts, and why she'd travelled miles to sit there solo, a woman with a wine glass eyeing the customers as they came through the door.

Then there were her papers. Neatly folded and positioned on the table, a whole wad of letters. If stopped and questioned, or approached by the manager, she could offer them as evidence. They were her best chance. In any case they were all she had. The result of contact, received after work and read straight through, they'd carried her with them.

The letters and the calls. For the last two weeks, daily on paper or lying on the sofa holding the receiver: his voice and hers. And now in person, their first face to face.

Hearing her own thoughts, Beth pulled back. She knew her own silliness, how it pushed and pressed and despite her best efforts wouldn't let her be. To be feeling kept her up. Thin-skinned, or crazy if allowed, that's how she was.

Because for so long now, she'd not been herself. She could feel it in the room. There was a cold bare space somewhere to one side, a place without warmth. Inside experience there was a door closed, a stop and a darkness.

And she'd lived there, hoping: late night in the kitchen, in the back room, writing, and alone in the lounge, staring at the TV.

Leaning forward, she pulled a mirror from her bag. Prising it open and turning side to side, she studied what she saw. The mouth was full, chin line sharp, the cheekbones high, the hair dyed red-brown with waves and thinning a little. Lines around the eyes and forehead, some of them deep, had been part-brushed out. The image she saw was grey-eyed, long-nosed, all rather *meant*, but also receptive and alert.

Folding the mirror, she glanced around the restaurant. To be here at all surprised her. She wondered quickly how many others were out there waiting. Dressed up women sitting in restaurants facing the door, believers and hopers rehearsing phrases, awaiting their cue. She wondered, too, if their mind-sets showed or if, like her, they'd adopted stillness and presence as some kind of cover, a shield to hide their thoughts.

Her attention narrowed, picking up on couple-talk with movement and faces listening – and how she might present. The room was warm, almost pressured, and illuminated by candles. From where she sat it was divided in two. The front part, a square, was shined up like a studio, with long, varnished tables, flowers in vases and multi-coloured tablecloths, while her area, running widthways at the back, was dark-lit and private. The two sections were split-level, linked by steps. At the front, the lower part, there were groups dressed up and talking, people checking watches, others fingering or studying menus, some disrobing, others on mobiles, some by the window glancing around, while a few sat in silence folding napkins and examining their bills. At the back it was empty, with spaced-out tables and softly floating, ambient music.

9

Picking out a letter, she unfolded and spot-checked for phrases. The handwriting, which was large, filled up the page. In it she could feel an outline, a suddenness of presence, imagined in the flesh. A shoulder she looked over without being seen. It was as if she'd discovered a page from a half-finished diary; not real, of course, but quick and alive, present in the writing. He was out there somewhere, approaching.

Again she saw the house with its clothes racks, hangers, dressing gowns and books in bed. Feeling for the light switch, then thinking in the dark.

She folded the letter, returning the wad to her handbag. Better, she thought, if no one saw it. There was too much there which might invite comment – odd thoughts, hesitations – those all-raw flights, many of them excessive. And now, for better or for worse, it seemed they were happening.

A waiter came up. He was short, neatly dressed and his child-round face was attentive and smiley. In one hand was a cream-coloured notepad which he held out like a gift. "Are you all right, madam? Can I get you anything?"

Beth glanced at the drink she'd been sipping. The liquid had reached bottom. Somehow, without her knowing, her past was in there, hidden. "Oh, yes. Thank you." She stopped, measuring her glass. "I'd like another. A small one, please."

The waiter confirmed, returning quickly with a glass on a tray. She thanked him, perhaps over-warmly. "Someone will be here," she told him and he smiled.

"Of course. Whenever you're ready, madam. No problem."

Noticing his accent she shifted slightly and smiled back. She felt a brief connection. "That'll be soon, I hope."

The waiter nodded, checked his pad and withdrew.

For a second, as he left, she saw herself sitting forward holding her glass, and wondered whether she should follow. Go up, make payment and slip off through the door. It might be the best way. Because after all, she couldn't be that certain, and being outside would be that much easier, without obligation. She'd just begun to imagine herself on the street and picture him arriving at an empty table, when the door opened suddenly, bringing her back.

The couple who entered struck her as unusual. The woman was small; the man stooped forward. They were careful and deliberate, with her head up to his shoulder and his face distanced, as if he wasn't there. Both wore high-buttoned coats and heavy boots. Beth felt for them slightly. They reminded her of what she used to be.

A waiter met them, hands to his sides, speaking quietly. He was offering and inquiring. The three paused, reverse-stepped slightly, then moved to a corner. Beth noticed, as they shuffled into place, how quickly the woman picked up the menu, busying herself turning the pages. Her skin was red and looked rather sore. A small tight muscle in her neck flickered and pulsed. The man sat opposite, with his hands placed loosely on the table, awaiting her decision.

They exchanged some words, without much expression. Beth thought the woman was trying to connect. The man, it seemed, wasn't really present. She could already see them, husband and wife, struggling to make do. Going through the motions, avoiding conflict, playing their part. Together but alone, in a house filled with silence. She was glad that was over.

She checked on her phone. Cupping her hand, she eyed it from the side then from above, as if was a puzzle. Her friends had warned her. There were no calls or messages, and her inbox hadn't changed, but having it close...

For a second time the door opened, this time a man alone, tallish, in black. Standing by the entrance and smiling vaguely as if on screen, he scanned the room. As she looked, Beth breathed in. His face was soft-skinned and open, with steel-rimmed glasses over rounded cheeks. Grey-white hair framed his face, curling around his ears and straggling at the back. His forehead was large, eyes thoughtful, mouth held firm. She noticed how he stood facing ahead; poised, it seemed, for things to develop. There was a brightness about his face, a pressure and intensity of nerves, or awareness, as if he'd a speech to deliver.

This, of course, was him. Feeling his doubt, Beth rose and called.

The man advanced, smiling. "Hello. You must be Beth?" he said, reaching the table. As she nodded he stepped up and touched her shoulder, lightly, descending to her arm before pulling back.

"And you must be James," she replied, remaining standing. For a

11

moment, she was stunned. It was as if he was sizing her for a dress, or she was sizing herself.

"The same, as in the late-night telephone calls."

She remembered his voice, clear and upbeat at the end of the line, and her breathing calmed.

"Can I join you?" he asked, glancing at her drink.

Catching his irony, something Jane Austen-ly popped into her head. "That, sir," she began. Then, stopping and colouring slightly, she invited him to sit.

Returning to her chair, Beth felt looked at; mainly, mirror-like, by herself, but also, gently, by the man who now sat opposite. Seen in close-up, he was fresh-faced and watchful. Although he'd lines – mainly light, barred across his forehead – his eyes were young, blue-grey and direct, but also understanding.

She wondered what he thought of her sequins and the tightness of her top.

"I hope I'm not late," he said.

"No, not at all. I was early."

James settled. "I was worried. This place was pretty hard to find."

"Oh, you mean my directions?"

"No, nothing like that. I just didn't allow... didn't realise how far it was."

"You came up from Trafalgar Square?"

Lowering his head, he grinned, "The long way round, after asking a few people. They all thought they knew but, when it came to it, couldn't quite remember."

Beth looked thoughtful. She hoped it hadn't been too difficult. "Would you like a drink?" she asked.

"Later, thank you," he said, unzipping his jacket. "Anyway," he continued quietly, "I'm here now."

"You could have rung me."

James agreed, smiling wryly: it seemed he knew. Leaning back, he talked her through his search, presenting his walkaround as an adventure. When Beth asked about getting cold he shrugged and rubbed his hands together. "Warm enough now," he said, and his head came up.

Beth blushed. The expression in his eyes made her breathless. She was back there by the window, watching in the dark. "Shall we order?" she asked, picking up a menu.

"Good idea," he answered, scanning *today's specials* printed on a card. He considered for a moment. "We could share something. A menu for two." His voice sounded firm; it steadied and calmed her. All they had to do was choose, simple as that.

They agreed on an all-in meal, lightly curried, with starter and main. Beth wanted popadums and James, when the waiter appeared, ordered water and a sweet lassi. In the break before service they both sat back. The music in the restaurant seemed closer now. Soft and insistent it filtered in, mixing with their voices. It was as if they were audience, watching themselves; the moment held them.

They talked and exchanged – speaking about work, things that had happened, describing their day – then Beth spotted movement.

"Is that what you wanted?" she asked as a tall, ice-white glass with a cream head of bubbles arrived at the table.

"That's it, goat's yogurt," he said, and mentioned a student trip to India while suggesting she try it. "It's good," he added. "There's a salt version, for the heat. But this is tastier." He held out his drink for her to sample.

Beth hesitated then accepted. As she took it in her hands, she felt the touch of his fingers passing and the cold at the bottom of the glass.

She drew down a mouthful. "Good," she said, compressing her lips.

"Have more if you like," he said, as she offered to pass back.

"That's all right, it's yours."

"If you want it, it belongs to you."

"I'm fine," she countered. "Really, I am," she said when he raised one eyebrow. "Really," she repeated, offering again.

James nodded. His eyes had focused and his expression had deepened; he was giving full attention.

"Oh dear," she said suddenly, pointing, "but I must do something about this." The edge of the glass was smeared with lipstick. "It's not nice," she said quietly, napkin-rubbing. A cold, hard ache was threatening to take over. Somewhere, on her own, she was running water, scrubbing metal, filling up cupboards.

"That's OK," he beamed, "I like it that way."

13

Beth double-checked his face. He seemed sincere. She finished her rubdown and held it to the light, dabbing vaguely and tut-tutting: "Well it's gone, mostly. I'm really sorry."

James shook his head, "No problem." He took the glass, turning it both ways. "No problem at all," he added then ducked his head forward to half-drain the glass.

Soon afterwards the food arrived. Brought on a trolley by the round-faced waiter, it was richly-scented and heated from below, green and yellow, bathed in sauces, with rice and veg piled in layers on oval-shaped dishes. The spread was laid, two plates were polished and a candle was lit at centre.

"Shall I serve?" asked James as the waiter withdrew. She nodded happily, and told him what she wanted. Checking as he went, James served them both, mixing ingredients. "For what we're about to receive," he said then stopped.

Beth examined his expression. His eyes had stilled and his mouth had tightened. "What is it?" she asked.

"Just the words."

"The words?"

"Well, I wondered..."

"You wondered? Something about me?"

"How you might feel about that phrase."

"Ah, you think I might be offended."

He looked at her. "Not sure," he said, appraisingly.

"Is it something I've said?"

"Not *said*. But I do remember reading…"

"You mean my letter, the one about faith?"

James hesitated; he didn't want to spoil it. "Romantic faith," he quoted. "It sounded rather fine. I couldn't help noticing." He laughed to one side, as if he'd caught himself out. "I suppose I did think you might be vaguely churchy."

"Well I'm not. Offended, I mean." She unfolded a napkin: "So perhaps we can start?"

"You mean break bread?"

"Eat what's here. Pure enjoyment, that sort of thing."

"Well, if music be…"

"Play on," she returned, picking up her fork.

He nodded and she smiled. Then, exchanging glances and remarking lightly on variety and taste, they began their meal.

They talked as they ate, filling in gaps and quoting letters. They recalled how they'd changed, in childhood, right through youth, and as adults in marriage – what had happened, what went wrong and where it had left them. Their stories, told slowly, were a mixture, some dark, some tentative, some surprising and some quite upbeat, developing into sideswipes and tongue-in-cheek remarks about battles in private and versions put round for the benefit of friends.

"In the end you come to expect it," he said, "so you say to yourself 'OK here we go again' and push straight through."

"Yes, it gets to a point," Beth replied, pausing between mouthfuls, "where it doesn't really matter. Whatever you say, it's always wrong."

James nodded.

"And *that's* when you get out," she added, surprising herself. And she realised that this was the point – she'd said it without thinking, found herself out. Because for Beth, things had moved on. Somewhere around her there had always been a gap or disconnection, a half-and-half feeling. Of course she'd had her moments – her children, her friendships, the café she'd built up – but behind that, in private, with the man she called her husband, it had never really happened.

But now, talking here together was different. It was as if she'd been reading a novel and, turning the pages, had found the right place. The action had started and she was being heard.

When they'd finished eating, with James forking portions, remarking on blended mixtures and food for thought, Beth brought out her letters. "What you sent me," she said simply. "All of them."

"I wrote that much?"

She fingered carefully: "Twenty two pages." To her, these said it all. They were what had brought her.

"Ah, but *you* wrote even more."

"I'm not sure about that."

"Definitely. I'll count them when I get home."

"You've kept them, then?"

"Of course." He laughed, "And reread them. You're a real writer."

15

"Well, if that's so, it's because I find it easier..."

James nodded as she returned the letters to her handbag.

"I suppose it's about words, and getting them on paper," she added.

"Words, words, words," he said lightly.

"Yes, that's what I use," she continued, meeting his eye.

"OK, so what would you do," he asked, "if we couldn't speak?"

She raised one eyebrow, "Sorry?"

"No words, only gestures."

"I don't quite follow."

James repeated.

"No words at all?"

He nodded.

"You mean sign language?"

James gave a thumbs-up.

"I'm not really sure."

"It's a game people play. People like us."

Beth considered, staring at her glass. "You mean you want to try?"

"Well, why not?"

"OK," she said, "let's have a go."

James placed one hand palm-up on the table. He looked down and up. Raising the other hand he air-drew a circle around the room. A mischievous expression crossed his face. His fingers closed on an imaginary microphone and he mimed a chorus from a song. Breaking off, he looked both ways then waved to the gallery, jazz-handed. By now he was fresh-faced, beaming into camera. With a smile, he ended pointing to himself, to her, then down towards the lines in his palm. His eyes met hers and he nodded. When Beth made a noise, he switched his finger to his lips.

Beth sat forward. For a second she blanked, then narrowing her eyes, looked right, looked left, dropped one shoulder and raised her arm in a rounded gesture. Her face shaped surprise. One hand came back to press against her forehead, feigning thought. She held her pose before straightening, turning out her arms to a chicken-wing position. She pushed herself to the edge of her seat. Her mouth dropped open and she froze for a second, looking down. When she flapped her hands, James began laughing.

"That's not allowed," she said, straightening in her chair.

"But I didn't speak."

In reply she rolled her eyes. Folding her arms, she adopted a quizzical expression.

He shrugged, "OK, point taken. But does laughing count?"

"Yes."

"You sure?"

"Absolutely."

James laughed again, this time more softly. Pushing upright, he raised one hand to his jaw. Turning his wrist and starting at a corner, he zipped up his mouth. In the pause that followed the room came closer. Suddenly he leaned forward and touched her hand. "I've just thought," he said. "We can do it another way."

Beth's eyebrows shot up.

"Listen," he raised one finger, "you know this track?" On the speakers, a warm, darkly sinuous female voice had just begun. Behind it, a deep bass rhythm was beating up. He rose, offering his hand: "Dance?" The one word, said nicely, filled up the air.

Beth flushed, about to speak. When James placed a warning finger to his lips, she paused. His offer was a lift... she'd not imagined... it was all so unexpected – but also, perhaps, a proof of commitment. It meant he was with her.

He asked again.

Beth looked around quickly then rose. The one word went with her, repeated. Dance, dance, dance: it was quite enough for her.

Allowing him to lead, she passed between tables to a floor space at the back. Here they took up position. In the half-dark, moving slowly, absorbed in warmth and breath and the closeness of flesh, they began.

As they slow-danced together, Beth felt his hands closed about her waist. She was touched and held and at one with herself; it was as if she'd come alive. They shuffled in step, rocking side to side, and she was full-length in the mirror, trying out her moves. The words came back from a dance show – *such a wonderful feeling* – and an idea struck her. She'd watched and cheered and given her support, but always at a distance, from the outside, and not like this: suddenly she was at centre.

The music ran on. They turned and stepped, moving without thought.

17

Their bodies, pressed close, were soft and loose and smoothly connected; it seemed they were afloat. And she knew, as she circled, what touch and excitement and bright lights and being on screen really meant.

When they sat down afterwards the waiters were laughing. Several diners had noticed and were turning in their seats. Somebody waved, calling encouragement. There was a brief, admiring smattering of applause.

"They like it," said James. "Floorshow."

Beth, catching her breath, poured herself a glass of water. She offered him the same and he accepted. Her body felt good; she wanted it to go on. "It's first night," she said brightly, sipping at her water, "and we're on the bill." She laughed, raising her drink; this was unreal, and yet it was happening. Watching from behind her hand, she smiled; he was warm and alert and full of excitement. With this man before her it seemed that anything was possible.

The waiter appeared, asking if they'd finished and how they'd found the meal.

"Just right," said James.

Beth agreed and the waiter cleared up. While the men exchanged remarks, she reached into her handbag, pulling out a lipstick. She twisted and a red, finger-sized cone pushed out.

James laughed, "Ah, I see it's colour time."

"You weren't supposed to notice."

He ducked his head towards her drink, "Remember?"

She smiled.

"Red on white," he continued, "your mark."

Beth took a breath. Words like *bright spot* and *bubbly* ran through her head. His attentions said it all. She was enjoying the challenge. "You'd like a sip of mine?" she asked, raising her glass.

"Maybe," he said quietly, "if…"

Pouting slightly, she caught his mood, "So you enjoyed it – your lipstick?"

"There wasn't really enough to tell. Now—"

Beth's chin rose. Suddenly she was quick and sparky and alive. "Very well, if you like, you can have more." This time when she drank she circled the rim. Where her lips touched the edge, the glass coloured up. Grinning to herself, she offered it without wiping.

"That's quite a mouthful," he said.

Beth half-closed her eyes. Her lips showed full and red.

"Which I shall have to sample," he continued, working round the rim and draining the liquid.

Camera-like, she watched him. His expression was little-boy, and impish.

"Am I red?" he asked at the end, touching his lips.

Beth nodded.

He held his expression. "Very red?"

"Pretty much, I suppose."

"Beetroot?"

She shook her head.

"What then, peachy?"

She pushed forward to take a good look, "You're part carrot, part rose."

Grinning, he met her eyes then dabbed with his napkin. "Then you know me already," he said.

They stayed an hour more. To anyone watching, they were oldies at a table. A woman, fifty-plus, still slim, wearing a pink sequined top, beads and bangles and contoured jeans, and a man in a leather jacket with a dad-rock look.

As the evening progressed their talk became a flow, a verbal retrospective, analysing marriage with nods and shrugs and measured observations, leading to comments about how much they'd learned.

For James things hadn't worked. He'd been so busy. With kids and job and DIY and household chores and problems to sort, all of them charged and apparently *expected*. He'd been there in the centre, arranging weekends, playing hero and doing everything, without much thanks. In fact he'd been ignored, or seen as an embarrassment. It was just like him, he said, to get himself hitched to someone who took advantage.

Beth was more resigned. For her it was sad. She spoke about the patterns, the signs there visible if only she'd taken notice, the lack of real contact. Her talk was quiet and thoughtful and full of low asides.

She'd tried, and fitted; she'd given what she could.

"Not that it did much good," she added, wryly. Her husband had been, she said, one of those obsessives, a born-again type who wouldn't talk or give and, whatever happened, wouldn't open up. "I should have realised," she said, "it wasn't a marriage." A picture returned of curtains drawn, a screen, a mug, a half-written story.

Putting down his drink, James frowned. "It seems so weird..." he began, passing one finger along the tablecloth edge.

Beth raised one eyebrow. "Yes?" she said quietly, watching his finger.

"You wonder why people do it." Reaching the corner, he flattened his hand. "I mean what's the point? If marriage stands for anything it's about partnership. Hold back and you get nothing."

Beth nodded.

"So yours was pretty much *nul points*?"

Again, she nodded.

"When you'd expected more?"

"I wish I'd seen what was coming."

"Was it bad?"

Her eyes remained fixed on a point beyond the table.

James asked what had happened.

"I suppose," she replied, "I wanted something he couldn't give." Colouring slightly, she looked around quickly. "I mean of course, affection – something personal – *human* commitment. What most people call plain straightforward love." Her lips pushed out. The final word re-echoed in the dark, it was soft and fully-formed. Like her mouth, it was inviting.

He studied his plate: "What you might call the missing ingredient... without which it's all tasteless?"

Beth followed his gaze. A quick bright calm was rising inside her. "But in the right mix," she said musingly, "preferably with lots of affection."

James raised his head to look across the table.

"Though in my case," she added, "I'd have settled for less. A lot less."

"Really? But would less have been any good?"

She asked him what he meant.

"With some people you have to keep the bar right up there. Otherwise..." he waved one hand, "you know what the kids say – don't ask, don't get."

"But there has to be a willingness—"

"On both sides."

"Perhaps you think," she asked suddenly, "I was to blame?"

"How?"

"By doing what you said, not asking?"

"But you've told me, there was nil interest on his side. With some people it's as if they want to make it hard. They just can't be bothered, or need the big stick. Whatever it is they don't *give*. In the end it brings the whole thing down."

Beth's forehead creased. "But I suppose it could have been different. I didn't make a fuss. Maybe if I had..." In the dark she found herself poised, halfway between doubt and some sort of defiant confessional. The words *soul loss* and *outcast* came up in her head.

Suddenly James reached over and took her hand. "You were fine," he said. "Fine, fine. Just fine. Really." The touch of his flesh was a shock; his smooth cool pressure closed around her palm. Soft-gripped and firm, it brought her to a stop.

When they left the restaurant it was hand in hand. The waiter thanked them, bowing slightly as they passed out through the door. Beth, who was smiling, answered politely. It was as if they were on curtain call and this was their show.

Outside was cold. The air was still and raw and the street lights glared. Walking slowly they stepped past stone-fronted buildings with columns and porticos and heavy double doors. They passed by signboards and photos with illuminated cast lists and quotes in red, then turned in through a metal archway. Before them was a square where people were emerging from a glassed-in forecourt. As they skirted a statue, a light wind got up and Beth huddled close. The square became a road with an arcade opposite. Reaching the kerb, she checked both ways. The road felt cold and bare, it was all brick and metal and shiny surfaces. Her grip shifted slightly as they crossed between traffic. The headlights glowed silver on tarmac. White lines and streaks cut through the dark.

When they reached the other side their fingers locked and they moved in step, arriving at stairs down to the tube. There were posters visible, a curved metal handrail, a dispenser with broadsheets and tiles in rows.

"Which way are you going?" she asked.

"To London Bridge, like you."

"You're sure? I thought it wasn't on your route."

"It is now."

"I don't want you to feel you *have* to."

"It's *want*, not have to," he laughed. "Which means I'm coming your way." He glanced quickly across at the stairs, "In any case it's late, so we'd better get moving, jump on a tube." His voice broke off as a group pushed past, descending.

"Well, as long as you're certain."

"I am." Narrowing his eyes he lifted her hand as if he was presenting her to an audience.

"I don't—"

Using both hands James led her, palm extended, to the stairs: "Even if I have to carry you down."

Beth reached out with her free hand and connected lightly, caressingly. "Well, if I can't persuade you otherwise," she whispered.

He pushed close, kissing one ear. "Allow me," he said and drew her to him. Arm-linked and smiling, he partnered her down.

Between tube stops he put his arm around her shoulders. "Warmer now?" he asked, and she nodded. Leaning back he saw her image in the window. In the glass she looked different. She was head to his shoulder, girlish, smaller than he thought. Her eyes had narrowed and her mouth was full-set and rounded. She was all depth and mood and reflection. "Our stop," he said, as the window paled to a platform view.

They stood and pushed forward to the door, joining a sizeable group of passengers, mostly young, who disembarked, some of them singing. When they reached the escalator James took the lower step and Beth half-turned, allowing his embrace. His hand felt her waist; she was smooth and supple and cinched in tightly beneath her coat. All the way up, absorbed in feeling, they stood holding on. At the top, the escalator cut off and they stepped onto flat. Beth led through the barriers, turning down a short connecting tunnel with adverts on both sides. Arm in arm they climbed a slope to arrive at a concourse with screens above and platforms ahead.

"Ten minutes to go," Beth said, checking her watch against the screen times.

He followed her gaze, "So, that gives us a little longer." His voice had smoothed and dropped low.

She turned and caught his eye, "Till just past the hour..."

James leaned close and they clenched. Now she was excited, her chin rose slightly and her mouth widened. She was all brightness and intention. The cold station air didn't touch her. "Ring me tomorrow," she said.

"When?"

"Evening, early as you like."

"Of course."

Their mouths came close; something automatic was drawing them in. Meeting slowly, their lips made contact. As his tongue pushed in, she fitted and squeezed back and the kiss took over. Between them it was dark, dark-light and somehow reflective. Their lips shifted and held, turned both ways, then softened. They were suddenly one person, joined by the mouth.

For James it was immediate, a dip into flesh. Deep throat and pressure, repeated.

For Beth it was without-thought and wordless. She was kissing, that was all. Her body was all give and touch and lightly-taken softness.

For both it was a fit.

They hung there kissing, locked together, moving and exploring, parting only when a clock chimed the hour. "I'll have to go," she said, pulling back.

James stepped up as she drew out a ticket and moved to the barrier.

"Early as you like," she repeated. He released her hand and she turned, slotting in her ticket.

"OK. Goodbye." For a second he wondered whether he should join her, disregard everything, push through to the platform and board the train.

Her ticket popped up. She called into air as she passed through the barrier, "Goodbye."

"Goodbye."

The train began to hum and a note sounded as lights flashed, the doors half-closed then shunted open. Beth called and ran. She arrived, turning, and held up her arm. As she pulled herself in, the hum returned and the doors hissed shut. Almost immediately the train began to move.

His last sight was her face at the window, waving and smiling as the carriage pulled away.

Chapter One

Dear Beth,

So now I know what you sound like! I was standing at the top of the stairs when you rang. I remember wondering 'Is this a cold-caller?' as I went down to take it. As my father would have said, probably as he pulled on a pair of heavy boots, 'phones are like bloody bosses, they make you jump'. I'll tell you more about him later. Quite a bit later, I imagine, because this letter's going to take time. But once I get started… I'll write when I can, bit by bit over the next few days, and keep posting.

Anyway, when I picked it up I recognised your voice from the recorded message. You sounded oh my goodness so warm. Chocolate, vanilla, strawberry, cherry. I think, to be honest, a bit edgy as well. I suppose anyone in your place would have felt the same.

I really enjoyed our talk. When I put down the phone there were so many words and ideas filling my head that I just had to start this letter. So I'm going to write as it comes, with a smile and a large cup of tea, and now. It's like that art quote: 'the chance meeting on a dissecting table of a sewing machine and an umbrella'. There's a lot to take in.

So I'm rerunning what we said, all that info and life material, then back to the start, to your ad, dialling that number and hearing your talk. I rang back twice to check what you'd said and each time it got better. One particular phrase stood out. When you said you were an open book that's when I thought, oh yes, I'll leave her a message. It sounded good. I suppose the honesty factor's pretty well top of my list. Being up front, speaking from the heart, owning up, that's what my ex really couldn't do. Or we both couldn't, mainly because we brought out the worst in each other. We were dug in, victim/perpetrator swapping roles, running a campaign, but trying not to show it.

I hope you don't mind if I write head-on like this, and things come out. It's how I am, or I'd like to be. It's a risk, I know, but I don't do well with too much politeness and things unsaid. So if I'm asked anything about myself I try not to dodge. I felt we were definitely moving in that direction by the end of the phone call, so I'd like to push it a bit further. I just reckon at this stage of life it's better to get things on the table so you know where you stand. I suppose I also secretly hope that you'll want to read more. But if not, please say.

I'm writing this, by the way, upstairs in my flat. It's warm, cheap for London and really large, which suits me. The outskirts of Mitcham are unexplored territory, out of the way and pretty messy. I like the view over the Common, which is fenced off and industrial to the south but wild around here in a dirty kind of way. It reminds me of the North. At this time of night you can only see the train lines and the lights of the station. And the pink-on-black glow of the London winter sky. The sign we live under.

Sandra and I lasted seventeen years on paper but you could say it was all over in five. We did the sticking-plaster week-on-week counselling thing without making headway. I can't help thinking of the scene near the start of Through The Looking Glass where Alice sets off from the door and the path bends and bends till she arrives back at the house. Though in my view Sandra blocked and I did the pushing, but then you always blame the other side, don't you. Anyway I'm divorced now five years on, no strings attached, done that and moved on, though we still argue about the kids.

I remember we talked about yours. I could tell how important they are. It was in your voice-tone, all hush-hush and soft-centred. Ruth and Naomi you said, one a daddy's girl, one a nurse.

I've got two, Hannah, 16, and George, 20. They're sparky, inner-city, lots of friends, very oral, still in education. Not kids really, but still willing to play off their parents, bid up for presents and holidays, quote their rights and shift between houses. Seems they've got the best of all possible worlds. The way it works Sandra's too soft and I'm middling, but like you and yours, I love 'em to bits, really.

26

I'm tired now. If you want a thumbnail sketch I suppose I'm an upfront type, pretty dogged but playful, with a fair dose of reflective. I enjoy talking, mainly deep stuff, meeting people, walking and reading novels like One Flew Over The Cuckoo's Nest, Chesil Beach, The English Patient, also I'm into classical music and rock, especially blues.

So what more can I say? Well one thing, perhaps, about this letter. I'm giving you an edit, a fair second copy. It's as close as I can get to the voice in the head but tidied for style. A mask that shows through. Which might seem a bit self-defeating, like the emperor's new clothes. On the other hand it can feel overdressy. All rather artificial, reading and writing with a dictionary to hand when we can pick up the telephone and talk.

Yes. Talk, talk, talk.

Hope you get this soon. I'll continue tomorrow, after posting. I really did enjoy our talk.

Best wishes
James

8.2.03

Dear Beth,

Next episode.

I said I'd tell you about my father. It's early morning and I'm at the desk, even though I haven't any jobs lined up today. In my mind I'm already busy. It's how I function, a useful habit which gets things done. Because, in general, who you are shows in what you do, but also the reverse. With choices and habits and promises, we make them, or they make us. Like my father when he retired from the railways. It was as if he'd lost an arm. Make or break, I suppose, which sounds like a bad joke when I think of him in bed with throat cancer. They kept him in hospital until there was nothing they could do, then my mother took over. He died six years ago.

I want to cross that out and start again. But I've decided to leave it. I had to do something so I walked around the house, sat outside and closed my eyes, but now I'm back.

Reading what I wrote, the truth is I wasn't reconciled to my father when he died. We lived in Chester-le-Street and he took on that Northern aggressive black humour, the chip on the shoulder depressive stuff about them and us and better off dead, a kind of inverted schadenfreude. That was later on, after he retired. Before that he was a joker, and a family teaser. But the signs were always there. There was an edge of hardness to his practical jokes, he was keeping a score. And he always disputed with bosses, shopkeepers, neighbours and especially with me, taking aim at anything creative, what he called bloody namby-pamby or airy-fairy. Sour grapes, I suppose. Because he knew he'd a brain and felt passed over. He was a man who read up on facts as if he was preparing for an exam, then turned them into weapons, taking on politics, war, history, North vs South, God and the church, till there were no truths left standing. Mind, hearing him now as I write, I realise it was an act, a put-on as he'd say – his own way of kidding or ribbing or reckoning. A part he played to impress the lads, even indoors where none of them could see him. It makes me think of Billy Elliot and bits of Lawrence. That all-out spoiler, bloody-minded, bring-down-the-temple business. So where did he get it from? Probably something passed down from big Daddy-O, his dad and his, men who stood apart.

But then Eddie Lavender had other sides as well. He'd a practical-joking, throwaway larkiness, doing Carry On voices and plum-voiced speeches… the Right Hon Harold Macmillan and The Queen… and a long-term passion for dogs. At various times he kept a spaniel, two collies, a red setter and a mongrel. I remember their names: Lenin, Trotsky, Stalin, Engels and Marx. When he walked them and I came along, he'd break into a whistle. Quick, fluting runs which I've not heard since. I think they were tunes he made up. We walked around the hills with him whistling and delivering speeches about Kronstadt and The Winter Palace while the dogs ran wild. He was, in his own way, a latter-day revolutionary, a sans-culotte. And he didn't want me to become a landscape gardener.

Well, I think that's probably enough about him. There are limits. Men on men can be such a bore. I remember watching The Deer Hunter and thinking how much blood, sweat and tears does it take to make a film? Two guys spilling everything. Talk about self-indulgent.

And I'm wondering what you're thinking about my first letter, or will be thinking as you read this. I'd like to be with you as you open it, to watch and interpret your expression, like a fly on the wall. Even better to climb inside, as in that film The Fantastic Voyage, and hear how you react, what you like and what you don't. Of course it's speculation, but I still find myself imagining meetings and having those conversations with people in the head. Like those niggly, blow-by-blow, finger-pointing dialogues when you make up different versions after a row.

I remember in childhood playing back voices. I was the listener, the boy on the landing hearing little scraps, words and laughter caught through doorways, imaginary dialogues running in my head. It took me to a world of thought, somewhere private, my own special place. A mirror-crazy land where I'd watch from the ceiling, slip out unnoticed through air vents and keyholes, picture myself sky-high, turning cartwheels or dancing on the roof. Pretty silly, eh? But then I was a soft boy and very much bottled.

Well, I think that's all for now. While I've been writing the sun has come up, picking out the frost on roads and cars. The sky's clear, bright and cold. Looking around, everything's hard-edged and made of polished steel. The pylons in the distance, the corrugated fences, the flat tin roofs on workshops and garages, even the bushes look like metal... all cold hard sticks and stripped-back branches.

But inside it's warm.

Best wishes

James

10.2.03

Dear Beth,

Oh yes. A couple of days, a long letter from you and a chat on the phone.

Opening that letter was one of those moments. I could see it was fat and knew it was you from the postmark, but I was still apprehensive. There's always a doubt, an unanswered question when a letter arrives. It's that time taken opening, when you don't know what's coming. So much seems to ride on it. You imagine different things, mostly painful, ranging from cool and ultra-careful to downright rejection. But that all disappeared as I read your letter.

You wrote about your life so beautifully, I could see every detail. Page after page, I wanted to keep reading, and when I reached the end I went straight back and read it again. I hadn't expected that you'd say so much, or describe your family in such detail. I had a strong sense of light and line, with you in the middle, what you believe in, your friendships, interests, things you enjoy and what you might be looking for. I loved all the scenes... the country walks, lighting fires, drawing birds, your dad painting eggs... but the best bit was at the end, because it was what I'd hoped for but didn't want to say. Men, as you know, are supposed to make the running, but not rush in, while women pull the strings. Though in my book, it's a bit of both. So yes, as you say, we should meet up. And I'm very happy, excited really, to eat out somewhere, so we'll sort out the details on the phone ASAP (but not, of course, rushing it...).

You ask about childhood. I've told you about my dad. My mum was what folk, aka people in the North, call a different kettle of fish. Theirs was a marriage of opposites, Eddie uppity, Doris calm. Dark and light, a balance of forces. Even now she's inclined to fit in, to see the other side and adapt to being pushed, but behind that's an independent woman who knows what she wants. To me, in her own quiet way, she's always been there. I remember watching her sewing, her hands on the covers stripping the bed, her slippered feet pushing the treadle, her floral dresses and fresh-faced smile. A lady and a housewife.

Our small side-return with its plant pots and boxes was where she grew her herbs. She taught me the names, pinched out stems and made me close my eyes. "Can you tell which is which?" she asked, passing different leaves beneath my nose. Then she'd make herself busy planting, using egg boxes. When the seedlings appeared she'd separate the shoots and root them in bowls. Heart-shaped lettuces and sprigs of cress, which she put in our sarnies.

I think she could have easily been veggie, but not in our household, not with my dad. He had an idea that meat was brain food and that grain made you fat. Given his style I imagine he insisted, but my mum either provided or ignored. She remained herself. What mattered to her was keeping people fed and clothed and happy and healthy, so she made do and put off and saved what she could, and when we moved she chose the house, what we took with us and how we handled money.

That move made a difference. Hastings never suited him. For her it was home, with family close by. But for my brother and me it was my playground, and his teenage hangout. Full of wind and sun and seagulls,

30

it offered its cliff drops, its quick-getaway walled-in steps down to the sea, its lights and rides and amusements and pier-cum-promenade with views of the bay and France. Mystery and adventure.

I always feel there's something special about the sea. Nostalgia if you like, but I think it works for our family. So in Hastings I felt close to Richard, my brother. We were young and crazy and acted out scenes from films with me as cop, him as hero on the run. Nowadays he's an inner-city type, a thinker and a teacher, and a bit of a rebel like Dad. If I'm honest, we're hardly in touch, which is my fault as much as his.

When Eddie moved back to Chester-le-Street, we lodged for a while with my mum's parents in St Leonards. And when Doris and Richard returned north I stayed on. After that, through youth, I paid Henry and Isobel regular visits over Easter and summer. I remember them as old-fashioned boarding house owners who provided quizzes and puzzles and soft toys and full English breakfasts, and were sweet on me. Whenever I'm by the sea I think of them.

Wish you were here.

James

13.2.03

Dear Beth,

I'm sitting at home playing Nirvana's 'Nevermind'. It's probably not your kind of music, but when I listen, eyes closed, it perks me up. I remember a stage when I'd drive to work singing along to John Lee Hooker, Buddy Guy, Howling Wolf, foot down, volume up. Nivarna's like them: strong, and power-packed. 'The bigger the problem the bigger the pill' as George Clinton said. If you ask me why I do it, I'd say it keeps me young. It's the kind of music which exposes all. But please don't worry, I know I'm not seventeen! Or if I am, that's a choice, something I accept in order to use it. To taste but not swallow. It lets out the child so I can be an adult.

I got into Nirvana in my first big gardening phase. That was when we moved. I'd rise at six to go out digging and planting with music in my ears. Front and back, with headphones, to the sound of crazy guitars. I still have those tracks on tape: Rock the Kasbah, My Generation, Voodoo Chile, hard-driven, swinging-from-the-gate stuff. And I know from travelling that The Stones can keep you going – energy, energy.

Sandra always said I couldn't sit still. It was one of her not-now-dear remarks. Anything I did made her feel threatened.

Now the music's stopped and the flat's gone quiet. And I'm happy with that, too. I can hear the rumble of a train, traffic passing and birdsong in the hedge. Someone next door is talking on the phone, while high up above, a plane drones over. Yes, in the quiet times I'm comfortable. Where the action pauses, the self can be heard. And after that music it's one-sound-at-a-time, like an icicle drip, or a stone into water.

So I sit, listening out. I'm waiting for a call. I've a project to start on a walled garden, working for what my dad would call 'the other side'. I'm designing for a rich CEO. As it happens, he's a rock fan, too. He has a roomful of electric guitars. Gibsons, Fenders, Les Pauls, they're his trophies hanging on a wall.

When I look at my vinyl collection I remember Hannah as a baby. She'd crawl towards the bookshelf, chuckling, and drag them out. Before I could stop her, she'd scattered LPs across the floor. When I called out, "No!" she ignored me. If I tried putting up a fireguard and blocking with chairs, she climbed around the side. When I upended a table and cross-tied the legs with string, she simply burrowed under. I attempted distraction with toys and games, but she set off again. And every time I hauled her off she crawled back, chuckling determinedly.

Hannah was fearless. You couldn't take your eyes off her. Before you knew it she'd be up on a chair digging into cupboards and smearing cream all over. The bathroom was her play zone where she'd squeeze out tubes and chew down brushes. Out in the garden she'd pull up plants and hide behind bushes. I remember finding once, out shopping, that she'd escaped from her pushchair. The shop was small, it was a hot day and the doors were open. When I realised that she'd turned the aisle and was already halfway through the exit, I ran calling out. I could see her outside, crossing the pavement, heading for the road. Fearful images ran through my head. A car came close, and I shouted. She hesitated slightly and I just had time to scoop her up.

Later, in the middle of the night, she'd cry for hours. I remember picking her up and stroking her head till she nodded off, nestling in my arms. But when I put her back, she'd stir. As her head touched the pillow she'd take a breath then break out crying. Very soon she'd be yelling and I'd have to pick her up and start again. I can still see myself sitting there, stroking, lowering, drawing her back up. In the end I'd creep out like a thief, willing her to sleep. Then afterwards, lying awake, I'd picture the animal shapes and cartoon faces printed on her wall.

There were other struggles, too. I remember how Hannah would climb out of her cot and push into our bedroom, wanting to join us. For Sandra that was fine. She liked the warmth and could sleep through anything, but I'd had enough of nocturnal visits with George. He'd appear, crawl in between us and kick me awake. Weeks of that and I was tired out. So when Hannah came in I'd a mattress on the carpet, ready to receive her. And when I intercepted, to my surprise, she settled without complaint. I think it might have been how I moved, maybe how I spoke, or the near-total darkness. Whatever it was, she slept through peacefully, and so did I.

What I remember about that period was the urgency and the exhaustion. Having kids takes over completely. It's about non-stop juggling and stamina. Before I had children I had so much time on my hands. But, as you know, once you're a parent you have to make choices. It's a question of what you want to hold on to. Above all, of course, you hold on tight to your children. After that, listening late at night in a small dark corner with the volume turned down, I held on to my music.

And the kids are all right.

James

16.2.03

Dear Beth,

Your letter this morning was a shock. I thought our meeting was definitely on. Now it's off, or might be. I'm confused and, I have to say, feeling sore. I've read what you wrote, recognise it's difficult, but I thought we'd agreed, and in any case…

But then again, I suppose if that's how you want it. Or if it's mañana… and I see you're not offering a date… well, maybe that's best. Or maybe not, who knows?

I've made a cup of tea, it helps! I've so many thoughts going around, mainly attempts to make you change your mind. Rereading your words I see it's not definite, the door's not shut yet. So, OK, OK, reasons for/reasons against, one side/the other, I'll draw up a chart.

For	Against
Having got this far, everything's set up. Adventure, what's round the corner. It's worth a try. I'm a decent guy. It doesn't hurt, could be fun. OK it's a challenge but there's no obligation. You really shouldn't treat me this way. You owe it to me and yourself.	It might be a disappointment but then it might not. Yes, there's risk and you're right about families, but we know so much already and we're not blind. If we put off it may never happen. As adults we choose.

Best wishes
James

17.2.03

Dear Beth,

I see now. I'm glad we talked. Of course I do understand, a phrase you used often, and your apologies. Yes, glad. Genuinely so, for now it's clearer and I think it's like standing on the beach... the long lines ahead, the view, blue-grey to white.

The sea's so uncluttered, it reminds me of youth. It bears down in a rush, or slowly in a clean sweep to the horizon, where ships go by.

I'll be there on Friday.
Best wishes
James

Chapter Two

Beth loved her dad.

From the beginning John Jarvis was there, a bookish man in tie and glasses standing by the window. Tall and slight, with prominent ears and a toothy smile, he listened and explained, so she understood. But also he picked up on why, why not, and what really mattered. And for Beth he was always there, close by, observing, an all-weather man taking in the garden and examining earth, checking for plant growth with a life-interest in birds. All sorts of birds, mainly blackbirds but also dunnocks, starlings, robins, finches.

"Watch carefully," he said, speaking quietly, as they nodded and danced, hanging on the feeder. "Birds are fierce," he told her, pointing.

Pecking into brown, the birds drilled the feed.

"It's a different world," he said, touching Beth's shoulder.

Wingtip to wingtip, the birds wheeled and spun.

"They all have their stories," he added, playing with her hair. And she looked and she nodded, taking in everything. His words were what she needed.

Another day she joined him just outside the door. They were sitting on a groundsheet spread across the wall. Her dad had a sketch book open in his hands. It was brown and cream and filled with birds, all hand-drawn and copied from black-and-white photos.

"Rara avis," he said, finger-tapping a picture.

Beth smiled. She liked his words, they gave her ideas. Strange as they were, for her they had meaning. She waved into air, "Are there r-r-ravis here?"

"I think not. Or if so, like angels they're invisible."

"Come on, cheep-cheeps."

"And no birds sing," he said, looking up.

Beth followed his gaze, saying nothing.

"Ah well," he added more brightly, "just have to wait."

The sky was grey, silver at the edges and softened by mist, the trees were still, the air felt damp and a few green-yellow weeds sprouted around the borders. The garden was empty. Exchanging glances, they scanned the lawn and peered at the telegraph wires then tried imitating calls. But the birds, it seemed, were fast asleep or in hiding.

John marked the page, closing the book. If you were patient, he whispered, they all came out. Hidden in leaves or gathered around the feeder, they were always there.

Close to his shoulder, Beth looked ahead. He was her dad; he made things happen.

"They're my *flights of fancy*," he told her, quietly – a phrase he repeated, on wet days watching by the window, and on half-and-half days (ghost-grey, like today) sitting together just outside the door.

Afterwards, remembering his face, Beth realised that he'd something more, a depth of sadness, a down-mouth in his smiles. Behind it all, he wasn't of this world. He observed, he spotted, he imagined and, like St Francis, talked to the birds. He knew all their names, told her how they lived, made up anecdotes about soul-birds on fire and journeys from the north, and invented conversations that he tried out in private, at bedtime, adding to his stories from one night to the next.

Often long and sometimes unfinished, his tales developed into Aesop-type fables with worldly-wise animals offering life-thoughts and commentaries, and humans who ignored them. The stories were fun, but gently barbed. Using nicknames and jokes and unlikely settings that half-mirrored life, they filled up the evening with improvised plot twists and verbal adventures.

And it was his stories, invented on the spot and delivered in private, together with his characters – both animal and human – that Beth kept with her, hearing him often as she played out her life. He was always there.

From the start she was Beth. Christened Elizabeth Mary Jarvis, she was the first of two, born near Bury St Edmunds to non-conformist parents.

She was B, the beautiful daughter of Louise and John, a well-respected couple who were seen by those who knew them as 'the double act' and 'the perfect pair'. Paired by habit – like-minded, vegetarian, anti-materialist and involved in causes – but also by choice, as lifetime partners who registered and stood out, their closeness kept them different. Not just different but pacifist, Methodist and, in their own way, independent thinkers: John researching local history which he turned into pamphlets while Louise collected sayings, Victorian, mainly, which she stitched into cloth.

And Beautiful Beth, who had Brains as well, was their joy. They called her Elizabeth after Louise's mother, a big-jawed woman whose sepia-tinted photo stood on the cabinet beside Beth's bed. She, too, was different. Wide-mouthed, high-voiced, impassioned, she'd written several stories – *kiddies' stuff* she called them – and shared them, smiling, in stop-go episodes where she closed her eyes, waiting, it seemed, for something more to come, then flicked on several pages to end with a frown. A woman of feeling, Beth's jolly gran whose OTT gestures resembled the young-girl heroines who appeared in frocks, dancing or declaiming on the covers of her books. Illustrated volumes that Beth read, when older, feeling the frustration of a large-jawed woman whose husband, sitting in the background playing cards, had never really taken notice. Or if he did, wasn't that bothered.

"Blooming books," Jim called out, yawning.

And Beth took against. She didn't like his voice, his tics and narrow-eyed quips, his self-regarding grin. In her thoughts and in hindsight this man wasn't good.

"Give us a pint," he declared, scanning his cards. "More use than *making up*." – a phrase she'd been surprised by, hinting at differences Beth didn't understand.

At other times he seemed puzzled. What, he asked flatly, was the point? Chapters, sequels, words on paper, he'd had that at school, kept quiet at the back, got lost off.

Pushing out her jaw, his wife thought otherwise. Books, she said, were a pleasure; they fed the mind. For children they were everything.

Beth agreed. Her gran's words, heard in passing and memorised carefully, were often repeated. Said quietly below breath, persistently to her mum, in confidence to her dad and written up, round-script in a corner, each boxed and numbered in blue felt pen and displayed by way of reinforcement behind her bedroom door, she called them her sayings.

They were:

1. YOU ARE WHAT YOU READ.
2. STORY BEATS REAL.
3. MADE-UP IS SO.
4. WITHOUT STORIES WE'RE BORING.
5. A BOOK IS AN ADVENTURE.

When asked where they came from, she coloured slightly. When pressed by her dad, she smiled. "It's what *we* think," she said, inviting him to view them. "All of us," she went on, standing at the bed end. The pronoun included herself and John, her mother, her brother, even old Jim, but most of all the image of her now-deceased grandmother.

"She wrote because of you," her dad said another time, pointing to the photo.

Beth fell silent as she looked. The long-faced woman was standing tall, with swept back hair and a thoughtful expression. Framed by a window, she was gazing out on an overgrown garden.

"It was her gift," added John.

His daughter nodded. Her white-faced gran belonged, it seemed, to one of Beth's own stories: tales of daring and one-time adventures which she'd written in her sketchbooks then back-flipped and spread to begin a new story.

And as Beth grew older she voiced her tales, setting them outdoors. Under her direction, with herself as protagonist and featuring her brother, she plotted and scripted and staged them in the garden.

"Toby," she called, "this part's for you." And if he didn't want it or walked off to a corner, she simply delivered solo then started something else.

Because outdoors she could do anything. As Beth she was half-lady, half-outlaw, switching between stories and mixing genre. Her parents didn't know it, but she'd horses and spacesuits and teacups and binoculars which she air-drew and named, directing their use as prompts in her story.

The main game was *Shipwreck*, with Captain Beth, standing on the rockery, sighting dolphins and navigating channels as she directed forward. "Land ahoy!" she called and Toby echoed, leaning into the wind. As the waves became taller they swayed side to side and mimed their parts, shouting. When the water took over they ran downhill, taking to the lifeboats.

"Abandon ship!" she shouted. Reaching her boat, Beth began air-rowing, advancing at a crouch. "We're washed up!" she called when she arrived at the lawn.

Toby joined her saying nothing. Without even noticing he'd walked untouched across a wide stretch of path. In the story this was water.

"Toby!" she cried, pointing. "You drowned."

The boy flushed.

"You can't do that."

"Can."

"Well, you shouldn't."

The boy stepped back, planting both feet on the path.

"You're spoiling."

"No."

"I'm the captain and I say so."

Eyes down, Toby returned to the lawn.

Beth sighed. "Now we'll explore inland," she said, leading down-lawn to a dogleg at the back. Toby followed in silence. Here they took shelter beneath some overhanging branches. Screened by leaves they peered across grass. Blackbirds and finches were hopping around the edges. "It's an island," she called, "with treasure and wild animals." The patch beyond was damp and leafy and spread with growth. There were fruit trees and climbers, weeds under bushes and mildewed roses.

Toby blinked. "And that's HQ," he announced, pointing upwards. In the tree above, a series of ladders with halfway landings led to a wood-and-canvas platform.

Beth shook her head, "It's the Wendy House, where the castaways live."

The boy made himself busy. He was jerking at a branch.

"So now," she added, approaching the ladder, "we're the lost boys. Which means, yes, we can fly..." Beth back-swung and began to climb. With a springy, bunched-up movement, Toby followed.

They clambered up to a flat run of boards divided by a wooden partition. There were support struts both sides, a door between, and a grey, stretchy, holed-through canvas roof. It looked like a cross between a hut and a tent. Ducking forward they passed through the door. Inside was messy. In the centre was a bamboo table covered with flaking chalks, two battered slates and a blue plastic tea set. Beads on strings hung down from the sides. Two orange box seats were stacked underneath.

Beth pulled out a crate then picked up a pole from the floor. Mounting the crate, she applied the pole end to her eye, turning a circle. "Nothing on the horizon," she said, expressionless. "Or on the island," she added, swinging round.

At the table, Toby was spot-testing chalks, breaking them in half and scrubbing the ends, before drawing.

Beth continued scanning then dropped her head.

Toby had completed a scrawly, pear-shaped outline with shaded-in areas. "It's a map," he mumbled when questioned from above.

"That's where we are?"

Toby continued drawing.

"Of course, it's a story," she said slowly. "And this is how it goes..." Speaking quietly, as if from memory, Beth began.

Directing her voice, she named her characters as Beth and Toby and described a shipwreck with the girl rowing clear and the boy treading water. The Wendy House followed, with treasure and wild animals. Next was their landing, the move inland, an island tree house – her lookout, his HQ – leading to a bamboo table with chalks and crates. Here her expression softened as she spoke about the place, the castaways together, mentioning the boy, the maps, the girl as captain, who made it all happen...

"And that's their story," she ended with a lilt. "And as long as they keep telling it, they'll never leave the island."

****

The morning after meeting James, Beth had what she called her Desert Island Dream. It was just before she woke. In the dream she and James were radio guests. Speaking into an old-fashioned mike, they described their tastes and answered questions about what they valued most.

40

Although it was a dream, Beth could feel James's hand touching hers gently.

When she was young, she'd had much the same dream and shared it with her dad. He'd read her *Treasure Island*. Later they'd played at *Survival*, inventing crazy uses for objects that they imagined being left over from a shipwreck. While Beth had drawn rope-and-plastic wings, John had made up a game using keys and coins. When Toby joined them, a coconut-football had been added.

In the dream the radio presenter, who wore glasses like her dad, asked them a question. "Tell me," he said, "what two objects would you save to take in your Ark?"

Beth smiled, "One each?"

"That's right."

"Easy," she said, "my lipstick."

"And your... choice?" asked the presenter. Although she couldn't be certain, Beth thought she heard the word "husband's" slipped into the middle of his question.

In answer James drew out some stacked papers. "The letters," he said. He selected one which he folded and tightened at the corners, till it sat in his hand like a bird. There were four exposed surfaces, divided by two crossing slits. Inserting thumb and finger below, he moved it back and forth. It gaped then closed. Beth thought it must be hungry.

"Give me a letter," he said.

"J," she replied.

"Now two letters."

"A-M."

"Two more."

"E-S."

Each time she spelled out a letter James finger-shuffled his whirlybird. It stretched and collapsed, then pulled itself tall, bowing to an imaginary audience. It was his puppet.

"Now choose a flap," he said, holding it wide open.

Beth looked down into the folds. The paper inside was covered with writing.

"Any flap?"

James nodded.

There were four to choose from so she ip-dipped, selecting one which she peeled back. The paper felt alive. It reminded her of opening a window on the advent calendar.

Inside were four words, printed in red, with green and purple highlights. Leaning forward she read them to herself. The words said: YOU WILL FIND LOVE.

****

As a schoolgirl, Beth wrote stories for her friends. Tales of children who sneaked out of houses and ran through woods, children who camped out or time-switched nightly into Victorian schoolrooms, oddball children with super-sight and wings or youthful savants in touch with other worlds, and simple everyday children in stories where small events mattered, loyalties were strong and just-so things were said. "It's all true," she said, if asked to explain. "Really-real."

And to her it was. Writing often, she told of incidents in the classroom – objects disappearing, ink marks and scribbles and whispered messages – and playground spaces where strange things happened.

Head down, excited, she made up what she could, thinking of her gran.

And people liked her stories. Written at speed and added to daily with oddly-worded phrases and sudden exclamations, their twists and turns and unexpected shifts impressed her friends. *Their* friends liked them too. Word got around and Beth wrote more. Mysteries, mainly, with thick fog and ice and faces at windows, followed by cries, footsteps leading nowhere and strange disappearances, or sometimes accidents with freak winds and thunder and glimpses of ghosts. And everything she wrote was creepy or puzzling or absurd or full of crazy action.

"Surprise, surprise," she hissed, as she offered her latest.

"Horrible, isn't it," she teased, huddled with her friends.

"You have to b-e-l-i-e-v-e," she added pointing to a just-written story, "whatever it says."

Later still, in the lower fourth, she told her friends she'd stopped. The stories, she said, weren't there. She read, of course, and wrote in class, producing as required – mainly exercises and tests on meaning –

and kept up her grades with an emphasis on corrections and preparing for exams.

But in secret, in her bedroom most evenings, closing her eyes and picturing her friends, Beth was a writer. It recalled, in shadow form, her dad's stories.

And she wrote from what she knew: school scenes, home scenes, tales set in small towns, with girls who went together. Hers were clever girls who read, said things and looked around seriously, while talking *people*.

First off was Charlotte. Wide-eyed Charlie with her short hair and freckles, the all-go girl with her tales of inventions and records broken, using coin piles and card towers that she balanced on tables and matchstick boats for visits to the park.

"It's magic," she claimed proudly, siphoning coloured water to run between glasses.

Sometimes she sent messages written in reverse or coded by reference to well-known books. She could add up in a blink, drew well, sight-read on piano and had reached grade four.

In the story she was 'C', the jump-in expert, whose feet-first reactions made everyone laugh. Her clown-girl mishaps occurring everywhere, in parks and streets and on and off buses, but chiefly in the classroom, together with her tendency to appeal to the gallery and gesture wildly, made for entertainment. "Can't help it!" was her catch phrase, or: "Watch O... Watch O... Watch Out!" which came out straight, in a single breath. As madcap joker she overshot the mark or simply ignored, went into overdrive and got by in a tangle. But also, by degrees, she changed and developed, taking on the role of tongue-in-cheek commentator and clever-clever watcher who saw, took stock and signalled by example.

But in life she was different. The real girl Charlie gave up her interests to focus on admirers, on what she called her *types*. Past sixteen, she said, you could straightaway tell. Either they'd got there or were promising. Whichever way, boys were it.

At other times she was careful; she knew just how it was. As a girl of the world, she could hold her own. "I like them simple," she said confidingly – meaning, she said, boys who didn't put up – office juniors and bookshop assistants who knew what a girl needed, how far and how much, and what was expected. She wanted boys who went deep.

Beth sat listening with her head to one side. Although they'd placed themselves beneath trees at the end of the garden, her friend's talk, half-boastful, half-breathless, wasn't really safe. What if Charlie's words got back to her parents? If someone told, or they overheard in passing? And what if something happened, if her friend cut off or fell ill, or even, as in the newspapers, her nice girl Charlie ran away to get married and ended as a hostage, tied up in a basement by one these boys?

Charlie smiled. "I'm a choosy girl," she said, narrowing her eyes. Reaching to one side, she teased out a grass stem and bent it around her finger.

Beth stared off into air.

"See, it fits," her friend said, binding her flesh.

Beth's expression had flattened to a politely-held smile. Now, the thoughts she'd had seemed rather foolish.

Her friend repeated the word choosy.

"That's how girls should be," declared Beth, holding her expression.

Charlie showed her hands. "Look. It's my ring," she said, knotting the stem.

"That's nice."

"See, I'm engaged."

"You're engaged?"

"Oh, yes."

"So who's the lucky boy?"

"You."

"Me?"

"Ha, ha, not really."

"So who is it?"

"Oh, I don't know. Anyone you like."

"Anyone?"

Charlie considered, tugging at her ring. "Any boy as long as he's tall, owns a car and isn't called Fred."

"And that's all?"

"Oh, he has to be a fab kisser," Charlie added, gazing past her friend. It seemed she could see things Beth couldn't. "And a virgin."

Beth remained still. The last word wasn't nice; it was one of those expressions found in dictionaries which she'd seen girls looking up. A conversation stopper, certainly with parents. A word like a switch, set to go off.

That evening, addressing the photo of her gran, Beth told her story. What she said was a summary, changed in certain parts; it offered the true feel, the air-light surface and the shadow underneath. Because life had its dangers. Something unseen was approaching, as if she'd been out walking, alone in darkness, and heard someone following. And Charlotte, she realised, wasn't there to help her.

So Beth preferred 'C'. Her on-the-page protagonist, though clumsy and reckless, hadn't that self-willed edge or it's-me presence. In the story, she was brightly engaging and framed within limits. Seen as a character, her words and appearance were that much more attractive, more rounded, more truly human than her boy-obsessed friend. For Beth, as a teenager and secret bedroom writer, the story was the person.

There were other friends too. Girls of spirit with interests and individual viewpoints, get-up-and-go types with spark and life adapted into writing. Girls like Meg in her hand-designed frocks and multi-coloured hairbands who took on parts no one else wanted, stepping in to sing if someone dropped out at the end-of-term service.

Meg was sweet. Round-faced and fringed, she was everyone's friend, a listener and supporter who advised on hairstyles, helped out with homework, gave little presents and asked about feelings. She put herself last. Quick at Art, she would dish out stock, sketch in outlines for girls who couldn't get started, mix paint with water in just the right proportions, then complete her own work with a few rapid brushstrokes. "That's lovely," she'd say, as she pinned up a picture by a classmate. "It's the sort of thing you do really well." Then she'd store her work in the art room cupboard, pressed between cardboard and slipped in behind an unlabelled plan chest.

In the story Meg was wild, a Pre-Raphaelite siren living by the sea in a tide-swept cave. Between songs she'd improvise melodies, running her fingers through her all-gold hair. As Morgan Le Fay she came in with the mists and appeared on beaches where she lay in the sun. When she swam out to a rock her body turned silver. She was finned and scaled and gleamed all over.

Beth called her Selkie – a name she'd learned from her dad – imagining her friend switching persona from wild-girl explorer to fresh-faced helper. As Selkie, or Silky, she was hard to read.

And once, in a contest, Meg had been both. With Beth there watching, she'd swum freestyle for the school, breaking a record and passing all her rivals.

"Hey hey, here comes the dolphin!" cried Beth, as her friend climbed out to the poolside.

"You think that was fast?" Meg said, turning her head. Her cheeks were flushed and her hair was running water.

"You beat them all."

A cheer went up as Meg waved to the crowd.

Beth laughed. "I think you enjoyed that."

Meg smiled sweetly. As she reached for a towel her eye caught another swimmer flopped across a block. The girl, who was thin and shivery, was staring into water. She looked worn out. "Are you all right?" Meg asked quickly, crouching down. She repeated her request. When the girl said nothing, Meg removed her towel. "Here, take this," she said, wrapping it around the girl's shoulders. Patting the towel, she examined the girl carefully. "And listen," she added, "I'm going to give you a present."

The girl's eyes widened. "Oh, thank you," she said, as Meg helped her up.

An announcement boomed out, calling for the winners.

"Just wait," said Meg, "I'll be back."

She returned a few minutes later, holding her medal. It was gold and polished, with a red silk cord threaded through a hole at the top. "Here," she said, throwing the cord over the girl's head, "I want you to have it."

The girl blushed, "But I can't, it's yours."

"It's yours now," said Meg, gazing across the water, "I'm not racing anymore."

"You don't want it?"

"No."

The girl considered, fingering the silk, "You really don't?"

Meg nodded.

"And you won't be swimming?"

"Oh, I'll swim all right with friends. But only for fun."

When Beth arrived, Meg was sitting with the girl, dangling her feet in the pool. They were both wrapped in towels. Meg's face, reflected in water, was calmly smooth. With her gentle, unthinking smile, she reminded Beth of Ellie in the Water Babes. And the girl beside her with a medal, whose water reflection seemed joined onto Meg's, was a Selkie.

Two other girls were close to Beth. One was Rachael, nicknamed Brainbox, a tall thin girl who bike-rode to school wearing long grey socks and a Mackintosh. Everyone knew her. She was the girl who could calculate without paper, measure within inches by eye, recite the periodic table and name all 190 countries, with their capitals. To Rachael what seemed obvious and straightforwardly interesting – numbers, science and all things factual – was simply how it was. She *knew*, didn't see the gap, and took herself, without any real evidence, to be some sort of norm.

Rachael entered Beth's stories as a teacher-lover. She sat at the front training her 20/20 vision on the new maths master. She viewed him like a specimen, logging all his habits. She verified his timings and routes down the corridor. Writing in her notebook, she recorded what he said, repeating his words and checking all the facts, before scanning him for shape, bit-parts and physical make-up. His dimensions were marked off, plotted on axes and turned into data. His looks were a formula; gestures equations; his self made up the universal theory.

In the end, as herself, with her blend of specifics and individual elements, like all of Beth's friends, Rachael was different.

Then there was Amy who appeared in both worlds simply as herself. She was what the others called plain. Young and slight with soft grey eyes and a down-to-earth smile, she talked about lessons, ticking off her homework and preparing for exams. As *Eveready Amy* and *Amy-The-Doer* she kept her own notes, recording her marks and filling up daily schedules. She was the girl who organised societies – quiz groups and revision clubs and debates in the library – and issued handmade cards, using words like 'bona fide' and 'fully paid up'. She put things in place, was reasonable, thoughtfully pragmatic and functioned well. *Ordinary*

Amy, in story as in life.

And for all Beth's friends, to figure in her stories made them more alive. Inside her books they could change, develop and try out different acts, test for properties and switch between characters. They could be anyone: lead, support, good girl, bad girl, talker, dodger. For them, like her, a book was an adventure.

****

"What's your favourite colour?" asked James.

Beth was back in the Desert Island Dream. After three hours' sleep and a full day working in the café, she'd left early, intending to write. Her excitement had carried her until she reached the sofa but then she'd nodded off. In her dream she was warm. The studio was comfortable and softly-cushioned. Images rose up of flesh in water. She could have been floating in a fish tank.

The show was live. Its theme was relationships, and how pleasure and survival were linked. They'd talked about interests shared and now, with James as the presenter, they were discussing likes.

"What's yours?" she said quietly, inviting his gaze.

"Any colour?"

"Your fave."

"Pink."

"Pink?"

"The colour of your top."

"Any others?"

"Red."

"Like my lipstick?"

"Yes, mine as well."

"On your glass?"

"…*on my collar*…"

Beth's face was glowing, "Mine's blue-grey."

"Eyes?"

"Sea, skies, as well."

"Anything else?"

"Hopkins."

"Hopkins?"

"Like Pied Beauty."

"Mixtures, combinations."

"Clashes as well."

"But what about blues?"

Beth's gaze softened, she was giving him the look. "Music, you mean?"

"Oh *yes…yes…yes.*"

"They're sad."

"Very."

"You often feel sad?"

"Sometimes, when I'm alone."

"So what do you do?"

"Play music, or sing."

"You sing?"

"Singalong, bathroom stuff."

"I think I'd like that."

"*O Sole Mio*, that sort of thing?"

"If that's what you sing."

"Or *Straight from your heart*, perhaps?"

"Ah, I love those lyrics."

"*Keep us so near while apart...*"

"Yes… *I'm not alone in the night…*"

"Is that your favourite song?"

Beth coloured as she shook her head. "Blue Moon."

James said a few words, wrapping up the programme. He switched off the microphone and let out a breath.

Beth was watching him carefully, "So who do you sing to?"

"The girl of my dreams."

****

When she was fourteen Beth became Saffron. "Call me Saf," she said to Meg, examining an art book spread across her bedroom floor, "or Saffy. Saffron if you have to."

Her friend turned a page. "Saf's best," she said, pausing at a print of a raven-haired woman with one hand wrapped around a pomegranate.

"You like it?"

Both girls stared at the picture. The woman was red-lipped, blue-eyed, wearing a loose, grey-green robe. Her skin was smooth and pale as water.

"Why Saffron?"

"It's a girl in a book."

"Like her?"

Beth shook her head. "One of my gran's books. She wrote it, about Saffron."

"Your gran wrote books?"

Beth confirmed. "For children," she added, "with girls dancing and poetry."

"Were they fun?"

"Jolly – or meant to be."

Meg bent forward peering at the picture, "But not jolly." The long-necked woman in the art book was gazing at smoke rising from a burner. Her double-jointed hands were artist-thin and wasted. Behind her the light from a window spread across some ivy on a wall.

"Supposed to be. But sad… very sad to me."

"Don't say that."

Suddenly Beth was crying.

Meg placed her hand on her friend's wrist, "You loved your gran."

Saffron Alexander was the title of Beth's first book. She wrote for herself, alone in her bedroom, staying up late then rising early and putting pen to paper. Written as it came, quickly, then divided into sections, it fell into three parts, each headed in red, with boxed-in paragraphs and arrows back and forth.

The sections were:

A.   SCHOOLSCHOOLSCHOOL – a close-up study of friendships and incidents and exchanges about families, particularly brothers (How Annoying Can They Be) as well as teacher profiles and homework set (not explained) and UNEQUAL TREATMENT. A succession of rumours and fall-outs and larks between lessons with moments touching feelings and cheeks sucked in while fingering notes found in pockets and hair stroked gently while lying in the sun.

In this part, the longest and densest on the page, Saffron was a mix. When she led from the front, her assembled cast – a bit-part collection of faces from the classroom, book-life, shop life and remembered family members – were subject to her whim. But when she played spy or classroom assistant, her characters, who jumped all over and never seemed to listen, went off at tangents and made themselves the story, filling up the pages. Either they fidgeted or wouldn't stop talking. As characters they were out there, on paper, both independent and shaped by the story.

B.   THE ROMANCE (PART 1) – the tale of a family appearing three doors down, beginning with a boy seen passing, returning from school. A boy without a name, soft-faced, light-haired, with thin arms and shoulders and a loose-limbed walk. A boy Saffron liked, watching daily for his fresh-faced blushes and eyes looking around. And the story developing, with her overheard comments, leading to a name, a school, and some sort of background. Then a meeting by chance, Saturday in the park, with the parents shaking hands, while the boy (called Tom) was sent off with Saffron to buy ice creams.

In the weeks that followed she showed Tom her places. In her mind they did it all: walking the garden on out-of-view paths, visiting the churchyard then crossing the playing fields to the mill, the stream and swans by the lake. As they toured she talked, the sky cleared and he admired what he saw. Their story was a dream, a song at a window, a lightly-crooned ditty which she'd picked up from the radio, a boy-meets-girl, low-volume, summer-sun ballad which repeated and repeated…

C.   THE ROMANCE (PART 2) – suddenly a page break, a large-print heading, a switch in style and shift up tempo, with Saf and Tom as fugitives in a runaway story, outside time. At first by train, full speed to the sea, arriving in a mist where they slipped along the front then out across sand in thick clouds of spray. Finding a beach hut sheltered by rock; warm inside, with tinned food and candles, and the boy listening carefully to her whispered stories. Then sleep, then dreams.

Next on horseback, a Lorna Doone gallop, riding to a hideout in an ivy-thick wood. And the underleaf darkness following a path leading to a waterfall and an iris over green, where they dismounted. Then words in the margin, a list, a box and arrows all over as the writing faltered and boy plus girl walked off into shoulder-high ferns...

The book's last sentence was a single-line statement describing Saf waking, surprised and safe in her white-walled bedroom, returning from her dream.

Saffron Alexander, signed by the author, was finally completed in June 1967. By then Beth had lost all interest. There were regrets, mainly for the task, but as a first-time attempt, it had served its purpose. Sealed in an envelope marked 'strictly private', it went to the bottom of a box beneath her bed where it lay around for years. Because Beth was moving on. She was changing in ways she wrote up in her diary, using as headings a long-list of qualities which described her growing up.

- *Physically*, in the mirror she was taller, slimmer, with breasts and curves filling out. But also uneven with far-from-perfect teeth, hair she couldn't manage, skin-flush patches and a tendency towards voice loss when talking with boys.
- *Emotionally* she watched her own habits, found herself out, reacted and covered up, was driven, impulsive, get-up-and-go. But also sympathetic, she listened well.
- *Socially* aware, with a conscience, she held her friends close; they were her lifeline.
- *Intellectually* she counted her marks, topped most subjects and picked up at once on anything heard.
- *Report-wise* Beth, they said, was promising, conscientious, a pleasing pupil. Her mock exams were good. She was on target.
- *Imaginatively*, in herself, Beth progressed. She changed her approach from twice-daily drills – a tightly-controlled, necessary succession of tests, dates, memorised facts and thumbnail answers – to options, and a new stage of learning.

She'd entered a phase which took her from studying 'Os' to developing her own taste, particularly in reading. She was quick and adaptable, switching between magazine short stories, classic novels and a shortlist of poets – Wordsworth, Hardy and Edward Thomas – following leads that her teacher suggested, approved by her dad. And, as her taste developed, she branched out in verse, picking out favourites copied to her notebook, reread daily, and studied like a script. Poems she recited, at first to herself, mouthing in the mirror, next with John together in the garden, then trying out her friends, beginning with Meg then accompanied by Amy, ending with Rachael. Their responses ranged from listening carefully, to joining in word-perfect, to talking about puzzles and formulae to unpick.

And during that period Beth wrote poems set in nature, looking at landscapes and the passing of the seasons. Composing daily, she recorded her sensations: sunrise and the sounds around the house, the changes in the light, her within-walls routines, as she watched and imagined, writing-in her family together with the keepsakes, objects and pictures which they shared. She listened and she felt good. There were birdcalls, viewpoints and the red-stripe sunsets that glared across the fence. Everywhere, everywhere there was poetry.

And in verse she could say things in a glow, in sing-song, about truth and intercession and global inequality. Because what she called poetry, with its half-tones and waits, feel for loss and uplift shifts, was very close to worship. It touched on something larger. Her poems were for God.

There had always been poetry in what Beth felt in church. It showed in the candles, the flowers on cloth, the light through glass. The people who attended, all friends of her parents, had an elevated, child-round softness to their smiles. Of course they were ordinary as well. Her mother always said that they were free-thinkers who saw all sides, and the church was a home, an almost-private space where they gathered as friends. There was poetry in that as well. In the small things large, the everyday talk, the lack of all pretence. As her mother once said, it was cleanly simple, beautiful and colourful, but not overdone.

"Church is for family," Louise said, as she entered the porch with an armful of flowers on a Saturday afternoon. Behind her Beth, who had a bag across her shoulder, was the bearer of two tightly-wrapped inflorescent bunches.

"So here we are," called Louise. Her voice was firm and expressive with a vaguely northern accent. With her big hips, rounded cheeks and wide-mouthed smile, she filled up the entrance.

Inside the building was large and light. It was brick-built and carpeted in red. There were rows of cushioned seats, a central font, and an apse at the back with children's playthings. At the front was a huge, polished wooden cross which hung above the altar. It was ship's-figurehead-size, handmade, and fitted exactly into a projecting ring of bricks.

"We'll take them to the hall," Louise called, shielding her flowers as she sidestepped through a mock-Gothic door. She held it open with her foot while Beth followed. The room they entered was high-walled and recessed on one side with blue felt boards full of children's artwork. Their pictures included paper-cut rainbows and glitter-smeared angels, moon-faced flowers, stars with arms, houses with teeth plus strange-looking animals in multi-coloured inks. The next wall was plainer, with typed-out notices, a cork board with photos and a shuttered hatch. The other two corners held furniture, including an old scratched piano, a trolley, several folding tables, and between them and backed into the wall, some stacked-up piles of steel-and-canvas chairs.

"Now," said Louise, when they'd laid out the flowers on a table, "do you want to help me? Or...?" She glanced sideways towards a glass door which led upstairs.

"I'd like..." Beth said and paused. She wanted and intended, but when she was with her mother she found herself thinking other things.

Louise smiled, "You go along up there. Then I'll know where you'll be."

When Beth didn't move, Louise called, waving gently, "Go on. I'll be in and out with these." She pointed to the flowers. "And you'll be upstairs, so we can always see each other and call if we need to."

In reply Beth nodded, said her thanks and went out to the staircase. As she climbed to the gallery she could hear Louise winding up the hatch and entering the kitchen. The sounds were familiar: a key in a lock, a cupboard being opened, vases on tiles, a gush of water then a knife edge, scraping. It made her feel oddly restless.

Halfway up, by the hall above, Beth paused to think. She felt her mother's presence, like a hand on her arm. She could hear her below, singing to herself. A sense of separation was urging her on.

At the top, where the staircase doubled back, Beth entered a white-walled corridor. It was cool and narrow and twisted slightly as it ran back to the church. Her bag scraped the wall as she passed by a cross-shaped window; it looked like an arrow-slit in a fort. Reaching the end, she turned down and left, to arrive in a dusty, double-seated space. This was the gallery. It was narrow, wooden-pewed, barred in front, and hung above the porch like a theatre box. From here, seen lengthwise, the whole church was visible. Beth called it the bird's nest.

Sitting, she unzipped her bag and drew out a hand-sized notebook with thick, grey-grained pages. Fingered lightly, they felt like tissue. She leafed through, sampling. The book began with poems, some short, some unfinished, others extending over two or three pages. Carefully decorated with scrolls and stars, they were dated and signed *Elizabeth Jarvis*. After that it was empty.

Her heart fluttered slightly. She could feel the quiet.

In the church below, her mother appeared. She was carrying two cast iron stands with projecting, tray-like ledges. Green squares of oasis filled up the trays. Holding the stands both sides, balanced like torches, Louise placed them. "All right?" she called.

Beth called back, repeating her mother's words as a statement. She didn't want an audience. Louise nodded then disappeared off.

In her absence the church-hush returned. The air was cool and still, and Beth, feeling the silence, returned to her notebook. She stared at a page. There were sounds in her mind, turns and phrases, feelings, expressions and half-heard voices. A poem was coming.

Downstairs her mother reappeared with a spray of brightly-coloured flowers. She laid them in the font and began arranging.

On the balcony Beth was fingering her pen. Beginning slowly, the words began to form; they were shy and evasive but invisibly strong.

Below, using long-stemmed trailers and bulbs, Louise was placing colour against colour: red and red-pink, mixed with purple, offset by creamy-grey and white. Her stands were filling up.

Upstairs there were words, in a line. The poem was developing, with a space around the edges.

"Nearly done," said Louise, stepping back. She considered, then picked out some orange-yellow stems which she moved elsewhere.

Beth kept writing, trying out words. When the last line came, she signed and dated, then put down the pen.

Placing her last flower, Louise faced the altar. "A thing of beauty," she called softly, with a understated smile, "is a joy…"

The lines came back, filling Beth's mind. She knew them by heart.

For both, for now, this was their offering.

Chapter Three

12.2.03

Hello.

Is that you, Beth?

Yes.

It's James. How are you?

Oh, I'm fine. And you?

Pretty good... in fact, very good. And how's the weather?

Not so great, really. Misty, dull, then dull again. What about yours?

Much the same, cloudy and wet. I did some work, but rain stopped play. So how were things at the café?

Very quiet, hardly saw a soul. But that's normal, this time of year. Things don't pick up till nearer Easter.

Yes, I remember, you said. It's a bit like that with gardens, you know. People have to see things flowering before they'll call you.

They do? Well, maybe you should try down here. We've got crocuses and snowdrops everywhere – oh, and the daffs are up.

Sounds like Folkestone's quite far ahead. You've got primroses as well?

Hmm yes, we've had them for a month or two, growing wild around the café. We pick them and put them on the tables. I know we shouldn't, but there are so many. Sometimes I feel a bit mean about it. But then I look out the next day, and they're all flowering again. Maybe it brings them on. What do you think?

Well, that rather depends. With my gardener's hat on I'd say be careful this time of year, don't take too many off. With my own hat on I'd say, go for it.

So you think if we're careful...?

But I'm sure you are.

Well, I'm not so certain about that. The plants get damaged.

Why – are you telling me you're *not* careful?

I am, very! But sometimes, when I'm picking on my own, they get squashed.

Ah, I know the business, I do the same. You have to remember, though, plants are survivors, especially in winter. But are you, if you don't mind me asking, right *in* there amongst the flowers? Can't you choose where you put your feet?

You'd think so, but not really. You see, don't be surprised, but when I pick flowers, I dance. I mean really dance, wildly, all over.

That's interesting. What kind of dance?

Oh, nothing with a name, just bits and pieces. I make up the moves as I go.

Without music? So what do you hear, I mean in your head? Is it like that tune in The Nutcracker – just trying to get it – The Waltz of the Flowers?

Not really. More Cha Cha Cha with the crocuses. Expressive dance really, my own kind, with the sea and the gulls. Sometimes in slow motion.

Wow. Does anyone see you?

I hope… Well, no, I don't think so. Not too many, anyway. I do it early morning and the café's under the cliffs. The staff know, they've told me, but they don't mind. My deputy Sarah's joined me a few times.

So, it's party-on. But seriously, is it every day? Even on a day like this?

Not always, but I did this morning. It was clear first thing, and the moon – I think it woke me up – so I danced – I know this sounds crazy – reciting a poem. Keats's Endymion. A few lines, anyway. It's about the imagination.

Yes, I know it, and I can just see you there. Spring with dancers. Like that Botticelli picture, what's it called… Primavera.

You like that? My dad used to show it to me, in a book. It's very special. I've got a copy he gave me, hanging so I can see it.

My Dad would call it arty-farty. He'd say bin it or chuck it on the fire.

He didn't like it?

Never heard of it. Or maybe that's unfair, because he did read in his own lefty kind of way, but only what *he* wanted to hear about. Anyway, whether or not he'd seen it, he reckoned all art was rubbish. Absolute, total rubbish... He did like Lowry, though. Called it proletarian. I told you about him in a letter.

Yes, I remember. I'm sorry.

That's OK, no need to apologise. I remember I went through a *who the hell does he think he is* phase – my daughter's going through it now – but in the end, it's just fathers and sons. As he would say, 'It's about bringing 'em up, then getting 'em out the door'. That reminds me, have I told you about the youth project I work for?

No, I don't think so. Is that a second job?

Not exactly, I'm there once a month on a Saturday. It's a scheme for what they call disaffected youth, meaning kids with tags, that sort of thing. Nearly all boys, of course. Some of them have done time in prison. They're on probation and have to attend, or go back inside, at least that's the theory. Mostly they do as they please, while I do the gardening.

Oh, that sounds rather difficult. What are they like?

Well, they're not as special as you might think, just ordinary kids. You'd be surprised how sharp some of them are. Half the time they've been bored at school, and that's how they've got into trouble. They're the kind who've bust through everything, so you don't really have anything over them. If they don't feel like it they'll walk away and there's nothing you can do about it.

And you're alone with them?

No, that's not allowed, we're always in pairs. In any case they generally don't turn up, so it's usually just the keen ones. We've been down to one at times, and then we end up talking. Which is what they want, really. There's one boy in particular, I can't say his name, but he's a character. We see him quite a lot. Shall I tell you about him?

Go on. Please.

OK, let's call him K. K always turns up late – one hour, two, it varies. Often we call his mobile, or we knock him up, literally doorstep him, like the press. K's a clown. A gangly, toothy joker. He sings James Brown, badly. The others yell at him to shut up or tell him to rap, so he does, and goes into mime. K's a break-in kid. I remember one story he told about being out all night squeezing through windows, getting so tired he fell asleep in someone's living room. When he woke up he found he'd broken into his own house. I don't know how true that is of course. I do remember him bringing in a stag beetle that climbed all over him, even his face. K didn't seem to mind. He called it Archie and claimed it crawled into houses to bring back jewels. He fed it on cake and dark chocolate. In the end they fell out. He said they'd had a row and Archie did a runner.

Archie sounds a bit like him.

That's true. When K sings, he sticks his arms out like a beetle. I reckon that's how he squeezes into houses.

And how does he do with gardening?

Not much, if he can help it. But he does have his methods. He talks to the plants, seems to want to get to know them. I think they're a substitute family. But you can't get him to pick up a spade. Not that I really care what he does, but you have to go through the motions. My dad used to talk about showing willing, and now I think he had a point. You know, how things come round. I hear myself saying 'kids these days', and 'no respect', and I recognise it's *his* voice I'm using.

I think it changes once you've had children.

Absolutely. You see yourself differently, and them. You know that Bette Davis quote, 'If you've never been hated by your child, you've never been a parent'?

No, I can't say I've heard that one. But I do like her line, 'It should all be bigger than life'.

Yes, 'We don't need the moon, we've got the stars already' – something like that. She's a classic. I can't say I ever liked her, but then she's there to be admired, not loved, I suppose. A bad case of what they call inflation. I hope you're not a fan?

Not much. I do like that one line, but the whole relationship with Joan Crawford was awful.

Bad, bad, then worse. It's the danger of living out your art. Like Ted Hughes and Sylvia Plath – do you like them?

Oh yes. Which reminds me of something I didn't tell you. I wrote a story based on their first meeting and got it published, in a small magazine.

Wow, you must be proud. So you write?

I did, years ago. I suppose I dabble occasionally, even now.

You do? Tell me.

Well, it's not something I think about much, just another of those habits. I write notes to myself about people I see in the café. What he said, she said, where they met, that sort of thing.

Right. So you play consequences.

Doesn't everyone? In their heads, I mean... I just use paper and make it small, so I can stick it on playing cards. I've made up a whole pack. It's a game, a kind of patience where I shuffle and deal, matching them up. Pairs, I call it.

That's interesting.

It's just a game, really.

Sounds like something I used to play. A memory game. Only now, of course, I've completely forgotten... It does have a name.

Pelmanism?

That's it. Thank you, I needed that. Though there's a certain irony there, of course. Anyway – and I hope you don't mind if I say this – I think, with the cards and the dancing, you've got something important, your own private world, and that's great.

Thank you. But James...?

Yes?

Please understand, I may be imaginative but I'm easily hurt. And that means, be careful.

Oh yes, understood. It's all or nothing. That's another thing my dad used to say that I've come round to as I've got older. You show who you are, then it's take it or leave it. But perhaps I should say I want to be careful as well. It does take time.

That's right.

And one other thing...

Yes?

I'm not easily put off. Knock me down and I bounce back.

I think that's good.

And once I commit, that's it.

Me as well.

So on *that* note... As I'm getting tired, and I'm sure you must be, I shall think about everything... But for now, goodnight.

And you'll sleep?

Not for a while, probably. But tomorrow's work so I'll have to. Will you ring tomorrow, or shall I ring you?

I'll ring.

OK.

Goodnight, James.

Goodnight, Beth. By the way…

Yes?

No dancing in the dark. Those crocuses deserve a night off.

Yes, I run them ragged… Tomorrow, then.

Tomorrow.

Goodnight.

Yes, goodnight.

Chapter Four

When Beth first saw the boy, she was seated with Meg and Toby around a fold-out table in the upstairs hall. Placed at the centre of the space, the table was bare, the chairs pushed together and the group – five in all – were gathered like rest-stop travellers. Snatches of organ and voices in unison drifted through the walls.

They were being led in discussion by two softly-spoken women. Annie, the taller, was pale-skinned and watchful with silver-grey hair and perfect teeth. She spoke about the Bible as if it was a picture, a story full of love and passion that she witnessed daily. Clare, who was younger, interjected quietly about world inequality and the efforts of the church.

They'd arrived at the point, usually towards the end, where Beth found herself arguing with her brother. "I know what you think," she called. "You see him as some sort of super referee, up there with a whistle and a book, taking names and sending people off."

"You don't know."

"But isn't that what you think?"

"Not much."

"So how *do* you see God?"

"More like a big sis."

"Oh, Toby, that's not fair."

Annie intervened, explaining that people in the world held different views, mentioning the gospels and inviting reflection.

Clare, who was polishing her glasses, replaced them on her nose. "Of course," she said quietly, "for some football's a religion, they worship their team."

"But isn't that all wrong?" asked Beth. She looked quickly about the room, checking for listeners. When she was with the group, words popped out before she knew it.

"Quite harsh, yes," responded Clare. "I'm saying it's a vanity, which isn't very nice."

Beth coloured. "I was talking about football, it being so important. I wasn't criticising what you said..."

Again Annie mediated, talking about feelings and strongly-held views.

"But it's *so* competitive," said Meg, wrinkling her brow.

"What do you think, Toby?" invited Annie.

Toby hesitated. He was round-faced and serious with brown curly hair and a rash across his forehead. "You want to know about football?"

"About football and faith. Do some people take it too far? Are they using it as a kind of religion?"

Toby stared at his questioner. His eyes were large and red around the rims. "Football's a game," he said slowly, "but religion's different. One's in two halves, the other's all the time."

The group fell silent.

"Short-term, and long-term," said Clare.

"That's good Toby, good," put in Meg.

"So one's for show," added Beth, "the other's hidden."

And it was then, as she spoke, that the new boy arrived.

He was light-haired and slight and held himself forward, at an angle, with his grey-green eyes turned to one side. His face was narrow, long in the chin and slightly mischievous. As he entered he ducked, in a semi-humorous gesture, as if the door was low. Behind him, his mother followed. She wore a pink knee-length dress, cut to her figure and tightly belted. Her small round face was gently smiley.

"Ah, Mrs Bright?" asked Annie, rising in her seat and extending her hand. The women greeted with Clare joining in and the mother responding, waving vaguely towards her son.

"So sorry. I'm Neane, by the way, and this is Conrad. So sorry if we're late!" Here she directed a look towards her son, who had steered to one side, attaching himself to the radiator.

Clare drew up an empty chair, urging Conrad to join them. Beth watched the mother apologise again, and offer her son a coat, coupled with a caution, before bowing out.

"Please join us," Clare repeated, gently.

Looking surprised, the boy came forward. "May I?" he asked, glancing around.

"Please do."

He nodded. Suddenly he was older, long-faced and alert, and he dropped his head, smiling. "Thank you," he said, confidingly.

Annie welcomed, using first names, and reminded the group of their discussion. "So what do we think," she asked, "is sport these days all fine and healthy, or far too aggressive?"

Beth felt the pressure to answer. She'd views of course, mainly about tennis, and she knew the other two probably wouldn't offer, but the new boy's presence made her wary. She wondered how her words might sound, taken out of context. Or what might come up. Even though his eyes were turned away, suddenly she was out there, in public.

"What do *you* think, Beth?" prompted Annie.

The question brought her back. "It depends on the person," she replied, "who's doing it and why."

"I see. Do you mean it's a matter of temperament?"

"Well, I think so. A lot of sport is against the clock, isn't it? Or it's about doing it super-well."

Conrad looked up, "When I run, I run against myself."

"That's interesting," said Clare. "Do you run a lot?"

"I do, when I feel like it, but sometimes I don't."

"I see. So would I be right in thinking that you run alone?"

"Yes, when no one's around," he replied, and Beth felt the pause. There was a coiled up silence somewhere inside, a wait in the dark.

Annie put in a thought about training, comparing it to prayer. "It doesn't always come that easily," she said. "Sometimes you have to build up to it."

Meg chipped in, "I swim with a club," she said, looking at Clare. "It does us good, and we all get on. Anyone can come along."

"I like football," Toby grinned, "when we win."

Beth heard herself objecting. She began, using words like 'tribal' and 'ritual' then stopped. "But I suppose you could say football's just a game," she added, glancing at her brother.

The new boy smiled, "My mother says it's all about money. Money instead of God."

"But do you want money?" Beth found herself asking.

Conrad looked straight across the table. "Not instead."

She nodded.

"Because I'd rather run," he added, speaking quietly as if they were alone. "It's out of the ordinary." His voice sounded firm but also rather child-like. Behind his words was a range of possibilities, something with shape and promise. They were the first line to a poem.

OUT OF THE ORDINARY

Out of the ordinary,
you came
when least expected,
after the swordplay,
the brother-sister cut and thrust,
into the sunlight.

Autumn boy,
your colours came too soon
too rich for naming,
too soft to touch
too light to catch.

No fuss, no flourish,
Your business
Was as natural as the forest,
You're A to B
Like season to season,
A steady pace,
Oblivious.

I know you saw me
because as you ran
you breathed a "Hiya,"
that made your rhythm falter.
But I'm the one
left breathless
by the smile in your eyes.

Somewhere you're running on,
the silence behind you
is full now.

Your tracks
cut deep.

Elizabeth Jarvis

"So it's nothing to do with competition – the other runners don't count?"

Beth and Conrad were jogging by a hedge along a brown-yellow farm track between a cornfield and a thin clump of trees. It was early morning, the sky was clear and the air was cold and still. A rabbit scuttled away beneath bushes.

"Not when it's distance," he called back. His thin, elastic body moved easily over stone and mud. Beth ran with effort.

"But you time yourself?"

Conrad flashed a wristwatch.

"So it's about difficulty?"

"Only a bit," he called.

Their feet broke step, taking turns to jump-stride a ditch. As they reached a low ridge, Beth dropped back. The boy waved on and they cut across grass to arrive at a gate into trees. A thin yellow arrow painted on a post pointed forward.

"Or is it... about the route?" She was sweating now.

Conrad nodded, as he reached over wood to fumble with a metal catch. "Cross-country," he said, hauling back the gate, "is about getting there."

Entering the trees, they slowed slightly as they sidestepped a pool then ran side by side down a cool, shadowy avenue. Here they were alone.

"This way?" she gasped, as they arrived at a clearing and a fork.

"Long or short?"

Beth stood, hands on hips, gathering her breath, "Could you wait?" Her request sounded edgy.

Conrad stared forward, jogging on the spot.

"OK," she said, looking upward, searching for colour. There were cloud-streaks now with breaks, a low-level sun and a still-visible, gibbous moon. Like her feelings, the weather wasn't certain.

"The long way," she said.

They moved to the right following a line of twisted fence posts. The trees thinned out and they emerged above a scooped-out pit. It was grey and stony, tufted with grass. At the bottom was a mud-patch and a circle of standing water.

"Watch out!" called Conrad as he scrambled over a rotted stump. Beth followed, struggling slightly. They curved around the pit, following an uneven, rock-strewn track. On one side it was steep; on the other there were nettles and loose twists of wire.

As they came to a dip, Beth mis-stepped and stumbled forward. She gave a short, yelping shout as she lost her footing. The stones gave way and she slid into the pit. "Oh... oh!" she called, rolling sideways. Throwing out her arms, she slewed down, hitting rocks as she went. At the bottom she landed with one leg in the pool. Dust swirled up as she lay there, unmoving.

Conrad turned and scrambled down, shouting. There was blood smeared across her arms and down her leg. Her breath was shallow and her eyes were shut. "Beth! Beth!" he cried, shaking her shoulder.

She groaned.

"Are you all right?"

Her face remained pale and closed.

"Beth! Say something!"

Her eyes flicked open. They searched across his face. "Doesn't hurt," she said softly.

His hand touched her cheek. "You've got to be all right," he said, fiercely.

A slow smile passed across her face, "Don't worry, I'm OK."

"You sure?"

"Yes. You helped."

"Thank goodness." His head dipped forward and he kissed her on the brow.

Beth's arms came up and closed around his shoulders. "Thank you," she said quietly, allowing him to lift her.

****

"But you don't run anymore?" said James, sitting by the window of The Shorespot Café.

Beth smiled, "Walking's good enough for me."

Outside the sun was rising on a silver-blue sea. The air was clear and they could see down the slope, looking out across trees and bushes to a long sweep of gravel and a concrete jetty. White-flecked waves were lapping around its sides.

"Well, this is the place," he said. "Just chill out, enjoy the view."

"You should have seen it before, it was a greasy spoon."

"Really? You must have done a lot to make it like this."

"Money, time, effort. I practically lived here when I set it up."

"Sounds hard. But I guess it was something else to think about."

"Could say."

"So, everything I see here is *you*, in a way?"

She nodded, "My business, yes."

James looked around the café. Where they were sitting, soft light flowed in from the long picture window, further back the chairs and tables were lit from above by a skylight. On the tables there were flowers in vases, scented candles and leaflets advertising local exhibitions. The walls were hung with original artworks. "And those are yours?" asked James, pointing to a laminated photo-collage showing plants and birds, people laughing and overgrown, sunlit paths.

"Taken on my walks."

He rose to take a look, "Customers, perhaps?"

"Those are my girls, at the front. Behind, friends."

She ran through the names then answered questions. His eyes absorbed it all. "And these paths? Are they close by?"

"Why yes, all round the café." She looked out at the sea. It was stirring and shining. The horizon was streaked with grey-white sunlight.

"Would you care to take a walk?" she asked, head to one side. She was playing him now, judging his mood. "The views are good."

"Definitely," he nodded, staring ahead. "But first, I'd like to try something." Dropping his eyes, James frowned. He seemed to be looking inward, searching for a clue. "There's no music," he began, raising his eyes, "but then again, there is the sea…"

They both looked out. "Care to dance?" he asked suddenly, offering

69

his hand.

Beth smiled and accepted. She allowed herself to be led to a small, shiny, square-tiled dance floor.

"You have to imagine," he said.

Beth angled back her head: "I can hear the track." An arm went around her waist, and breathing together they began to dance.

"You remember?" he said quietly.

She answered, but her words seemed unimportant. Of course, whatever they said, it was all about feel – only that, and the actions. Her body, like his, was circling quietly.

So they turned and shuffled, swaying slightly, linked without thought. They were on the dance floor, moving in silence, watching the sea.

When they left the café it was still early. There was ice in the hollows concealed beneath bushes and the grass was white. They followed a road that turned into gravel. Reaching a track that ran beneath the cliffs, they stepped across patches of frost-hardened mud.

"Do you walk this often?" asked James.

"In the summer, yes. Not when it's like this."

On the flat they paused looking out then moved on holding hands, adjusting as they went. When the path narrowed they kept in touch by talking or pointing out features, sometimes stopping to look back where they'd come.

"It's a wild spot," said James, and Beth nodded. Walking with him was an adventure.

They turned a corner and entered an area full of boulders and mud slides and prickly vegetation. The path dropped suddenly. Looking down, they could make out a rock-fringed bay with a stream to the sea.

"Do you want to go on?" Beth asked.

"Of course, as long as you do."

The sun had clouded over. A wind had got up and the sea was cresting. The cries of seagulls echoed from the rocks.

Helping each other, they descended. The path was slippery and the ground in places had hollowed to a drop. At one point James stumbled, steadying himself against a tree, at another Beth led across a stream, halfway down they zigzagged over scree to arrive at a ridge, below which, at a rest spot, they caught their breath.

"Let's sit," she said, hitching side-saddle onto rock, "and enjoy."

James joined her. "Happy?" he asked, squeezing her hand.

"Oh yes."

"Mind, it's still quite a drop," he said, stretching sideways to peer to the bottom.

Beth leaned over, holding his arm. The rock here was sheer. Below, it opened to a thin strip of water caught between cliffs. At the sea end a huge, steeply-sloping block held out the waves. Behind it the inlet was still. Its dark, enclosed surface seemed almost lifeless.

James looked up. "So what's the story there?" he asked, pointing along a fenced-off spur. A faded sign said *Danger* and, beneath that, *Lover's Leap*.

Beth's expression flattened. "A woman who drowned, I believe."

"You mean she jumped?"

"Not exactly, the story is she climbed down to a boat."

"To escape with her lover?"

"She tried."

"So what happened?"

Beth shook her head. "The weather changed as they rowed out to sea, at least that's the story, and they both drowned."

"Ah, doomed love."

"Well, romantic, anyway," she said, shivering slightly.

The wind was gusting. It came and went, funnelled by the rocks. A deep, insistent surf-noise was rising up the cliff.

"But do you think it really happened?" he asked.

"Probably, but then does it matter? It's true to life, that's all."

"You think so?"

"Don't you?"

"Well, I'm not a cynic. But I do think we should take nothing for granted."

"So you don't believe the stories?"

"Of course, all lovers *have* to die."

Beth laughed. "But not..." she said, cutting herself off.

"Or at least, it's like that in youth," he continued. "...*trust me*."

She smiled and pushed in closer, "But then sometimes... not often, but sometimes…" She paused, searching for words, "People meet and surprise-surprise, things happen."

In reply James touched her lightly. At first on her hand, saying nothing; then palm-flat, grinning, smoothing back her hair, shifting to her cheek, her shoulder and dropping to her breast, as his mouth met hers.

They rocked back and forth, kissing; then repeated, in a clench. Their faces had softened and their movements slowed. They were there, together, and nothing seemed to matter. No one could see them and they touched and they kissed, searching for pleasure, simply, as it happened, and because they could.

The tide was going out when they reached the shoreline. They followed the stream, sliding on gravel. The wind now was blustery and the clouds were low. In the distance the surf was kicking up. Bare rafts of rock showed around the headland.

"We can go out there," said Beth, waving forward. A few spots of rain mixed with spray flew in from the sea.

"Is that wise?" asked James, holding out his hand.

"We can get round the point to the café."

"If that's quicker."

Beth confirmed. She kissed him, once, twice and led onto the rocks. To begin with they simply stood, plotting a route, but when the cold drove them on they made their way out. Firstly on the flat and then, braced against the wind, across cracked, uneven surfaces. There were flurries now, some of them hail, driving from the sea. They called out and laughed, braving the weather. At a channel they slowed, choosing a detour, by a stack they ducked down, when they neared the headland they looked about – mostly they kept on. Reaching the point, they were absorbed by sound: the surf-roar, the wind, the seabirds crying. They were out there, alone.

As they entered the next bay, Beth waved towards the cliffs: "There's a place here," she called, "out of the wind."

She steered to one side, closing on rock. As she pointed towards an overhang, the rain grew heavier. "This way!" she yelled, pushing on. Water filled the air. Whipped up by the wind, it soaked through their hair, beating on their backs. They scrambled for the cliffs, reaching the overhang where Beth pulled him in. "We're here!" she shouted, and her voice echoed briefly. Suddenly it was quiet.

Blinking, James looked about. They'd arrived in a short, scooped-out cave with a double-pillared entrance. It was tall and egg-shaped, and level underfoot. Along one side the rock dipped to a shadowy pool. A small vase of withered flowers stood by the poolside. Beside it a burnt-down candle had hardened onto rock. A few dead flowers had fallen into water.

"What is this place?" James asked. "Does it have a name?" His voice echoed slightly in the dark.

Beth hushed him. She motioned to the opposite wall where a fold in the rock acted as a seat. Beside it a squared-off stone doubled as a table. At one end, incised into rock, the stone was decorated with an Ichthys.

"The Chapel," she said quietly.

****

A banner behind the stage read LIVE LIFE FOR JESUS. Stretched like a sail, it was gold on black, bordered by red. A web of wires, fixed to the edges, led back to wall hooks. Lit from all sides, the banner appeared to be afloat.

Front stage was the show. It had begun with recorded hymns, followed by an organ fanfare and the entry of a woman in a high-necked gown. She'd called on the Lord quoting scripture then welcomed the choir: all long-sleeved, smiling and shiny, in white.

"Oh yes, hear the Gospel," the woman cried, and the choir launched off into an upbeat number, driven from behind by floor-shaking notes punched out from the organ.

They ran through three more, a high-voiced solo sung by a boy in a suit, a foot-tapping, handclapping acapella and a stand-up rerun of the big-tune opener.

"And now," cried the woman, unclipping her mike, "I'd like you to welcome the man you've all been waiting for, please put your hands together for your testifying preacher, Luke Patrick Martin!"

At the back, Beth and Conrad were applauding. The audience roar had brought them to their feet.

A dance of coloured lights wheeled across the stage, the organ struck up and a tall man with a long-faced stare strode to the microphone. He was wearing a white jacket speckled with gold, a loose red shirt and black flares. His thick, wavy, silver-blond hair fell to his shoulders. He raised one hand, pronouncing a blessing. "You are the children of light. Let the Love and the Truth and the Power of the Good Lord Jesus come upon you."

A man called out, throwing up his arms. His words set off others, shouting to the ceiling. A girl next to Beth went down on her knees, sobbing.

Backed by the organ, the preacher began. His voice was low-toned and deeply resonant, pausing between questions and inviting thought. As he worked his theme – the great clash of opposites – his delivery sharpened: there was danger in what he said. Using words like *shameful* and *unwholesome*, he spoke of exposure, of falling and failing and being cast out. Raising his arms, he issued warnings of the world led astray, the wrong path chosen, the opportunities lost and the judgement soon to come. "It has to stop!" he cried, standing tall. The organ faded as he invited them to pray.

Beth felt pressure in the gap that followed. There was power here and calm. The hall was full of fear and hurt and locked-down excitement. She wondered about Conrad: was he shivering like her?

The prayers were for healing. The voice from the front dropped to a silk-smooth whisper, delivered close-mike. His heartfelt words filled the hall. Afterwards he stood back, absorbed in thought, while the long-gowned woman cued in the choir. They sang in parts, arm-swinging gently while a collection was taken. He blessed their gifts as some flowers appeared, added a few prayers then left the stage, waving.

When the interval arrived, Beth and Conrad stepped outside.

"What do you think?" she asked, sipping lemon barley.

Conrad grinned: "It's good. Very." His face, half-lit by a streetlamp, was focused forward.

"So, you think we're winning," she said.

"How do you mean?"

"Just a way of speaking, that's all. You're enjoying it?"

"Absolutely. Aren't you?"

"It's all right. If you are, I am."

74

"I thought you were moved."

"Oh yes. It's a bit footbally, but I'm getting there."

"I found it an experience."

"Well, yes, it *is* exciting."

"Yes, the Living Word."

Beth drained her glass, saying nothing.

Conrad smiled. "God's judgement," he said quietly, regarding her with a fixed expression, "sees all. Nothing, absolutely nothing, ever escapes him."

In her dreams that night Beth heard her dad talking about God. He was with her, by her side. They were together in the garden, sitting on the wall – but also in a painting, a scene from the past with eyes behind leaves, green men carved in stone and bird-faced creatures peeping out of holes. The lawn smelled damp.

"His wildness and wisdom…" began John, and she saw herself climbing. He was there as her guide, leading upward. "Silent and unknown," he continued as they spread their wings, rising up a cliff.

The dream switched to church. They were upstairs in what she called the bird's nest. Looking down they saw purple and red. An organ began playing, leading a hymn. "Many colours, many faces," her father sang, as balloon-mouthed notes floated up. The congregation followed, ascending slowly. Each in a bubble, they were shaped like flowers.

"The great as-if," sang John and the scene changed to water. There were images, reflections and shadows on the surface. Beneath that, in the depths, there were thin-faced ghosts. They swayed back and forth, touching gently. She was down there, and she wasn't, and the shades were all around.

A prayer began. The words were simple, but repeated: "We thank you Father for our dreams." Then John read the lesson. It came out as a story of birds and animals, chatting. A warm glow of candles filled the air, mixed with roses, richly scented. They were at home, at supper, and their plates were full of petals.

John stood up, reciting a poem, and took her in his arms. He was carrying her, lifted like a bride, up, up. Then air, then sun, then birdsong beginning, and eyes opening slowly, turning slowly like the pages of a book.

"In a different world," said her dad, quietly, and they walked out in the garden, with sunlight all around, as they listened to the silence…

The next day, Beth's birthday, Conrad was there. He'd sneaked into college and slept on her floor staying there as a friend, without of course anything happening. They trusted all the way. Because what others called dating they saw as sharing, an intimate, honest, truth-seeking openness. A togetherness before God.

When Beth first woke, Conrad was standing by the steps just outside the window. He was still and impressive with his face angled back and his eyes half-closed. There was uplift about him and a weight of intention, watching for the way. She was aware of him out there, calmly separate and self-directed. And when he came back in, he still seemed to be thinking. Hoping for a surprise, she didn't remind him.

Over breakfast Beth held back. The dream, though backgrounded, was still half with her. It came between them, softly, making her uneasy. So when they talked about the gathering, she was careful. It was almost as if the service hadn't really happened. The moment had passed, she'd been there, taken in the feeling and now was moving on. "Well, it *was* an experience," she said, trying to catch his eye. "And I did feel the love, by the end."

"I'm pleased," he replied, and they shared a short reading before going out.

In the morning they walked. Beth led off, following a route which she hoped might interest him. They passed by colleges with Beth naming some and crossed a park, with the weather brightening, to turn down some steps and arrive at the riverside. Here they wandered by trees to reach a built-out platform with huts and a boathouse. She noticed how his mood seemed to lighten as they looked across water.

Conrad took a fancy to hiring a boat, calling out "Watch me," when she asked about rowing. He paid a man in leather for oars and a ticket then pretended to be wobbly as they pushed off from land.

"Back by twelve," the man called, flatly. Conrad frowned and dipped the oars.

"So you *can* row," Beth said slyly as they rounded a bend and passed beneath a willow. Its fingers brushed her lightly, like a web.

"Good exercise," he said, shifting position. His knuckles gleamed white where he gripped the oars.

Beth fell silent. They were face to face, with Conrad pulling strokes. He was calm and easy and kept his breathing low. An ironic smile played about his lips, almost as if he was awaiting orders. Beth wondered whether the boat trip, without anything being said, was his way of taking notice. They passed beneath a brick-built bridge, forking off along a backwater to arrive at a lake. Screened by trees, its surface was absolutely still. There were small tussocks both sides, some flat-leaved water plants and an overgrown island at the centre.

Conrad raised the oars. As the boat began to turn, he gazed across the water. "To the island?" he asked and Beth nodded. He had rolled up his sleeves exposing flesh. His long, loosely-jointed body was whiplash thin.

"We can land there," she said, "round the back."

"You want to?"

"If you don't mind the rowing."

Conrad grunted. "Just tell me one of your stories."

"You'd like that?"

He dipped in his oars, "Go ahead."

Beth lowered her fingers into water. Its coolness tingled slightly. The sun was there filling up her head. She sat back, picturing her other birthdays and her dad in the garden. It reminded her of worship.

"It's called Shipwreck," she began. "It's a dream about a brother and sister playing in a garden. They're sailing, with the girl as captain, on the rockery. When a storm gets up the ship goes down. But the children, as children always do, escape. They end up as castaways on the lawn." She paused, watching the ripples, while Conrad pulled on the oars. "And because they believe, things happen. So they climb to the tree house and while they're up there, a cloud comes over. And suddenly, as if they're asleep, everything blacks out. They hear a warning cry and the flap of wings, and realise it's a bird. A huge, fire-crested one they've heard about in stories." She laughed. Conrad kept rowing. "So the bird carries them up, up, to a boat in the sky. And they sail away for a year and a day, or something like that." She paused again, hand in water, while Conrad swung the oars. "Then – let me think – the bird returns, the cry come back and a storm gets up. It all blacks out, and lightning strikes.

Everything burns up completely, the ship, the bird, all wiped out in a fireball. But of course it's a story, so the children escape. They end up as castaways back on the lawn. And it all begins again with the girl as captain standing on the rockery, looking out across the garden..."

Beth's hand trailed in water. Conrad continued rowing. By the time they arrived, it was lunchtime, the sun was shining and they were alone on the island.

It seemed best now if she didn't mention her birthday.

****

When Beth and James left The Chapel the rain had stopped. A thin white glare was spreading over water. There were faint flecks and spills on rocks. Further out, the sea was greyly smooth, like linen. "I'm drying out," she called as they scrambled across pebbles to the sea's edge. Their feet slipped and scrunched and they held on to each other with a sense of release, as if they'd been rescued. They were outdoors, the sky was clearing and they'd made it through.

Facing the water, James put his arm around her waist. "Tide's high," he said, "soon be turning."

Beth examined the view. It was much like a painting. "It's as if everything's hanging, just for a second."

James laughed, "Well, let's keep watching." He looked down to where the waves were hissing and bubbling over stones. "Remember water's different, it doesn't settle."

"Yes," said Beth. She leaned into his side: "It makes you want to get into a boat and row – go way, way out to the horizon." A silver-grey shaft of sunlight cut across the bay. Birds called out and the air seemed to shine.

James squeezed her hand then crouched down, fingering the stones.

"What're you doing?" she asked.

"Looking for skimmers," he said, scooping up a handful of coin-shaped pebbles. Choosing one, he leaned sideways and flicked it across the waves. The stone hop-skip-jumped before disappearing into water.

"That's fun," she said.

He picked up another and threw. Hitting a swell, it bounced high, spun, and dropped out of sight. "Only one jump," he said, shaking his head. He tried a few more skims, kicking up a line of white splashes. Beth, counting the hits, urged him on. He varied his methods from underarm to overarm then, twisting, curled a throw behind his back.

"Tricky," she cried, clapping her hands. "But what about distance?" she asked, pointing to the horizon. "Can you do that?"

James scooped up a handful and rocked back on his heels. "Up and under," he called and scattered his pebbles in one clean throw. They sailed out and landed in a group, plopping and pricking the surface.

Beth laughed. "I couldn't do that. It's too far."

"Maybe you could, with practice."

"I doubt it."

"I think you could."

"Not me, I was never any good at things like that." Her mind flashed back to a scene in a field with her dad.

"Why not? I could show you."

"No, I'd rather... But wait," she said, "there is something, from childhood," she stepped up to the water's edge. "How about if I do this?" she called, shifting back and forward to avoid the waves. As she called and shifted, a soft spluttering wash pooled about her feet. "Can't catch me, Mr Sea," she sang, dodging. "It's a great game," she called again, as a white line ebbed and flowed, hissing on shingle.

A larger wave rolled in, driving her back. It broke in a rush, spraying her heels and causing her to jump. "Oh!" she cried, slipping on weed. As she went down, James stretched out and pulled her up. "Thank you, my knight," she called and dusted herself off. She was by his side now, breathing hard, with her eyes fixed on water.

"Shall we take a dip?" he asked suddenly.

Beth stared from James to the sea, "Isn't it freezing?"

"Almost certainly, but I'm willing."

She looked around quickly. The beach was empty and suddenly it seemed they were out there with the elements, alone and free, in a world without people. "You really want to?"

"As long as you're up for it."

"That's crazy."

"Yes."

A wave rushed in, rising on gravel. It filled and foamed and boiled over, then with an abrupt, gurgling hiss sank back to nothing.

"OK," she said, "you're on."

As they pulled off their clothes the sea swell dropped and a faint glow widened across the surface. The sky was clearing and the air was thin and dream-like. Above them a small flock of birds cried out. Their shadows moved like ghosts on water. There was no one with them.

When they waded out, the first shock of cold took away Beth's breath. Holding his arm, she stepped across stones. The stones turned to sand and she moved more easily. As the water deepened her body firmed up. Her feet went forward, pushing into softness. Her toes and her fingertips tingled; she was in the flow. If there was exposure, it had left her now. She was out here with him, feeling the love, and the tide-change had begun. The cold below had become a kind of wrap-around warmth. The sea, and her excitement, was filling her up. It closed around her thighs and pushed her off. Suddenly she was lifted and her insides freed; the waters held her. For her this was everything – passion in action, desire for James and the fullness of God. She was swimming out naked, with the sun on her back, and only he could see her.

****

After leading all the way in the Baptist College run, Conrad stood on the seminary steps, bowing his head. The applause fed his smile, kept hidden, as he gave thanks through prayer. He'd done his personal best. It made him glad to be.

"You were great," said Beth as he joined her in the crowd. "I watched you from the roof."

Conrad towelled down his cheeks. He was half a head higher than her; his jaw was long, sweat bathed his forehead and he'd part-shaved his head. With his sucked-in cheeks and faraway look, he seemed like a cross between a monk and a soldier.

He thanked her, unsmilingly.

"First by a mile. You must have flown."

"Good, eh?" he flashed.

Beth nodded shyly.

"I imagined I'd jets on my feet," he added. A little-boy niceness had entered his voice.

"They say it's a record," she said, taking his towel.

"Thank you. I'm grateful," he replied, lowering his head.

Beth glanced over. She wondered how he felt. He was staring rather blankly towards the ground. His face suggested prayer.

"Run with endurance the race set before us," he said quietly, rubbing his legs, "Hebrews 12:1."

His tutor came up, a small, unkempt man with horn-rimmed glasses, and they shook hands. Antony used the phrase *ne plus ultra*, eyeing his protégé. He hoped he would see him, he said, at the forefront of the movement. When introduced to Beth, he held out his hand, offering an enthusiastic welcome. Two other men appeared, both young. Like Conrad, they were tall and rangy. As they talked their eyes shifted around. They joked with Conrad, calling him 'the kid' and admiring his fitness.

A bell rang. "Time to eat," Antony declared. His eyes were twinkly and directed towards Conrad. Beth thought him fun, and surprising.

In the refectory they all bowed their heads while grace was said. Over the meal Conrad answered questions, emphasising his thoughts with tongue-in-cheek gestures. "It all comes back," he told his tutor, "to beliefs and habits, and how we are with God."

Later, after eating, he went quiet. While the others told stories he played with his placemat then reached beneath the table and held Beth's hand. They sat there undetected, showing nothing. It was as if they were plugged in to an invisible circuit. While the plates were cleared they remained linked until another bell rang and they unhanded. Conrad leaned close to her ear. "Shall we go?" he said quietly, as if he was asking her to a party.

They rose, made their excuses and walked off together, pausing by the door. "Outside?" he enquired. She nodded and they slipped out quietly.

He led, at first without touching, along a curving path between shrubs and borders. When they reached a building he turned through an arch and they entered a walled-in garden. "This way," he said, taking her hand. "You'll see."

They walked between walls of bamboo and head-high hedges. Turning right, they climbed some shallow steps. Somewhere in the leaves a bird cried out. The path went deeper, arriving at an enclosure. Here, at the centre, screened-off by branches, they came across a polished steel sculpture.

"This is where I come," he said, "when I want to think."

The sculpture seemed to glow. It was flat on top with a small, bubbling jet and a swirl of slowly turning water. The pool ran out, flooding down the sides to a basin below. It passed down the metal in a smoothly shifting, silent curtain. They stood side by side watching the flow.

Conrad lifted his head, "I've plans, things I'm working on." He smiled. "Let me show you." Stepping forward, he rolled up his sleeves and shoved his hands into water, holding them there with a fixed expression. His flesh turned white, dividing the flow. "I mean to stand up," he called, "and speak out, make an impression, get people thinking." He spread his hands wider. The water spurted out, soaking his strong, sinewy arms. It bubbled and ran, dripping from his elbows. "It's a promise I made," he said, stepping back suddenly, "in the sight of God."

Beth felt his passion. It was hot and cold and shivery all over. He was making his vow.

Conrad held his arms out, rocking slightly. "Do you think that's possible, as a minister, to change hearts and minds?"

"Oh yes," she replied, breathing quickly. "Definitely."

"And would you – can you find it in your heart – to help me do that?"

Beth's eyes widened, "Of course, I'll do anything. But how?"

"A joint project, for life. We'd manage it together."

"Conrad, you mean…?"

He dropped his arms to his sides. Speaking hoarsely, he addressed her: "I'd like to ask, invite you, if it's possible. Can we be engaged?"

Beth blushed. "It's a surprise, I didn't expect…" Suddenly she rallied, "A lovely one, though."

He stood there, unmoving. She reached out and placed one hand in the fountain.

"Together," she said, as the water parted and Conrad joined her. They locked hands in the flow "We're engaged," she said as the silent rush of water curled and bubbled, pulling at their flesh.

It was God's will, he told her, on the first day of their honeymoon. "He

---

Isaiah 40:31 'But they that wait upon the Lord
shall renew their strength'

Elizabeth Mary Jarvis
and
Conrad Mark Bright

request the pleasure of your company
at the Christian celebration of their sacred union
in the eyes of God

Saturday, the sixth of September
nineteen hundred and seventy five
eleven o'clock in the morning
St Martha's Church
Old Lane Hedbury
IP29OT

Reception to follow

---

chose us to be here," Conrad said as they left the hotel.

His tone surprised her. They'd arranged it in a rush, with talk about the beach: unspoilt, Conrad said, with deep clean water and runs to the point. He'd checked it with friends and knew it would be right. In any case, as he said, this was their moment. But when they arrived it had turned out rather differently. It seemed there was a week-long evangelical gathering, and suddenly they were booked in.

Their route to the meeting ran along the front. On the way there, Beth walked slowly. She looked over at her husband: his eyes were fixed forward, talking as he went.

Turning her head, she could feel the wind playing on her face. It sharpened her awareness. Last night's gale was gradually dying down. A fine drift of sand had lodged itself in cracks and was now blowing loose, across the pavement. As they passed a shelter she noticed large-print posters with headshots of worshippers. They were all smiling nicely. On one wall, a half-torn white-and-red banner announced this year's line-up.

By Conrad's remarks she'd understood something: he'd come here with intention. "So you *know* where it is," she said as he led to a large glass building decorated with cloth-strip crosses.

"See, it's busy," he declared, pointing to the people on the steps. There was music issuing from a balcony above. Every so often a door opened and voices blared out.

"Conrad, please," said Beth, stopping, "I don't know about this."

He angled his head away. "You don't know?" he repeated, suddenly quiet. "You mean you don't want to go on?"

She struggled for words. In her heart she was divided, part of her was willing – this was their honeymoon so she wanted it to work – and part of her was astonished. It seemed like he'd carried her off, "I'm just not sure."

He turned his grey-green eyes in her direction; they were red-rimmed and watery. "It's important. God understands everything we do. It hurts when we deny Him."

Beth bowed her head and held out her hand. Conrad took it, unsmiling, and they walked in together saying nothing.

It was God's will, she told herself for the next five years.

When she visited her dad she didn't talk about *him*. Sometimes, on their walks, she touched on arrangements, on calendar events and festivals with readings and services and meetings in their house, or she told of vigils and late-night prayers. But when John took her hand and they looked out for animals or name-checked plants, she felt something moving – tears or something deeper – and, remembering her poetry, dropped into silence.

When she saw Louise, she didn't mention marriage. At church they kept themselves busy cleaning into corners, putting up notices and cutting flowers. Now she was older she could see how things were: the new life, and the old. The church she'd come from was a home, a place she could sit and think and dream of understanding, where ideas were welcome and people shared. She could see it in her mother with her ease of acceptance and eye out for others, and in all those who remembered and took time to greet her, especially her old teachers, Annie and Clare.

Also, on the phone or in letters, she talked about commitment. To her brother she hinted at effort and the struggle to stay up. With Meg she shared faith, how Conrad had the Call, how his ministry was expanding. For Rachael and Amy she focused on the new house in Folkestone and having children. And even with Charlie she talked about girlhood, and the difference she was finding.

It was God's will, too, that Conrad was angry.

A raw, dark anger not seen by others, a spark of excitement or outrage, a sudden switch in tone and fist to the table. And immediately the words, the not-me excuses of a little boy wronged. Then the chair back and door shut, followed by footsteps on gravel and the car driven off.

And the darkness, cornered; long days apart or together without feeling, and the household, still divided, in silence, with its tasks and its routines.

Then the next five years writing stories, in secret, for herself. Drafts on paper kept in envelopes and moved between drawers – all dark, all unfinished – with dead-end settings and out-of-sorts talk. Stories of domestics that broke off mid-sentence, meetings with strangers, and one-page diaries about women abandoned. In them she was alone.

And then came a piece that she handwrote slowly, and kept well-hidden, a journey into otherness which she thought about so often it almost took her over, a place she'd finally come to, full of simple fear.

And that was God's will as well.

A HOUSEKEEPER'S TALE   by Saffron A

Theresa was a housekeeper. She worked in her master's house but she lived below in a small dark basement. Often at night she heard him, walking overhead. It wasn't just the slow shuffling tread that made her shiver. She knew he was up there, eyes to the floor, peering through the cracks. In her dreams she saw a big-bodied animal, sniffing; the paws against ice, the claws breaking through.

She had never met her master. But in his absence she heard him all around. He was a singer who had trained his voice to imitate life. As part of his practice, he sang against the birds, and his grace notes were perfect. With the animals he could growl and go low, grunt warnings, chatter, purr, or trumpet in chorus. It seemed he was everywhere, rustling in the bushes or white-water gurgling, running with the flow. Not just in the footfalls and breathings that stirred the empty house, but in the other songs, more mysterious and wild. He could call across the hills, dark to light; by day he was the wind, shifting through branches; at evening, by the sea, he drifted with the spray.

His name was A. She'd read it on his letters. Holding the envelopes to the light and studying the postcodes, she wondered. People wrote, repeatedly it seemed. Sometimes she speculated just what they knew, or wanted. Were they admirers who had once heard his voice? Did they owe him or want some sort of return? Was he what they hoped for, without knowing why? It made her uneasy. In his own letters, did he tell them about her, and her life in darkness? Or was she his secret, one of many?

Theresa never saw him. She worked around the house, cleaning, cooking, tidying, and in the evening she sat alone in the quietness, hoping he'd appear. She imagined him phoning with a word about work, a brief explanation, but the call never came. So she went to bed early, listened, but only ever heard him, or so it seemed to her, after sleep when his footsteps woke her, circling slowly.

For a long time she waited. There were messages about payment, notes and reminders, but all short and strictly instructional.

Theresa wanted more. Taking his notes, she finger-traced the loops and curls. She whispered answers to questions he hadn't asked. She tried different ways of describing her feelings and then, putting them together, composed a long letter. It was full of hope and belief and ideas for the future. The reply, when it came, was impersonal, merely pointing out that there were documents to check, a surveyor due and that the piano needed tuning.

So she searched the house for some faint sense of him, opening drawers and peering into cupboards. Nothing but clothes, shoes, socks, hankies and a broken watch. Checking the shelves, the books were old and vaguely theological, with a few historical volumes, all second-hand

and apparently unread. She dared, for the first time, to lift the lid on the piano and press a key. But the sound was cold. Its hardness hung heavy in the silence it broke, but it told no story.

Upstairs she drew the curtains as instructed, and felt the coolness as she shut out the light. The bed was as she'd left it and the en-suite bathroom was bare and cold. There was nothing to go by, no trace of the spirit that inhabits a house when its owner is away.

It was as she cleaned behind the fridge that she found a feather, caught in the grill. She had to use a knife to prise it out. When she examined it, her hands shook a little. Its size surprised her. Long and soft, it was semi-transparent and almost weightless. It could have been a leaf, dried by the sun.

Later she wrote in her diary:

> 'Did I uncover it, or was it left for me to find? Either way, it was more than evidence. It seemed like paw marks in earth. But I could hold it and keep it safe, and when I stroked the softness, it felt like air. It made me think of beauty, colour and flight: of fable, or dream. It felt unearthly.
>
> I kept it for a while underneath my bed where it was safe, and mine alone. Whoever it belonged to wouldn't know I had it. But now I've decided to put it out where he can find it. It's a kind of offering, a counter in a game. I hope my master will accept it...'

That night, after moving slowly to a spot above Theresa's head, the footsteps stopped. In the silence that followed she could feel a kind of shadow pressing on her face. She imagined eyes staring through the dark, sizing her up. In a second, it seemed, the plaster might crack and a God-like claw might reach out and grab her. There was nothing she could do. Inside her, the fear cried out. There was some kind of mistake, a throwback or distortion. It would all pass over. Perhaps if she lay there, perfectly still, holding her breath...

In the morning, the feather had gone. In its place was a small, round cage with a silver handle, no bigger than a lamp. Wedged between the bars was a neatly-folded note. Opening it slowly, Theresa shivered. It began by telling her not to fear and not to resist, for all would be well. Tonight, it said, her master would come. The rest was practical, mentioning timings, readiness, what she must do and what to expect.

And finally there were conditions: the silence and the darkness must be absolute.

During the day she prepared without thought, keeping busy. As the evening approached she started to count down. She could sense his closeness. The house was in his gaze, and she was his target.

That night, when he came, his presence filled the house. In her diary, she described it:

> 'I was shivering, hot and restless, intensely aware; the room seemed both close and open to the skies. I only wanted it over. My chest felt tight and my breath was straining.
>
> Suddenly it changed. The darkness of the room deepened and swelled. A breeze passed through and he *was*, I could feel him. Then he was gone.
>
> Afterwards I fell asleep, almost at once. In my dream I was drifting into silence, in a still, cold nothingness of glass, of space. There was no one there, only myself and the void.
>
> In the morning, rising, I went upstairs and stood by the window, waiting.'

That evening, he came again. This time Theresa was prepared. She'd changed the sheets and scattered a few petals on an extra pillow. As the air stirred she felt him enter. In the dark she could sense the tide of his breath. For a second the room quivered like leaves in breeze. Then, again, he was gone.

Over the next week he came every night. Each visit was a single breath, a shadow on the wall, almost without contact. And each encounter, lasting only seconds on the clock, yet lingering afterwards, felt quite final.

And then she realised. There were no rules or limits. He was her master but she was his mistress too. She could hold on to him, if she chose, and only then decide to let him go. Because he came with her breath. He lived inside her.

So she practised breathing, like a swimmer. As soon as he arrived she took in air. They were there, together, floating in a bubble. She could live for two.

Her purpose made her proud. They were lovers of a sort, at night, in silence. And like all lovers they lived their connection, a brief, nocturnal moment of closeness that passed unseen, something otherworldly, a shot in the dark.

The next day was different. Theresa had a feeling that someone or something was there, inside her mind. There were eyes trained on her, voices somewhere, peripheral figures just outside her view. As the evening came on, it seemed they were gathering. The house was alive with unseen watchers.

Awake in darkness, she could hear the music, singing in her head. Things passed before her: the piano, the birdcage, the notes through the door.

This time, when he came, she could feel him in there, groping. When she breathed out he remained in her body, filling up her lungs. She wasn't in control. As he squeezed still harder, she knew this was final. He'd closed his arms around her, and left no air. This time his stay would be forever.

Chapter Five

What R U up to honeybird? Still awake? xx Sent: 03-March-2003 22:12:05
Wide awake 4 U mon ange xx Sent: 03-March-2003 22:12:57
U rock me baby aaaall niiiight loooong
B with me now my flower man xx
And U my queen bee
Buzz buzz buzz xx
Crazy about your sugar, sugar mama
Branches of a tree, birds in a nest, peas in a pod
Shall I compare thee to a summer's day? xx
Annihilating all that's made…
U R strawberry mango guava peach
And U my green man
My iris lily night scented stocks
U John Brown me Queen Vic
A rose is a rose is a rose is U
Will dream of U 2night xx
Sleep well my sweet lady xx
And U my chevalier xxxxxxxxxx

Next morning when he woke James checked his watch. Holding it up to the grey-white window he could just make out the clock face. The fingers were pointing down. He thought about Beth as he rose and drew back the curtains. He missed her. Picturing her mouth, he heard her voice faintly, like music remembered. The restaurant came back, with the feel of her body, close up, dancing. She was soft and smooth and hot to touch. Pulling on his dressing gown he imagined their next meeting and what they'd say. He'd ask and she'd reply directly, without hesitation. He missed her face, her quick shy smiles and hands held out, her clear-eyed answers.

He realised on the landing how much things had changed. Up till now he'd believed in mutual self-interest, in an equal, calculated, rational relationship where both sides made bids, held their ground then settled in the middle on what they called fair shares. With Sandra, it had been like that. All about balance and space and lines of agreement. They'd needed rules – then, of course, ignored them. But now, quite suddenly, he'd returned to that place where the waiting ends, someone walks in and the couples start dancing.

In the shower he sang an on-the-road song. Though inside the flow, he sang quietly, in snatches, staying cool. In the bedroom, while dressing, he mimed to the mirror, playing air guitar. He enjoyed it as drama. This one was for everyone, his workday blues. On the steps down to the kitchen he high-fived and waved, imagined Hannah's comments, then smiled to himself as he switched to adult.

As he boiled the kettle his thoughts returned to Beth. She intrigued him. She made him think of candles and letters and poems in a drawer. Her goodness showed through. When they were apart he could still feel her in the room, a gap and a presence, a woman who spoke to him with back and forth messages, dream stuff, youth talk, kisses.

Picking up his phone, he paused, examining the screen. He wondered what to say. Oddly, he could feel her. She was waiting for a message, or so he imagined, alone like him, maybe at a table, reading his letters. A song went through his head, *Sun, sun, sun, here it comes.* Looking outside he could see it, beginning, a half arc to the horizon. As his fingers touched the keys another line came back, *Little darling it feels like years...* Not that it had been really, he thought.

When James pressed Send, the song was repeating, the sky was clear and their day was just beginning.

Morning oh girl oh!
Bonjour. Comment ça va? xx
Blue skies. Bright eyes. Coffee cup. Et toi?
Accounts. Invoices. Calculator. Ugh!
Just to try and earn a dollar (SHOUT girl HOLLER)

O O O O Stay'n' alive
Yeah oh yeah. Bittersweet xx
What U doing 2day?
Down with the kids digging borders
With crazy K? xx
If and when he shows. No holding breath.
Love U. Have 2 work now xx
Get down! Me 2. Love love love xx

All that morning Beth was lit up. She carried out her tasks quickly, with ease, thinking of him. When Sarah entered the café Beth greeted, talked as friends and planned the day ahead, but didn't mention James. Partly she was shy – it seemed so sudden and hard to explain – but also Sarah might jump in and ask awkward questions.

Returning to the laptop she continued her spreadsheet, feeling that today nothing could touch her. Hearing Sarah singing in the kitchen she tried out a few words, poetic expressions, offered in play. The words were enduring, she'd used them in letters and, though familiar, she felt their truth. She heard them, repeated with emphasis, filling up the song. They were all about love.

As Beth went around laying tables she thought back to their meeting. She remembered how she'd stepped in from the cold, and the wait inside. She could still feel herself glowing. Frame by frame, she ran through what had happened. His hand on her shoulder, their talk, his sudden invitation then circling the floor with the chorus starting up, *Oh show me heaven, cover me leave me breathless, oh show me heaven please.*

Holding a water jug she toured the room, topping up vases. The flowers had lasted: she'd selected them carefully at yesterday's market. They were white and cream and faintly scented. Touching their softness made her think of him.

During the morning she unpacked orders and took turns in the kitchen. The café was quiet and when Sarah offered, she left her to serve and went outside with an apple and a sandwich.

On the footpath to the beach she sat down on a rock. Eating slowly she looked out to sea. Since his first visit the weather had changed. The wind had dropped and the sun had come out. She remembered his remark about *Primavera*. He'd be in the garden working with his students. The kids, he'd said, were OK. It amazed her really the way he told it, joking about tags and criminal records. It underlined the difference between them. While she'd been on her own, dreaming of passages from a half-finished novel, he'd walked in. There was edge there and excitement, but uncertainty as well. And all of a sudden she wanted to hold him.

Taking out her phone, she held back, thinking. She wondered why she'd not told Sarah. Maybe it showed she didn't want to share him. Part of her was out there, felt the connection, and didn't want him spoilt. He was her flame: a quick, bright flicker, a light she'd walked into, concealed within her heart. And she loved him absurdly.

As she turned back to the phone remembering their dance song, with love words and promises running through her head, his text arrived.

What U doing now crazy gal? xx
Lunch break sun by the sea holidayish
Sunny here no students (K ill!) thinking of U
Can see us walking madcap in rain. Lover's Leap from me 2 U xx
My my my. Loonie is good. xx
U2 love is the sweetest thing
Have U seen narcissi? White orange yellow gold
Dancers. They flash upon the inward eye xx
Good 4 names. U and Me. Milk and Honey. Billet Doux.
U know all their names?
Some. Lemon Belle. Lollipop. Lucky Dip xx
I can C U now Adam digging xxxxx
Who was then a gentleman? PS This Sunday outing 2 garden?
Oh yes. U decide where. Take me there.
Thinking. Kissing. C U Sun xxxx

Chapter Six

During her marriage Beth kept up by telephone and letter with her school friends, arranging meetings where they shared their feelings and the stories behind them, talking about home life and work life, and how they'd changed.

From the start their stories, and views on couples, made her think. Theirs were the voices that she heard in her head urging her to stand up. They told her to be careful, ask questions, be critical and measure what was happening. They also told her that she'd been treated badly: a thought she blocked, fearing it would show. But the voices returned, creeping into everything, whatever she did. They filled up a hole. And though they disturbed her, her friends' remarks, heard in the dark, couldn't be ignored. Looking back later, she realised that they'd helped her.

Of the four, she saw Meg the most. They'd kept in touch, going out to films and theatre and, after saying yes, they'd been there as bridesmaids, giving thanks for their blessings while helping with straps and adjusting hairdos.

After their weddings, when they met in a café, they both brought pictures. "Let's see yours," Meg said, leaning forward as her friend pulled out a plastic wallet. They enjoyed being together, able to talk.

"They're only a selection," Beth said, clearing a space on the table top. "Most of these were taken by my brother," she added, spreading them out.

"Ah," said Meg, "you must be pleased."

"I am, though I haven't looked at them properly yet."

Meg examined the snaps, "Do you mind if I group them?"

Beth agreed. While she went the toilet, Meg held them to the light, matching and comparing, laying out two piles, with one photo kept separate.

"I see you've been busy," said Beth when she returned.

Nodding, Meg picked up a picture from the first pile, "See, the church ones are so-o-o romantic."

"You think so?" asked Beth, fingering a back view of herself with her dad. "Maybe she's running for it."

Meg laughed. "And here she comes again," she half-spoke, half-sang, "the blushing bride." This time she pointed to a scene from the second group. It showed Beth in her bedroom half made-up, peering closely at the order of service.

It was when they turned to the separate photo that Beth, thinking it through afterwards, realised that something wasn't right. When she saw it, she recognised her pose, and the fear of going under. It had been taken by her dad a day before the wedding. In it she was kneeling by the font with her face cast down, reflected in water. The picture was romantic, a young woman waiting, or praying, in late-Victorian style. But what touched Beth – and, perhaps, her dad – was the sadness of the picture.

At the end of their meet-up the photos went back to the white-yellow wallet. Beth kissed her friend and then carried them off. Slipped in between plastic they felt, already, part of something invisible. They remained there hidden, at the bottom of a drawer, only ever viewed behind closed doors when she told herself stories, alone with her feelings, on their wedding anniversary.

Years later she expressed it in a letter to Meg. Written late at night, it began with news about friends and family, mentioned illness and matters of faith then shifted abruptly. She reminded Meg of her father's photo. Asking for God's forgiveness and confessing how she struggled, she declared her unhappiness then admitted that she didn't know what to say. Finally, writing slowly, she shared her thoughts about the picture by the font.

She wrote:

INTERCESSION

O Lord, hear my prayer.

Put your gentle arms around this girl. Whisper in her ear. Bring her close to the fullness of your love. Deliver her from loss, make her whole. Roll back the fears, raise her, lead her, tell her to stand up.

O Lord, hear my prayer.

Return her to life. Do not allow her promise to be taken and nothing given; but, hand-in-hand, show her the way. Give love, breathe life; lift her, gently.

O Lord, hear my prayer.

Comforter, Inspirer, Face-to-Face God, touch her there. Release her from the cold, the wait in darkness. Open your arms and move her to be strong. Warm her, delight her in your spirit, and in the flesh. Be with this girl, this woman, all-known, knowing, and known by you.

O Lord, hear my prayer.

Beth soon came to realise, when she met up with Amy and Rachael, that most of their talk was about money. They described themselves as ordinary, middle-income, and not at all showy. Compared to some, their needs were simple. All they really wanted was to wine and dine and have nice things, to spend and be happy. And being well off, even though they denied it, kept them on the lookout. Whatever was current – must-have clothes, tasteful decorations, apps and accessories – it was never enough.

In the world they lived in, it seemed that everything was, or should be, theirs for the taking. So Amy was settled with well-schooled children, lived nicely in a beautiful house and went on holidays in Crete and Corfu, but wasn't at all pleased by the cost of her weekly shop-up. And Rachael had a liking for the latest gadgets, buying them online and changing them monthly. She called them her playthings, joking loudly she was OD'd again on all her cards.

When they met up over coffee Beth listened carefully. She could tell, although they didn't say it, they saw her as odd. A church mouse woman married to a man of the cloth. She suspected when they left they'd talk about her as if she'd missed out. Because for them, she realised, it was obvious, a husband was a catch. His job was to provide. If he was fit he had to be sweet-talked, given his head then harnessed. In their world men liked *doing* things; the challenge was to train them.

"Blokes have to be handled," Rachael said, raising her voice. They were sat inside a roped-off area watching shoppers crossing an echoey, glass-roofed square. It was afternoon, the mall was busy and the air was full of music and passing conversations.

"And good to look at," called Amy, nodding towards an advert showing a larger-than-life sportsman.

"It's how you speak to them," Rachael replied, eyeing the advert. "You have to make what you want ab-so-lute-ly clear." She glanced sideways, checking on Beth and smiling encouragement. "You OK?" she asked. When her friend nodded, she went back to sipping from her cup.

"Is your husband like that?" asked Beth, pointing to the picture. The sportsman was wearing a skin-tight outfit, padded in places. She knew he was a racing driver but not the name, and didn't want to ask.

Rachael laughed. "In my dreams," she said and paused, examining Beth carefully. "Not really, of course."

Beth studied the man in the advert. He was blank-faced and serious with a slight twist of the mouth. Staring straight over the shoppers' heads, he seemed to belong to another age. She could see him in a film, giving orders as a Roman emperor.

"They like to be heroes," said Amy, rolling her eyes. "You have to laugh. They're all in the business of playing Terminator."

"Or Johnny Depp," added Rachael, pulling out a magazine.

"But yours is different?" asked Beth.

"Yes, as long as I remind him who he is, daily."

Beth held her gaze. Behind the bravado, her friend was reaching out. "So how do you do that?"

Rachael hesitated then held up a page from her magazine. It pictured models in black wearing expensive jewellery. "See this," she said pointing to a filigree necklace with a single iris-like stone. "If I ask him nicely, he tells me I can have anything. So I choose the best."

"Hey, that's top of the range," said Amy, scanning the small print. "Did he really say you could have that?"

Rachael confirmed then offered the catalogue to Beth. Suddenly her voice tone dropped, as if they were one-to-one. "I know it's not your sort of thing, but I do think it shows something."

Yes, but what? thought Beth, glancing at the pictures. There were stones in rings, on chains, embedded in bracelets and set into clothes. At the bottom of each page, a close-up showed them. Blue-white and purple, or pink and glowing, they were glass-cut, petal-like and almost-liquid. She had to admit they were beautiful.

Handing back the magazine, Beth took a breath. "So, is he the man for you?" Behind her question was alarm. Was it really like this in people's marriages?

"Oh, Guy? He's a good man. I know. He respects me."

Amy nodded, "You can tell from his eyes. He looks at you that way."

"So he cares about you," Beth said, leaning forward.

"He knows how to keep me happy."

Beth looked doubtful, "But does he ever say I love you?"

"Oh no, he'd never say anything like that. It's in his actions."

"You mean buying beautiful things?" Beth pointed to the catalogue.

Rachael laughed, "Yes. It's like that song, diamonds are a girl's best friend."

"So, he plays by the rules."

Rachael confirmed. She stirred her coffee and smiled. "What you have to do is make a man understand ev-er-y-thing you want. Money, love, sex or whatever, as long as he gives it to you, then that's fine." She gazed quietly at the photo of the necklace, "So that way, what you get is what you want."

"It's a fact," put in Amy, "they have to be told." Checking her watch, she announced she had to go. "Keeps them on their toes," she added, glancing up at the picture of the sportsman.

Beth looked too. She knew he was important, people admired him, but to her, although he was up there, he wasn't of much interest. She saw him as a boy, coming first, winning races. He was all self-confidence and look-at-me poses.

"Back to life," said Rachael, closing her magazine.

Beth eyed her friend. "Back to reality," she said, and her disappointment made her smiley.

When they left, the concourse had cleared and the high glass roof had darkened. The three of them moved across the square, talking. It wasn't till the door that Beth remembered something about the sportsman. It came back in a flash. Now she realised why all through their talk she'd felt him watching. His surname was Conrad.

But of all Beth's friends it was Charlie, whom she saw the least, who registered most.

They got together twice. The first was while Beth was young, meeting at a gig. To her the place felt exposed, but intimate as well. A lights-down basement full of talk and passion, which her friend seemed to like. Charlie knew people, or they knew her because she'd been with a band touring America, sleeping in hotels and living on chocolate and pills. For a while, she said, she'd rubbed shoulders with celebs: men she'd fought off, sworn at, slept with and ended calling friends.

But Beth noticed how, beneath the surface and despite her talk, Charlie wanted more. At quiet moments she spoke of romance. Backstage, all night, on the road, she was out there, looking. The tough talk was her B-side, adopted for effect.

"It's all about hype," Charlie said, filling up her glass. "You should see me, I'm all over the place. I hate being mouthy, but I do it."

Then for most of the evening, Charlie talked tough. Beth listened patiently while she spoke about addiction and burn-out and ego and people being real. Near the end, they chatted about childhood and Beth, when asked about Conrad, described her feelings. Then Charlie left, saying they must meet again.

After that she'd gone to ground. At first Beth thought her friend might be busy. She wrote a newsy letter, but nothing came back. As time went on she began to suspect that Charlie wasn't interested. Perhaps she'd been offended? Maybe she'd thought better and decided to cut off? But also there was the worry that something had happened, that Charlie was hurt or ill or even on the run. All she had to go on was her remembered voice and gestures. So for two years there was nothing. Then a birthday card arrived, and Beth was relieved. It was followed, at odd intervals, by an unsigned postcard, a box containing sweets, some heart-shaped earrings, a child's worry doll and then, a year later, by a phone call from the station to suggest meeting up.

Beth, when she picked up the receiver, recognised the voice. She hadn't forgotten the stories, and had prayed for Charlie often, at bedtime and in the dark, and in any case she was curious. So they met within the hour, sharing breakfast, alone in a corner of The Shorespot Café.

Her first impression was that her friend had changed. She seemed stronger and more grounded, less in need of comfort. "Now, let's talk men," she said, after touring the building and catching up. "So yours is a reverend?"

"He's a low-church minister."

"You mean he's a happy-clappy?"

"Not exactly, he has his convictions, important ones."

"But he believes in saving people like me?"

"No. I think, in fairness, he does a lot to help people, no strings attached."

Charlie threw one end of a black-gold scarf back across her shoulder: "All right, tell me then, what does he do to help you?"

"He tries."

"But what does he do?"

"Prays and takes services, visits people, goes around other churches…"

"Ah, but who comes first, you or God?"

Beth felt her face tighten, "I really don't think that's a fair question."

"From the way you say that, there's something wrong."

Beth's eyebrows shot up.

"I know," said Charlie, "I've been studying with a psychic counsellor." She tugged at a purple-dyed plait woven into her hair. "Now, tell me, how does he treat you?"

"Not badly."

"But not well?"

"I don't really know."

"Would you say he loves you? Really loves you, from the heart."

Beth declined to answer. Her forehead was hot and her palms felt swollen. Voices in the air were telling her to end this now.

"Or is he too busy with himself and being a minister?" Charlie was sitting back, twisting the tassels of her scarf. Her darkly-shadowed eyes were closely attentive. "I can see there's an answer you don't want to give." Suddenly she lifted the scarf above her head, leaned forward and wrapped it around her friend. "There, that'll help. Keep it. It'll protect you."

"Oh, but I can't."

"It's yours now, a gift."

"Really, I can't."

Charlie continued to watch her friend. She was speaking gently. "You've been upset by my words – is that right?"

Beth blushed.

"But you know, if you're honest with yourself, what I said's true." When Beth lowered her eyes, she pointed at the scarf: "Go on, I'd like you to have it. Please."

Beth felt the cloth; it was super-soft and silky. She thought of saying no, but gratitude won out. "Thank you," she said as she adjusted it on her shoulders. "It's beautiful," she added, fingering the tassels, "like a prayer shawl."

As she watched Charlie leave, Beth touched the scarf, hearing a line from Keats sounding in her head.

When Conrad saw the scarf he glowered. "What's that you're wearing?" he said, blocking the doorway. He was red-faced and sweaty, just back from his run.

"It's a scarf, from a friend."

Closing the door, he stood and stared before peeling off his shoes and climbing upstairs to take a shower. He moved slowly, as if he'd been injured. Beth could hear a few heavy thumps and the swish of running water. The pipes rattled until the flow cut off, followed by silence. When the bolt shot back, she jumped. Taking a breath, she checked in the mirror: the image told her she was still there. She shook her head, then opening a cupboard laid out breakfast.

When Conrad reappeared he was wearing a white shirt and grey flannel trousers. His expression was thin-lipped and very 1950s. Squeezing his long-limbed body between the table and the wall, he said grace and allowed her to serve him. Beth knew when he did that he wasn't happy.

"Black and gold," he said frowning, as he put down his toast. Beth remained silent, waiting. She could tell that inside himself he was asking for guidance.

He rose, avoiding her eye. It was as if he needed to escape from what he saw. "From Charlotte?" he asked, staring at the scarf. Wondering how he knew, Beth nodded. A wish to say something – anything – pushed into her head. She was about to speak when Conrad cut in. His voice filled the room. "Not her," he said, moving to the door, "not from that woman. Be warned, not her." As he stepped out, he repeated loudly, using her friend's full name. "Don't wear it," he added, standing in the hallway, then left.

The girls, on the other hand, liked it. Naomi called the colours cool and when Ruth touched it she smiled. "It's lovely," she said, 'like my friend's cat." Their approval was a lift. So she folded the scarf into her jacket pocket and kept it hidden, close to her body. In there, it warmed her and gave protection. Occasionally, when asked, she showed her daughters, but only for them, as a secret, when they were alone.

But Conrad, perhaps through Ruth, had his suspicions, and when he finally caught her, made his views known. "I particularly ask," he said stiffly, pointing to the scarf, "that you respect my feelings." He'd surprised her at the bottom of the garden where she went some evenings on her own. Thinking he was out, she'd left the girls to watch TV, slipped on her jacket and sneaked down the path. Guided by the house lights, she'd reached the corner seat and sat there, looking at the sky. It was quiet and cool and darkly poetic. She'd just pulled out the scarf when Conrad appeared.

His voice made her jump. It was as if he'd been there all along, hidden by the hedge. When she didn't reply, he flared up. "Give," he said, flicking his hand open. Beth stood up, saying nothing. "Give," he repeated, wriggling his fingers. Her lips had parted, showing her teeth. "I said *give*," he insisted, but his voice had thinned and his hand had closed up.

Beth cleared her throat then slowly raised the scarf. She stood there for a second at full stretch, staring into dark. "There," she said, dropping it. "Have it." The scarf slid sideways, caught on the hedge and hung there by a corner. "It's yours," she said quietly, stepping around and beyond him. As she walked up the path she could feel his presence. He was there behind her, watching. When she reached the house, he called, but she didn't turn back. Even at the doorway, when she heard her name and what sounded like *come back*, she went in without turning.

Next morning looking out, Beth saw that the scarf had gone. After breakfast she went outside to check around the hedge, finding nothing. Thinking back, she'd not seen it with Conrad. She was fairly sure he hadn't brought it in, but while he was out running she searched the bedroom. Again, she drew blank. When he returned, she didn't want to ask; it was better she thought, after last night, to leave him be. But to her surprise at breakfast, Conrad asked if she knew where it had gone. He spoke quietly with an inquiring smile. It seemed, from their exchange, that he hadn't seen it.

Later when Ruth asked after it, Beth said she didn't know. When Naomi pressed her she said it must have walked. "It's a mystery," she told them both as if it didn't matter. She did look again but, despite her search, it was nowhere to be found – except, perhaps, in her thoughts about Charlie.

But when she told Meg her feelings came back. "I was sad to lose it," she said as they climbed past the clock tower to the upper town gardens. "Charlie gave it, to protect me."

"That was kind," said Meg. She glanced quickly across the flowerbeds. They were end-of-year and straggly. "Have you any idea what happened to it?"

Beth shook her head.

As they walked through a gap in a low wall, Meg's face tightened: "Perhaps he took it?"

Beth's head went back, "He? You mean…?"

"You said there was an argument. He didn't want you to have it."

"I'd know if Conrad had touched it."

"But how do you know? He might've done it without you seeing. Because if it's really bad between you…"

Beth glanced round, seeking help. "Well, if that's so, I'm a bit to blame myself,"

Meg stopped her at a viewpoint. "You sure of that?" she asked. Below them some winding wooden steps dropped steeply down the hillside.

Beth looked out. Her friend's questioning came as a surprise. She and Meg were sharers: they swopped experiences, spoke the same language and read the same books. On almost everything they backed each other up. "You don't agree?" she asked.

Meg shook her head, "You take too much on yourself."

Looking down beyond the steps, Beth could see a line of shrubs and The Shorespot Café. A few faint wisps of cloud had gathered on the roof. "I do that?"

"Definitely." Meg moved closer. "Remember the photo, the one by the font."

Beth shivered, "Ah yes, I wrote about that."

"Your intercession?"

Beth nodded.

"When I read that, I prayed for you."

"You did? Oh, thank you."

"I prayed every day after that. I didn't want to tell you, but I had you

103

on my list for ages."

They embraced in silence. When they separated, Beth looked back along the path. "Maybe, if you'd said... but I suppose you didn't know how I'd take it." She forced a smile: "When it's bad, it's easier just to close your eyes, forget about things and pretend it isn't happening."

"You needed help."

"I think, maybe I still do."

"You really shouldn't be so unhappy. It's not your fault."

Beth gazed out to sea. A soft grey haze was spreading over water. She felt it advancing. For a long time now, it had been creeping up. This, she could tell, was a quiet kind of crisis. "So what should I do?"

Meg breathed in sharply, "It depends on how strong you feel."

They stood there in silence. The sea was still, the sky had closed up and the air was cold. Fine threads of mist were filling up the hollows.

Beth turned away. Her voice, when it came, didn't sound like hers. "You think I should leave him, don't you..."

"Maybe," said Meg, facing forward. "If you can."

"There isn't any other way?"

Meg shook her head. The mist now had covered the bottom of the steps.

Beth looked down. She felt invisible, and cold inside herself. The white advancing tide was blotting out everything.

"I suppose," she said, bleakly, "that's what I'll have to do."

But first, she had to see her dad.

She used, as an excuse, his recent condition. He'd caught a dose of 'flu which she told Conrad, not untruthfully, might be still around. She knew he didn't like illness, talking about how he saw too much on his rounds and didn't trust medicine, so she went without him, taking the girls.

Being on a journey brought them together. She had Ruth and Naomi to talk to and played games, told them stories then slept part of the way, and when they arrived Louise was there waiting on the platform. She drove them to the house, talking cheerily and questioning the girls. It was as if they'd always been with her. When they arrived, John waved from the doorstep and everyone embraced. His welcome, though jolly, seemed slightly awkward. Noticing his stoop and his sad-happy smile, Beth realised how much she missed him. She'd not kept up.

Over the weekend, Ruth and Naomi came first. Louise took charge, laying on hard-boiled eggs, jam sandwiches and bottled fizz, with elasticated hats and 3D glasses. Her taste was traditional, but the girls seemed to like it. They went with her to turn out cupboards and put on masks, wearing backless shoes and pleated dresses. They looked at old photos, picking out groups and asking about names. They even allowed Louise to read out loud from her mother's books, laughing at the outdated talk and sketchy pictures. With no one watching, they forgot their ages and played at being girlie.

Being back with her parents made Beth happier. They both seemed to know just what she wanted. With Louise making space and John there listening, she could have her say. And her opportunity came when she walked out with her dad, taking a route she'd followed on her runs.

"So how's Conrad?" John asked, as they skirted a cornfield. Tall and slight, he moved quite slowly, almost as if he was half-asleep. He looked quite sad, but his eyes were quick and attentive.

"He's at home," replied Beth, dryly.

They stopped by a cattle trough. On the other side, tyre tracks had cut a trench along the side of the field. A red burst of poppies showed above the wheat.

"And how is he?"

At first her answer wouldn't come. She remembered her runs. At that time she'd been younger and had done everything she could, but now she needed air – air and light, and someone to talk to.

"He's all…" She cut herself off. "You know, Dad, I want to be honest with you."

John stopped and peered over his glasses, smiling. "That's what you must be, my love."

"It's not nice, Dad, not nice at all."

"You mean you're having difficulties?"

She nodded.

"Then we walk and talk. And you don't hold back."

They set out, following the line of the trench. It led to a low hedge. Beyond the hedge was another field which was bare and stony and full of weeds. As they passed through a gate a flight of pigeons rose and circled.

For Beth, his presence helped her say things. She talked about their honeymoon, the day-to-day frictions, Conrad's demands, his putdowns and dismissals, followed by the silence. "It's impossible," she ended. "Either he either ignores me completely, or he's finding fault."

"I know," John replied.

Beth stared, surprised. "You know?"

"Yes, it was always difficult."

"You realised all along…"

"Your mother and I could see you were unhappy."

"So when was that?"

"Oh, when you visited, without him."

"And then, when I stopped visiting."

Her dad remained silent.

"So you understood, but kept it to yourselves."

"Yes. We had to, for your sake."

Beth nodded.

John took her hand. The bones of his fingers pressed lightly against her palm. It reminded her of when he'd given her away. He'd been so gentle.

"Remember the birds," he said quietly.

They looked out together across the field. The pigeons at the centre were head down, pecking for seeds. To one side a group of finches were swarming the branches of a low tree. At the far end some seagulls were rising and circling slowly, outlined by the sun.

"They all have their stories," she said, knitting her brows. Her thoughts were filling up with girlhood memories. Her gran was there together with The Water Babes and Rossetti's picture. In her mind's eye she could see the title of her own first story, The Girl Who Began Again.

John's eyes searched the field, "Like us."

"But not always happily-ever-after."

"It all depends on where you choose to stop."

"I wish I'd done that earlier."

He shook his head sadly, "As for an ending, you must decide."

Beth blushed. Even after the move away and her lack of contact, her dad was there on her side. His generosity hurt.

"I know I've not always been the best daughter," she said, "but I'm here now." Before he could answer, she drew back: "I've not been in touch, not nearly enough, and it's because of this..." she held up her hand. "Look," she said, turning her wrist to display her ring. It was silver, flattened on top and inscribed with a cross. "His choice, not mine.

106

And useless. It never fitted. I tried hard – too hard really, and now I need to live."

John gazed at her. She was staring at her hand as if it hurt. "Very well," he said slowly, "if it doesn't fit, you know what to do."

A group of starlings passed close by. They were swooping and twittering like bats. It seemed to her they were urging her on.

Extending her finger, she rubbed and twisted till her ring came off. "Watch," she said, holding it up, "I shall give it back." She took a step forward and threw her wedding ring out, like a stone, across the field. "There. It's gone," she cried as it spun low in the air and dropped to the ground. It landed in a weed patch, kicking up dust and scattering a mass of wheeling pigeons.

They stood for a while watching. The pigeons circled then returned to their patch to resume their pecking. Their busy seesaw heads ducked and bobbed like puppets. When Beth walked forward, they took off again. They continued circling while she crouched, pushing aside leaves. Using both hands she scraped and dug until she brought up her ring. It was dust-streaked and grey. Squeezing hard, she fitted it back onto her finger.

She was crying.

Dear Conrad,

This letter may come as a shock. I hope not. But if it does, although this may not be easy, please read it several times. It comes from the heart.

I see this as the beginning of a new kind of relationship. A more open, honest one. As it says in Matthew, 'A healthy tree cannot bear bad fruit, nor can a diseased tree bear good fruit'.

For a long time now we've been out of touch. Although we share a house, children and a faith, we live as strangers, in different worlds. To me, it's like being in hiding in a dark cave, cut off from life. As if the world out there is somewhere far away. It's a cold, lonely, shut-in kind of place. It makes me think of Yeats's line, 'Too long a sacrifice can make a stone of the heart'.

I know your church life is different. I can see how it lights you up. It's what you call The Glory. But to me, light and shadow come together, and where it's dark the truth is hard to see. So please don't be angry if I say our home life is dark: very, very dark.

Before we married we were full of light and energy, we ran together and trusted each other, living our beliefs. We were young and we were blessed. And equal in the eyes of God. I didn't agree with everything you said, but I respected your views and married with your kind of service. I wanted to make you a good wife.

But a shadow came between us. Whatever we did, we couldn't connect. Perhaps I should have reached out, made myself felt, but, starting with the honeymoon, it seemed as if everything was in your hands, and already decided. Maybe I pulled away or lost faith, but I knew you were busy and I turned towards the children.

I really didn't want to send this letter. I've been writing it for years in my head, while telling myself that it isn't true. I've tried, I really have, but now I know it is so, and I can't live this way. For years I got through by closing my eyes and blocking off. I was acting, of course. As it says in Romans 5:3, 'we know that suffering produces endurance'.

But denial, in the end, doesn't work. It sets up a barrier. So now I know that, right from the start, we weren't for each other. You were on a mission and I was afraid. Afraid of getting it wrong, of making mistakes and forfeiting your interest. And because of my fear I tried too hard, and did things that annoyed you.

So I've thought and prayed, but now I know. Because I believe that if God had intended us to be together then it would have shown by now. We took a wrong turning years ago. And now we're lost, stranded in a place where God can't help.

So I want us to separate.

Of course, it will be difficult. And we mustn't hurt the girls. But I do believe we have to be honest, more painfully honest than we've ever been before. If we can do that, then we'll come out stronger. Job 23:10 'when he has tried me, I shall come out as gold'.

Beth

She left the letter in Conrad's Bible. It was a Saturday morning just before dawn, the girls were away and she went to work early. As she closed the door, she shivered. The letter seemed so final. Walking downhill she tried not to think, but the words of the letter kept running in her head and she wanted to go back to remove it. She could imagine him returning from his run, reading it then chasing after her. On the steps down from the front, she felt so exposed. As she neared the café, the sky cleared and she began to slow down. Feeling a faint breeze, she stopped and looked back. There was no one following. The birds were singing and the waves were breaking quietly on the beach.

At the door Beth glanced up. *The Shorespot Café* – he'd not liked the name, said she shouldn't buy it and called it a vanity. There'd even been prayers and talk of Mammon. And yet she'd done it. Taken him on, told herself yes, made it her business. And people had liked it, she was Beth of The Caff. It felt like home.

During the day she kept herself busy. As Beth-in-charge she was brisk and cheerful, almost playful, but also the proprietor: judging, consulting, putting things in place. She laid out stock, chalked up specials, greeted everyone, cleared tables when necessary then sat down by herself to redo her spreadsheets. With her staff she was jolly, chatty, listening to all-action Sarah and agreeing shifts. With the customers, she served them with a smile. And with deliveries and enquiries her manner was attentively friendly but also managerial.

It was only later, when closing up, that she remembered the letter and her shakiness returned. She said goodbye to Sarah without revealing anything. On the way back she checked her bag and fingered her keys. Their numb smooth coldness kept down the sweats. As she walked downhill she counted each step, trying to stay calm. Entering the town, she saw herself reflected in a shop window and wondered who she was. She prayed, too, as she walked, trying to build strength. Several times she imagined Conrad's rage, or how he broke down, asking God's help. She saw his eyes, fixed on her letter and imagined him pacing, his voice crying out. And when she arrived at the front door, she held her breath then stepped inside quickly.

The hall was quiet. As she took off her shoes she was aware of him there, somewhere hidden. The doors were all closed. Feeling like an intruder, she stood for a moment before choosing the kitchen. As she entered, the room seemed empty, but then she saw him, sitting at the table. The letter was in front of him, half out of the envelope. His eyes were closed and his hands were together, gripping. His knuckles were white.

"Conrad," she said, flatly. It seemed he'd been there, praying in silence, for a very long time.

His eyes flicked open, "I say, no. It's out of the question."

She flushed, "So you've read it?"

Conrad stared. His long lean face was closed against her now. He'd said his piece.

"And that's what you think?"

"I said. It's impossible."

Beth looked away, "I'd hoped…"

Conrad stood up, "Marriage is from God."

"And so is love."

"For better or for worse."

"Then you don't see the problem?"

"We must live with what we are, husband and wife."

She found herself shaking, "And that's all? This has to go on, just as it is – on and on – and that's the end of it?"

Picking up the envelope, he shoved the letter inside and held it out. "Take this," he said, "and put it with your stories."

"I didn't think…" she began.

"Because I've read enough," Conrad cut in, walking to the door. He stood there, tall and wiry, blocking the frame.

"What does that mean?" she asked, and her eyebrows came together.

Conrad's face had smoothed to a mask. Nothing here could touch him. "You're making up," he said, shaking his head, "always making up." And he turned, strode into the hall and climbed the staircase without looking back.

They slept in separate rooms: Conrad sprawled full-length on the upstairs double bed, Beth curled up on the sofa. Although exhausted, she found herself lying awake, thinking. Their talk in the kitchen kept coming back. She was afraid of what he'd do, but angry as well. To be told she was making up brought back her gran and Jim. Like him, Conrad took advantage. She felt him prying into drawers, peering through darkness, overshadowing everything. For years he'd talked about God's call, while going behind her back. He didn't have the right.

During the night she heard him moving around. At first she just listened, plotting his movements. Then, as he paced round in circles, she became tetchy, wishing he'd settle. In the middle of the night a creaky, scraping sound disturbed her, as if he was opening a window. Finally, when the cold and discomfort drove her up, she sat down in the kitchen and pulled out a notebook.

Taking a pen, she drew two columns. One was headed *Reasons to*

Stay and one was headed *Leave*. Under the first she put Naomi and Ruth and some capitalised words – names of qualities, a few Christian values and some crossed-out feelings. Under the second she began with phrases that ran into sentences, continuing over into a double-sided spread. She wrote on, covering more pages, till her wrist began to hurt. It all came out, filling up the book. When she'd finished she realised that the writing had calmed her. Finding an envelope, she tore out the pages and slipped them in, adding a short covering note and addressing it to Meg.

Conrad, as usual, appeared at six, in time for his run. By then she'd had her breakfast and posted the letter. He was blank-faced and busy, saying nothing. As soon as he left she went to the bedroom. Taking a deep breath she stared in the mirror. The girls were at her parents' and she knew what she must do. Putting it on paper had proved it. Even so, when she pulled out the suitcase, she felt herself shaking.

She packed her clothes, her shoes, a few books and her writings, and carried the case downstairs. Glancing at the clock, she wrote a short note. She was about to place it on the hallstand when she heard a cough outside. "Oh," she said, ducking forward as Conrad came through the door. A white mist was filling up her head.

He eyed her oddly, pulling off his jacket, then stepped back against the wall. "What's going on?" he asked, staring at the suitcase. Beth shivered.

"You can't be," he whispered. His face had creased and fallen. One hand was shifting uneasily across wallpaper.

"I'm going," she said, moving towards the case.

"You're leaving?"

She nodded.

"Going – leaving – now?"

"I've decided."

"No, no. You can't," he said, lunging forward and taking the handle. "You mustn't," he hissed, "I won't allow it," and he pushed past her, carrying the case. "It's all wrong." He was shouting now, calling out to an invisible audience. "Don't let her do this!"

Beth stood back. Conrad turned on his heel and strode through the kitchen and out into the garden. As he headed down the path, she followed to the door. She was watching a scene that seemed unreal, yet couldn't be ignored; it forced itself on her, like the climax to a film. And he was playing lead role.

Reaching the bench she saw him stop. He sat down abruptly with his hands together and his body bent forward. He was staring at the ground. Her doubts came up, and with them a feeling that she'd been here before. Maybe he was ill. She had to stop herself from calling out. Flashing back to a run where he'd thrown up, she stepped into the garden. It was when he began to rock and his shoulders started shaking that she realised that he was crying.

As she approached the bench, she felt the white mist gathering inside. It chilled her right through. The case was by his feet and she wondered whether to take it. Part of her feared him and part of her wished she could make him understand.

"Conrad," she said quietly, standing a yard off.

He looked up. "No," he answered. His face had set firm and he picked up the case, standing to attention. "You must go," he said sternly, pushing the case towards her. Beth hesitated, eyeing his hand. "Go, go," he repeated, irritable now. Taking the handle, she felt the touch of his fingers then the jerk along her arm. As the weight pressed down she turned and lifted the case two-handed in front of her. She held it at chest height, like a shield, and began walking.

"Goodbye," she said hoarsely and found herself crying. She was worn and shaky, but relieved. In her mind she could see the gravel path ahead, the house, the road out to the station and, somewhere in the background, the last few strands of mist clearing.

Behind her she heard a voice calling out. The words were from a sermon. They brought back the darkness, the door shut, the cold, and the wait at the window. As she walked, the voice seemed to follow her. It was her master, calling. The voice was giving her a warning, requiring her to turn back "For a spirit of harlotry has led them astray," it cried, "departing from their God."

Beth walked.

Chapter Seven

The garden outing took Beth and James west on byroads, through unfamiliar countryside. They drove between hedgerows with blossom-white and green-leaf-shows, across single-track bridges over streams, past cow pools and gates and piled-up manure – then up through gorse to drive along the hilltops with a view out to sea.

With James at the wheel it was a full day's outing. Beth checked the food, changed the CDs and map-read. Inside, she was warm and tingly. Already it seemed they'd come a long way.

The ridgetop drive led to a square of gravel and a viewpoint. Here they left the car, walking forward with the wind in their faces. Two metal poles guarded the drop. "Like Thomas Hardy!" she called, pointing to cloud-shaped shadows spreading over downland.

James looked out. The hills were soft-sloped, with dry gulley strips and clumped-together thorns. At the bottom they were green, above that brown, streaked white in places, and treeless. He held up an imaginary camera: "And then, Julie Christie runs into view. L-o-n-g take."

"James."

"I'm only kidding."

She scanned the view. "Don't spoil things, it's beautiful."

"You're right." He took her by the hand and began to walk, swinging their joint arm. The sun came and went and the wind cooled their faces. "Do we know the name of this hill?" he asked as they followed the ridge, arriving at a circle of earthworks.

"I think it's called The Castle," she said as they passed between mounds. Her focus was ahead: this was her time.

The path they were following was bare, chalk-white and deeply rutted. James led to one end where they looked out across a crater-shaped drop, bisected by tracks. Beyond that there were roads and undulating farmland. The sky was clear and they could see to the coast, and beyond that the thin grey horizon.

"Up here!" he said, pointing to a steep-sided mound. They scrambled to the top, reaching a flat patch with a few scattered rocks. "We're kings of the castle," he sang, "or queens!"

The wind was beating up the hillside, colouring Beth's cheeks and tugging at her hair. "It's like a fairground," she called, circling her arm.

"How do you mean?"

"All rather wild and windy and crazy."

"Yes, I can see that. Anything else?"

She paused, eyeing the slope: "Well, you feel, if you could leap the wind might carry you down. Or up, up, into the clouds."

James followed her gaze, sighting a group of seabirds. They were wheeling and turning in loose formation. "That's the way to be," he said quietly.

She stepped to the edge. "Effortless, aren't they."

"You wonder how they do it. They just seem to hang there, as if they're afloat."

"Or asleep."

"Sweet... dream... babies."

"Well, perhaps. But they are *gulls*."

"I meant the song. How long must I dream, and so on."

"I suppose, looked at that way, they are a bit dreamy."

They stood, leaning on each other and swaying slightly. As James touched her cheek, Beth turned to face him. The wind blew raw and gentle around her face as she whispered his name. He fixed his eyes on hers, their heads came together and suddenly they were kissing.

At the end of their drive they turned in at a notice saying *Deanbury Sculpture Gardens*. The sun was shining and the air was fresh. After parking they followed the signs to the entrance. The path led to a high rainbow arch, cast in steel. It was stem-like and twisted, painted all over, and resembled a bouquet. "That's great," exclaimed Beth. "Looks Art Nouveau."

James ran his hand across its smoothly-curved surfaces. "If you look up here," he said, pointing, "it's got a row of eyelashes."

"You what – eyelashes?"

"Eyelashes."

"Well, I don't know about that. Aren't they supposed to be branches?"

James shrugged, "It's hard to tell."

"Maybe they're both."

"It's possible." There was a lilt in his voice: "You could use them to climb it."

"Climb it?"

"Why not? It can be done."

Beth rolled her eyes. "Not me, but you could try. Even better, you could *imagine* it. That way it's bound to come off."

James measured her with a look.

"You don't think so?"

He pointed upwards: "It's an idea. Jack did it with the Beanstalk."

Beth smiled to herself.

"Now you see me, now you don't," he added, taking her hand.

"So you'd like to try?"

"Don't know about that." James drew her to him, "I'd probably fall off."

They hugged, laughing, then stepped on and through to a sun-dappled wood. The light came in drifts, filling up the gaps. "So what's it make you think of?" he asked.

She peered both sides. The trees were still bare, there was moss between them, and fallen leaves. Small spikes of green were sprouting from the branches. She thought of her dad and talking in the garden. "A poem – or story, maybe."

"Like Goldilocks?"

They had reached a grey, weather-boarded house with shuttered windows. It was L-shaped, high at the front, sloping away to a brick-built extension. A handwritten notice outside said *Woodland Cottage*. Suddenly Beth had a feeling of being watched, as if they'd entered into someone else's territory.

"Looks more like the house that Jack built," added James.

She shushed him as a broad, bent-backed man appeared wearing a padded jacket. He was shuffling sideways, carrying a spherical object. When he reached the path he lowered it with a grunt and straightened, wiping his hands down his jacket. "I hope you enjoy this," he said, glancing at the sphere. "It's *art*."

"High or low?" James called. He seemed to be addressing the object.

"You're thinking of music?" asked Beth looking puzzled,

"Art," replied James. He turned to the man, "Does it have a name?" This time his question could have been about the jacket.

The man pulled out a programme to check. "Child's Play III – by someone called Angel."

"Sounds like a pop group," said James. "German, electronic."

Beth smiled. She could see him, head down at the keyboard, pumping chords.

"It says here it follows from Parts I and II," the man said, scratching his head. "You see I'm not much for art myself, but I reckon..." He paused, eyeing Beth.

"Go on," she prompted.

"Well, it's not how it looks. You try. Touch it."

Beth ran her hand gently across the surface: "Am I imagining, or is it warm?"

The man nodded.

"And smooth as well," James said, standing by her. "Baby's bottomish."

"I shall ignore that."

"Struck from the record – yes?"

"With immediate effect." Beth turned to the man, "So what's it made of?"

The man checked the programme, "It says here, graphene."

"But it feels like stone," James objected. "And what about the heat?"

"Some sort of mixture. I'm told it has chemicals stored inside."

James and Beth circled the ball. As they looked, the sun touched the object, spreading vein-like markings. Its surface was criss-crossed with hair-line tracks. "It's alive in a way," she said, "like an egg."

The sunlight disappeared and the ball turned grey.

"If you try playing doctor," said James, cupping the surface, "you can feel something. I don't know what it is, but it's alive *and* it's rock, or something like. It's all a bit left-field."

Beth placed her hands next to his. They both watched as the sunlight returned in a pink-white glow. "Yes, it feels organic," she said as the colour advanced, reaching her fingers.

The man nodded. "There are more. You'll see, if you follow the path." For a second he stood, outlined by the sun. "And they're all *arty*," he said, looking off. When the sun went in he straightened his shoulders and walked back towards the cottage. At the door, he stripped off his jacket, hung it on a nail then disappeared round the back. In his absence, the stone had lost all colour.

"He was absolutely right," said James as they toured the garden. They'd seen several curved pink-grey stones appearing at intervals along the path.

"Looks like they've just landed," he said, walking the line. At the end he touched Beth's arm. "Do you think they're watching us?"

Beth shook her head. Her face was lit by sun. At her feet, a disc-shaped artwork was glowing faintly.

James turned, "Would you do something for me?"

"Well, if I can. What do you have in mind?"

"It's something you've *talked* about…"

"Oh yes?"

He pointed to a grassy hollow beyond the trees. It was soft and smooth and screened on two sides by bushes. "If we went over there, would you dance, like you do round the café?"

"You mean with you watching?"

"Yes, if you're willing."

"I could. I really don't mind. But I'd need to warm up."

James reached out, "Text book method, of course." He drew her to him, touching and kissing once, twice, a third time, then pulled back.

"Very well," she said quietly, looking in his eyes.

With his arm around her waist they began to walk. When they reached the hollow they waited while a couple passed then Beth stepped forward. She put down her bag, kicked off her shoes and took up position next to a clump of white and yellow daffodils.

Her dance began, arms in the air, stretching and turning both ways. With James as audience, her body came alive. She'd entered, it seemed, a marked-out space where she shifted foot to foot, waving slowly. The wave became a drift as she advanced, before stepping back, bowing slightly. "Imagine, and then..." she said casually, extending once more, arms up, shaping an arch. Her fingers touched then fell to her sides.

Returning to first position, she flexed her shoulders and rocked side to side. She was calmly elevated and floaty. "Just be," she said, glancing at James.

Gradually her dance widened; there were flow-lines and shapes and a feeling of excitement; her arms, her legs, everything about her was signalling. She was at her best.

Reaching climax, she paused, head back, and drew breath. From here it was simple. The dance took over with one step, another, back towards the hedge then, touching the flowers, a full-body sweep and heel-down to a stop, facing James.

His applause brought her back. "That was great," he said.

Beth stood back, hunched slightly, with one hand on her side.

"You out of breath?"

"Just a little."

He waited then asked if she'd had lessons. When Beth shook her head he laughed. "But surely you must be following steps?"

"Not really, I just do what comes. Of course, being outside helps."

"But if I asked, could you do it again?"

"I could, if you joined me."

"Well in that case," he said, taking off his rucksack, "it's a deal." And he advanced, placing himself opposite, on the other side of the daffs. "You lead," he added, and stood waiting.

Beth took a breath. "You'll do as I do. Simple Simon – yes?"

He nodded.

"But now, here's an idea... Are you OK to use letters?"

"Sorry, letters?"

"Letter shapes, in the air."

"Ah, no problem."

"In that case, follow me," she said, raising her arms.

Hands above his head, he mirrored her pose.

"It begins with A," Beth called, narrowing her arms to an inverted V. Again, James copied.

"And ends in O." She outlined a circle in the air.

James drew the same.

"Then, of course, there's B," she continued, pointing to herself, "and J, who is L who is U." Her back-and-forth gestures ended with a sweep of the hand. "Or it's a combination, ABBA or ROCK or even L-O-V-E." She spelled out each letter with a quickly-changing, double-handed gesture.

"Hey, hold on," called James, "I'm losing track."

Beth stopped. "It's just feel. All you have to do is let go." When he nodded, she crouched down to the daffodils, touching their heads. They were soft, yellow-white and fully expanded.

"So perhaps we should do our own thing," she said, fingering a stem, "that might be best."

"Or take turns."

She cupped one hand around a flower: "Yes, that's good. I'll do a letter, then you do a letter and we'll go on that way. Alphabetical, if you like."

"Right," he said, "but are we copying?"

"Not unless you want to."

"OK, let's see how we go."

In the dance that followed Beth began by calling, illustrating her letters with a move or a gesture before James took his turn. His moves were in parts – first one arm, then the other, then both-ways stepping – quickly developing to a foot-turn, a shake and a fist in the air. Hers were smooth and connected. Their styles were different, yet related.

And then, after joking about fitness and gathering breath, they changed.

"Let's try numbers," called James, leading briefly, ten down to five.

"Or dates," she said, "using fingers."

"Together, now," he said, after signalling birthdays.

"OK," she replied, "X Y Z."

Afterwards, as they walked downhill, Beth felt him by her. Being this close made her more herself, more connected and alive. She felt the air, the flowers, the green life all around. They were here together as lovers.

As they moved through the garden, the sun came and went. Unseen animals rustled in the bushes. Where the path dipped down they came across a stream trickling slowly into brown-green pools. They stood by a bridge naming plants then crossed to a walkway laid across a bog. Here they passed by reed beds and rain-pitted mud. On the other side was a gate and a path uphill.

"You've been here before?" she asked, as they climbed to a view.

"Once, with the kids, and Sandra."

"Right here, with her?"

"The same." His head came up and he smiled.

"Oh look," she said, pointing, "there are lots of them." She hoped he'd take notice.

The hillside below was contoured. They could see, gazing down, a sculpture at each level. Mostly metal with wood and plastic add-ons, they were large, semi-industrial and glinted in the sun. Around them and between them in khaki and cottons, some nodding, some listening and others staring while talking on their phones, were the visitors.

"Now that's what I call popular," said James.

"Was it this busy, last time?"

"I'm not sure I remember."

She wanted him to say more, but he seemed distracted. "You don't remember anything?"

"Not much, just them running round. Oh, and Sandra talking."

"So you haven't forgotten that."

"Certainly not." James put his head on one side. "Even at this age, some things stick."

"Yes, and some people stay with us."

"You mean the telephone ex? She goes on and on. Still does, when she can."

Beth breathed in sharply. She wondered if, behind his words, he was comparing.

"She annoys you?" he asked.

"Not exactly. Not her, really."

His eyes widened slightly. "There's a problem?"

"No, not at all. Only me," she replied, and wished she hadn't.

James stepped closer, "So what is it?" He waited for a moment then touched her on the arm. "Is it something I said?"

"Not really, I think it's about this place."

"But I thought you were enjoying it."

"I am," she said shakily, "and I don't want to spoil it, but…"

"But what?"

Suddenly her voice broke. "I keep seeing you and her. Right here, in this place. And I don't think I can make you happy." She was crying now.

James reached forward. His eyes scanned her face. "Beth, please. I don't want you thinking that way. I've told you what it was like. It was impossible, every day a problem. This is different, and so much better, because I'm with you."

"But did you love her?" The question was a challenge.

"I told myself I did, that's why we married. But looking back, it wasn't love."

"So what was it?"

"Convenience. And a great deal of wishful thinking."

Beth brushed one hand across her cheek and shook her head. She was swallowing hard. "So, what about us? Are we OK?"

James smiled, "Really, we're a lot better than that."

"You sure?"

"Absolutely." He rocked her in his arms, "I'm with you, and don't you forget it. Ab-so-lut–ely." His hug was firm and gentle. It kept her with him.

"Thank you. I've been silly, haven't I?" She turned to her bag, searching for a hankie. It came out, white and lightly-scented, like a flower. Touching its softness was a help. When she'd dabbed her face she kissed him. "It's over," she said, "I'm myself again."

"We all have our moments."

"It's when you see yourself in another person's shoes."

"But there are no repeats, you know that? Especially us."

Beth thanked him again. She packed away her hankie and checked her watch. "Shall we eat?" she asked, pointing to a flat patch with a bench. Below it the slope dropped away in terraced strips, each a platform, connected by steps.

"Well, *I'm* hungry," James said, untying his rucksack. Inside were some bagged-up savouries, an apple and a square plastic food box.

Taking turns to dip into the sack, they shared the food while sipping coffee from a small metal thermos. "Lucky dip," he said, pulling out a bag of nuts.

"I'd like some," she asked, cupping her hands.

He laughed and kissed her forehead.

They picked at the contents, one by one. The nuts came in all sizes; they were whole, lightly roasted and unsalted. Dipping and munching, they shared what they had.

Afterwards they cleared up then took the steps down the hillside. It was bright and airy and the crowds had thinned out. At each terrace level Beth and James circled the sculptures, comparing reactions. There were nameplates with signatures, usually dated, some with commentary, mostly vague, which they read together. A few, untitled, had the artist's name, several had signs with painted numbers, and one, near the bottom, had a plan decorated with bubble-thoughts and doodles behind screwed-down Perspex.

"This one looks interesting," said Beth, eyeing the display board.

The sculpture was in parts and covered an area the size of a house. The gate was festive, with bunting and light bulbs strung between posts. A ramp led in to an open space. Behind it was an all-plastic dome covered in badges with a flag on top and multi-coloured, porthole-style windows.

"It's like a kids' playground," said Beth, pausing at the entrance. Beyond the dome there were outlying sections, mostly irregular, with slides and rope nets and wooden enclosures, all at different levels and connected by tunnels. "Let's go in, see what we can see," she added, dropping her voice.

Inside was shadowy like a cave. A vague, silvery haze filled the air: it came and went as if through water. "I wonder how that's done," said James, as their eyes adjusted. He noticed to his right a big-bodied couple walking the floor. The woman held an old-fashioned camera, the man's arm was heavily bandaged. They seemed slightly odd.

Beth stood close to James, watching. What she saw surprised her. The space ahead was filled with upended cardboard rolls tied in bundles. Between them were winding, maze-like passageways that crisscrossed the floor. It looked like a carpet warehouse. "Which way?" she asked.

"Wherever you like," he said, quietly.

They chose a corridor between rolls. At a twist where it narrowed, James took the lead, offering a hand behind his back. Beth held it, thinking of rescues. Reaching an intersection, they swung right to arrive at a white-walled chamber lit by lamps. At the centre was a large, concave reflector. It was ridged and glazed, dipped towards the centre, and faced them like an eye. "That's something," said James. Moving side to side he peered at his image. Like a ghost at a window his reflection came and went.

"It's strange," said Beth, stepping closer. A line in the mirror thickened to a block. As James joined her and they hugged, their reflections fused and spread. "We're in there," said Beth, "if you look."

"So which part is you, which is me?"

"Whichever part you want."

"No distinction, eh?"

"Well, there *is* a quote," she said, meeting his eye.

"Yes?"

"It begins with 'Anyone can talk love...'."

"And how does it finish?"

"I can't quite say it word for word."

"Give it a try."

"OK. It ends something like, 'but it takes a real lover to be silly'."

"That's good," he grinned, "two crazies are always better than one."

"You like the idea?"

"Oh yes. It's like The Beatles, I am the walrus."

"Not sure I get it."

"You don't have to. That's the point."

Beth leaned forward, watching her image.

"In any case," he added, as their reflections merged, "when you're on the inside," – he waved at the mirror – "you really can't tell one head case from another."

When they emerged from the dome James could see, looking downhill, the unlike couple. They were arguing. The woman was pointing to a path down the slope, the man had half-turned away. She was speaking like an actor, with an edge of defiance. Her words appeared in snatches as if forced out. His replies, when they came, were angry and deliberate.

Beth pressed a fist into her side.

"They don't seem to be getting on," James said, speaking quietly. The couple were now battling, with her voice up-and-down, his blocking, and both sides cutting in.

"I wish people wouldn't do that," Beth said, grimacing. The woman had turned and was walking off; the man was calling after her.

"Not in public, anyway."

"Not at all, ever."

"Yes, it's ugly," he said, "but some people seem to need it, or it's about having the final say."

She flushed. "But that doesn't make it right."

"No."

Beth stepped back, breathing hard, "I'd like to go somewhere, anywhere – another part of the garden."

"You're not happy?"

"I just don't want to be here and listen to *that*," she waved downhill to where the couple were still battling.

"I see what you mean. It sounds like a war zone."

The man was shouting and swearing.

Beth winced. "You wouldn't ever do that to me?"

"Absolutely not."

"You promise?"

"Promise. It's out of the question."

"I couldn't bear it."

He smiled. "Tell yourself, love talks."

"I will," she said, and they hugged.

Leaving the couple, they skirted the hill. A ridge led up through bushes to a hillside track that circled a lake. Here they were alone and they walked arm in arm, pausing at viewpoints. From above, the lake was a metallic silver-grey. It was long and thin and L-shaped at one end. As they descended to a bank, a scattering of white and purple flowers became visible. "What are those?" asked Beth, pointing to clump. When James said fritillary, she asked if she should pick them.

"Best not, I'd say. The gardener might not like it."

She laughed.

Their path dropped further, entering a mixture of dog's mercury and dwarf silver birches. Close by the water there were sunbeams through branches and insects circling. Now and then small shifting ripples appeared on the surface. At one point a squirrel scrambled up a tree. As they approached the lake head an army of crows flapped into action, cawing. "I don't think anyone comes here," said James.

"Are you sure?"

"Not often, anyway. You can tell by the track."

They'd reached a point where the path split. One track went down, dropping to water where it ended in mud, the other climbed, straight into bushes. Both routes were overgrown. Beth looked uphill, "Do you think there's anything up there?"

James shrugged, "Trees, bushes, time on our own."

"It looks the kind of place…"

He nodded and their fingertips touched. Something passed between them – a line and direction, a thought without words – and they set off together. They took the higher route, pushing through heather as they climbed to a wood. The trees were old and covered with lichen and ivy. At the edge there were elders and flowering thorns, further in there were oaks with twisted branches, beyond that holly and brambles and an isolated clearing. Here, in a corner, screened by laurels, they came across a large, tunnel-shaped shelter. It was barn-length and constructed entirely of woven branches. The wood had been trimmed and layered carefully, but was sprouting now.

James led to the door, which was arch-shaped, "I think it's a sculpture, or used to be."

Beth joined him, "You think so?"

He pointed silently to some peeled and faded, paint-streaked branches.

She passed one hand across wood and a few loose grains of colour flaked off. "But it could just have been a place to shelter," she said.

"Let's take a look," he replied, taking her hand as they stepped inside.

The space they entered was cave-like and still. In the semi-dark they could make out the walls. They were covered all over by a rough plaster mix. A faint blue light, spreading from the ceiling, seemed to fill the air.

"We could stay here for a while," Beth's question was framed as a statement. She was pointing past the entrance to a low, bed-style platform. It had a logroll edge, linked by wires; inside was dry and soft and covered with sheep's wool. Advancing, she prodded then lay down. "It's good," she said, offering her arm. "This is what we've come for. Our rest stop."

James heard the lift in her voice. Her eyes were on him, inviting. "James," she said quietly. She reached out to be touched, repeating his name as he pulled her close.

For him it was absorbing: a place quite private, an inside experience. They were all lips and tongues, kissing. For Beth it went deep; she could hang there forever, or so it felt. Now they were together, with time and opportunity, it reminded her of their kiss at the station.

His hands went free, circling her waist and down to her thighs. She sighed and they pressed in closer. There was heat now between them and a flesh-tight pressure.

"Yes," she said, fingering her buttons. As his hands began to fumble a rustle in the bushes made her sit up. "What's that?" she asked.

James rolled over. "It's a bird, I think."

"You're sure there's no one out there?"

"Listen," he said. The rustle continued, followed by an earth-scratching sound. "That's very close and too low for a person."

She shuddered, "I wouldn't want anyone coming in."

He drew her to him. "You remember how hard it was to get here?" She nodded. "And how overgrown it was?" She nodded again. "So if anyone was coming we'd hear them way off."

"You really think so?"

"Long before they got here. They'd have to parachute in, or we'd know it."

She lay back and listened, "Now you say it, that's a bird." She reached out to him: "I told you, didn't I, about Dad and bird watching?"

James said yes and repeated a few remembered phrases, speaking quietly. His calm took over and they both fell quiet. He touched her cheek, lightly, and stroked her hair while she lay back, smiling. She understood him now – right through, completely. He was what she wanted, that was all.

"Darling," she said, and an urgency entered. His tongue found her ear, lightly, and they began to undress, fumbling slightly. Each garment was rolled either down or up and slipped off by hand. They did it together.

"You happy?" he asked as he lay on his side circling her breasts then reached down to her thighs. She nodded and he touch-stroked lightly, while she explored his chest. Beth felt his warmth, his immediate closeness, and the shaking of his hands. Desire took over as he turned and positioned then climbed between her legs. As he entered a wave rose from below; it was as if she was underwater, swimming through light.

He began, moving in rhythm, rocking slowly. He eased in further, squeezing and pushing until he was deep inside, leading and led. He was in there, moving without effort. They floated and held each other loosely, in a grip. And then, driven from below, they tightened. His movement quickened, gradually building to a single, connected, all-in-one flow – speeding onward to a big-leap moment – and then they were squeezing and grunting and crying and shivering, till they came and came, releasing with a shout.

Afterwards they lay facing, in silence. Their bodies kept them warm. Above them a bird sang, whistling softly. The air through the door was cool and still.

When James reached out and pulled on a shirt, Beth sat up.

"Thank you," she said.

He smiled and stroked her cheek. They kissed.

"Well, it's a good place," she said, "but I suppose..." She began shifting about, gathering up her clothes.

James eyed her gently. As she dressed, he shuffled closer, handing over garments and kissing where he could.

"Yes, I like it," she said.

"Home from home?"

"It's our house in the woods," she answered, quietly.

James murmured agreement, touching her hair.

"And from now, it's our story," she added, smiling.

Part Two

If I'd known, I'd have memorised everything at the time. For James, for John and Louise, for my girls, for everyone.

I'd have captured each gesture – a light shift on glass, a face in passing, the weight of words – caught each turn as it appeared, fixed that expression (as exit? entrance? or something in between?) and recorded the whole thing, in detail, as it was.

A book is an adventure.

How could I have done it? On cards at table, coded, in the margin, or phrase by phrase carried in the head? In a flip book or chart, or maybe dance-wise with finely-balanced moves, developed by feel. Or perhaps as a snap, a second's impression, then mounted with captions and stuck down in a book.

Once, with dad, I named birds and talked. As we walked around the garden he told me their stories. I hear him now – we're in the bedroom – his thoughts, and the dreams that follow. It's him and me in private, like characters in a book.

Without stories we're boring.

Where I am now isn't easy. I try not to show it, but there's so much to think about. The past and how I've changed. I hear a high-up voice singing 'Demands my soul, my life, my all'. It's like looking out of the window, blank-faced and expressionless, on the last train home.

So this is my album, my gallery. Beginning, of course, with my husband and lover.

24.5.09

Waiting in the restaurant, I felt him coming. The blue-grey eyes, hair slightly curled, soft skin with wrinkles... he was searching for me. Of course your mind plays tricks, but this was different. What you remember is a glimpse, a pared-down image. The past is what we feel. But with James I knew straight away, as if it was now. In the restaurant he had presence.

I do remember the build-up. I thought of running because my nerves were singing out. Looking back, it all seems rather breathless. But it's one thing to say, another to be there. You try not show it, but you feel wide open. Turning up is a statement, and once you've done that, is it possible to back out?

I'd talked to friends beforehand. Of course I was starry, but I knew that trap. And Sarah had warned me, "It's the difference between shopping for a recipe and feeding kids," she said. "So *please* don't get burned."

That's how Sarah talks. In the café she makes a big entrance, calls out, says something quirky then sings from the charts as she cleans all over.

"You're dreaming what's on the menu," she went on, "but watch out for the bill."

We call her FSS: Full Speed Sarah. She's even more pumped-up than Toby at a match. I remember how she danced, first thing in the morning, calling out, "Olé! Olé!" and crazy-hand-clapping while running up and down.

But with me she's different. Perhaps it's how we've adapted, our French and Saunders on-stage thing. Or maybe it's by contrast: the dreamer and the doer.

On this occasion we were standing after work on the beach and Sarah was pressing her toe into a clump of seaweed. I remember her calling it *food for free*. While she talked about its uses, I listened and looked out. The sky was grey, shading to black, rimming the horizon. The wind was changeable and the tide was half in. It felt like the beginning of a film.

I thought of Dover Beach. That's what happens, give me a seascape or a big wide sky and I think of poetry. Celebration and consolation.

"Shall I meet him?" I asked.

The light on the sea glowed white. I'd a feeling of something moving, a bright spot within.

"You want to?"

129

I see it as a picture. Two women on the shoreline, one large, one skinny, with a world behind and a lifetime ahead. Or something shorter, more carpe diem. It's like that song in West Side Story, *Something's Coming*. Of course, begin a phrase and my mind fills the gap – *Down the block, on a beach* – which took me there and suddenly it was obvious. "Yes," I said, removing my shoes and stepping into water.

She joined me in the shallows. The waves lapped around us. They were clear and cold and tickly.

"Yes, yes," she said, taking my hand and we danced.

3.6.09

Recently I've been looking at Dali's *The Persistence of Memory*. The soft watches describe how I feel: caught in the glare and melted, in a quiet way. The view out to sea is sunny, while, in the foreground, the shadow of a mountain is filling up the picture. It's a clean bare place with sharp lines and spread flesh. A Gethsemane. It reminds me of my first experience of death.

I was eight at the time, the year I wrote The Girl Who Began Again. I was alone in the back garden. I don't know where my dad was, but I can still feel his absence. I was crouched down studying the path, seeing it as a jigsaw, an old one, with bits missing. Parts of it didn't fit. It was cracked and patched and smeared with concrete. Small, spiky weed-tufts showed around the cracks.

Taking a stick I began digging. I was poking at the side, exploring a crack, when a lump fell out. I remember sitting back in surprise. I can still feel it now, like an extraction. I was numb, trying to work things out. Had I done this, I wondered, and if I had, wasn't it by accident? At the same time I knew, and that made me jumpy. I had the stick in my hand and could see where the lump had landed, in the shadow of a bush. I hoped it wouldn't get noticed.

I glanced back at the house then checked the hole. Just one peek, I told myself, and I'd be done. But what I saw scared me. I could make out a rough, cave-like space filled with roots. It seemed to be alive at the bottom as if it was bleeding.

I looked again. This time I was prepared, but it still made me shiver. The roots were full of dark, wriggly shapes. They were running all over in lines and knots, filling up the cavity. It seemed like they might boil over.

Then I realised they were ants, nesting. And, in the middle, where they were busiest and blackest, they'd seized on something large. I watched in silence as they tore it apart. Body bits were held up, twirled in the air and cleared like rubbish. They were relentless. I began to turn away then realised suddenly what they'd got. The creature they were dismembering was a large, hollowed-out, silver-winged butterfly.

I was deeply shocked. How could they do that to something so beautiful? As if it was their prisoner. It was hard to understand. But also, by being the only witness, I'd got myself involved. And ants were ruthless, I knew that from school where a teacher had compared them to armies. I'd read about captive explorers being coated with honey and eaten by ants. But this was worse, their oddly-shaped, ritualistic movements were jungly, insistent and fiercely territorial. In them, for the first time, I glimpsed a different world.

For the rest of that day I could feel them with me. They were hiding in the toilet, inside the plughole and underneath the bed. Like the ants in Dali they kept reappearing, on plates, through cracks, and dreamed, in the mirror. At night I could feel them, tingling in my flesh. Even today, those ants are still with me. I can see them crawling on a clock in *The Persistence of Memory*.

I've read that Dali wanted to illustrate the theory of relativity. What I'd seen in action was the second law of thermodynamics.

15.6.09

I'm making my preparations. They're for me, in private, as a fall-back, but they're also for the others. For family and friends, if anything happens. I want it on record like a film or book, to be all in one place, like a CV. At the moment I've only told James. It's a matter of confidence. Telling the others would only set them off. They'd fear the worst, suppose I knew something then want reassurance, and there isn't much to offer, just a gut feeling.

Fortunately, James understood. In good-guy mode he listened before making a few suggestions. That's why I love him. He's a man, wants action, but always hears me out. He did ask for details and we talked about feelings, seeing doctors and what might happen. Later he looked up the symptoms online. And he played escort. So he walked me to the surgery and, when he could, drove me to hospital or collected me after tests. If I'd let him, I think he'd have taken my place.

So, encouraged by him, I'm preparing.

Firstly, I'm filling up a scrapbook as my aide mémoire. In it I've placed pictures of family, magazine cut-outs and pieces about animals, dance show programmes and catalogues from galleries. I've deliberately mixed it up, with a page for lyrics, a pressed-flowers page, another for cloth-scraps and bagged-up seeds, and a double-page spread with notes on card about people in the café. At the end I've added a section with certificates, a few poems and some ecumenical prayers.

Of course it's all about character, seen through a window. And it's for my daughters, to pass on what I can. So, on the cover I've added drawings: early ones of theirs, and one by me. On the inside I've dedicated it, signed and dated, to Ruth and Naomi. And I've given both a page, named at the top, with a one-line message asking them to fill it up.

Secondly, there's my bedside cabinet. It's rather fancy, striped and padded at the front with a cut-glass handle. I think of it as my allsorts collection. Inside, it's full of red-yellow ribbons, tie-dyed cloth and black and purple stones, and packed with goodies, like a gift shop. Of course they're a selection, so my drawers aren't me, not exactly. They're more about things and what they feel like. Everything in them has their own weight and specifics. They're there for themselves, and sometimes to surprise. Like art, they've been taken out of context, which changes their meanings. But first and foremost, they are what they are. And the history behind them is additional.

I keep up my drawers. I review what's in them, take things out, place them around the room, and make myself *see* them. Next I select, returning some, putting others on display. Then once a week I add in something new: a toy, a meditational text or an objet trouvé. I do this as a ceremony, taking time, sometimes with James, in silence. When he's there choosing, we mime. So, pointing to items, we nod or pull faces. Sometimes we give a thumbs-down, or we wave and laugh, setting each other off. Afterwards we stay silent.

It's like lighting candles, one from the other, in church. It's like our first meeting.

25.6.09

Inside myself I've always been a nun. Nuns are wild. They are lovers of gardens where bees hover around mint. The places where they pray are full of lilies and scented herbs. Their walks are like turning pages in a book.

I keep my nun hidden, most of the time. She calls herself Lucy. In her mind she's an expressionist painter. She's the one who stops on the path to talk to the birds. When no one's watching she climbs trees and swings on gates. As Lucy she's a dancer. When she's moving the world stands still.

The nun I am now is older and tougher. She lives on the edge. She's reached that point where her body drives her. Her mouth is dry and her insides ache. Her face is hollow and her bones show through. I call this nun Amanda. She still has faith.

In the dark she breathes heavily. There's a man by her side who keeps her going. He's her angel, cheering her on. She's against the clock and keeping focus. But what she has to do seems beyond her. The distance is telling. Although he's beside her, her strength is fading. The thoughts she has seem to vanish into air. What used to be her voice has become a whisper. Her arms, her legs are all giving out. She's a woman beginning Lent.

4.7.09

When I was young it all seemed simple.

I thought I could change things, have it my way, do everything at once. I was on the look-out. Like one of my characters I'd put myself together, a bit-part collection of film clips, life observations and aspects of soul. And I believed my own stories, because the truth was in the telling, and I lived inside my head, in whatever way I chose.

Made-up is so.

Now I know better. You watch as it goes on, try this, try that and laugh at your own absurdity, because anything can happen. It's how you frame yourself, and then stay in there, with effort. It's a bubble you blow.

Take my life with James. We began by telling all, the dos and don'ts, the things we'd learned and what we'd been through. For me, if it's a marriage, then both sides are obliged. It's like that theory about humans: looked at over time it's all about belief. Apply that theory to James and me. Right from the start we *chose* to be in love.

I think of it as a map, whatever route you follow, it's a one-way thing. The real risk is holding back, what they call 'letting things be'. But for us, with our history, it was about looking forward. So we'd say things in public, flaunt it, if you like. And we still keep it up – kind words in the morning, a cheek kiss, the L word – really we're on stage. Making our mark, telling all.

Which brings me to family, Hannah, and the problems.

17.7.09 – 30.9.09

I first met Hannah at a South Bank restaurant. James had showed me pictures, so I knew she was beautiful. What struck me was her child-round face and her scarf-like hair trained across a shoulder. She was long-limbed and slightly Romany. Young of course, and very photogenic. I noticed in a Facebook picture, posed next to her brother, how she looked into camera as cool as you like, as if she wasn't bothered.

James used the word 'lively' to sum up his children; he said they were 'smart kids' and 'perfectly wised-up'. The words that followed – London, the reconstructed family, college – should have made it easy. But maybe they were meant as a warning. After all, we do come from different worlds.

The meeting had been arranged on neutral ground. Not at James's and not by the sea. We needed space and an exit strategy. Also, we had to be careful. No looks, no handholds, and strictly functional talk. We knew we were on show.

"It's a bit like an audition," I told him, walking to our meeting along the riverside path. We were facing into sun, picking our way through groups of people talking into phones or pointing cameras, moving slowly, with a slightly distanced feel. On one side there was space with flags in the air and views over water, on the other side, glass and steel. In between were slatted benches and low concrete walls.

"Don't worry," James said, "they always like being paid for."

Looking at the crowd, I tried to spot his children approaching. I had their pictures in my head. Inside myself I was preparing what to say.

"In any case, I've told them," he continued, squeezing my hand.

"Told them what?"

"The rules," he replied, gazing ahead. A light, soft breeze was playing around our faces. "Don't worry, eating out will limit behaviour."

I know he meant well, but his words alarmed me slightly. I wondered what their unlimited behaviour might be like.

We arrived a few minutes early. The restaurant was modern with shop-sized windows and a view across water. Joining a queue at the door, we filed through an all-white entrance into an open-plan dining room. A waiter directed and we occupied one end of a cushioned bench.

"What are they like for timing?" I asked. By now I was feeling nervous.

"They're young," said James, dryly.

George arrived first. He was tall and hunched and softly-spoken. He had spots on his neck, a hairless chin and attentive, child-wide eyes. I felt for him.

We greeted, shaking hands.

"Han's coming, soon," he said gruffly, eyeing his mobile.

James checked for drinks, ordering juice.

I remember how they talked. They were deliberately low-key and careful of each other. There were gaps between phrases, words left hanging and the odd wry smile, as if they were side by side on a sofa, watching a film.

Then Hannah arrived.

"Is this, like, where we're eating?" she said, furrowing her brow.

"It's where you asked for," said James.

Hannah sat down, pulling out a silver-edged phone from her handbag. She laid it in front of her then touched the screen, sounding a bell tone, with her fingers dancing. While she was typing, I wondered just how much she noticed, and if she was with us.

"Shall we order?" asked James.

Hannah looked up, apparently puzzled: "You mean, like, now?"

"I intend to eat, I don't know about you."

"That's what people do in restaurants," put in George.

"You choose," she replied, returning to her phone, "I'll eat whatever."

It was a relief when the food arrived. I remember the rich, smooth smell and the soft/firm textures in piled-up bowls with sauces and garnish. It was fresh, slightly milky and herbal.

Hannah peered into her dish, shuddered, and pushed it away.

"You're not hungry?" asked James carefully. I could tell he was feeling blocked.

"I don't eat mixtures. You know that."

"Give it a go," he said coaxingly.

"Do I have to?"

"I'd like you to. Just try."

She glanced in my direction. Her eyes were dark brown and expanded. "How much am I expected to eat?" she asked, addressing her father.

"Whatever you feel like, and can manage."

"I might throw up."

"Well, do your best."

"Yes, I'm sure you can do it," I put in and James nodded, but Hannah looked away. I realised then it was safer to play audience.

"Han," George called out, "you remember our game with Dad, *it isn't happening*?"

She nodded.

"Well, do that. Eat, but tell yourself you aren't."

Hannah's face lit up, "Do you remember that, Dad?"

"As if it wasn't happening. Now."

"That means go for it, Sis," called George.

"And do you, like, think if I say this's a virtual meal...?"

James smiled: "If it helps, why not? Call it Zen eating. Do it for laughs."

Returning to her bowl, Hannah sampled around the edges, poked and prodded then stopped. "Feeling yuck," she said. A pink-red flush was spreading up her neck. I wondered for a moment if she'd some sort of allergy. Glancing over at an unconcerned George, I realised it was theatre.

"Gruesome," she added, sighing as she pushed back her chair. Rising to join her, James called her name.

"Need some space," she said, waving him off, "too hot." And she went to the loo, dabbing at her eyes and declaring herself sick.

In her absence, James asked the waiter to cover her plate. "Don't worry," he said, "Hannah'll be OK."

He said it as an aside, nodding slightly in my direction. It was one of his phrases. I knew when he said it, he wasn't happy.

"She's feeling it," said George, shrugging.

"That's Hannah for you," James said, waving his fork. "She'll be back, so eat up."

During the meal that followed, I remember thinking how well we played our parts. My role as girlfriend was all about appearances, and like any actor, my intention was to please. So I kept myself visible and agreed with things said. But also I was aware of how little I really figured.

The main show was at table. They took up their positions as father and son. James played lead, making suggestions and offering thoughts, while George held back, saying very little. I could see, as a double act, how they set each other off.

We'd nearly finished eating when Hannah returned. She appeared from the back and sat down abruptly, looking at the table. Her expression had stiffened to a doll-like stare.

"How are you feeling?" asked James.

Hannah murmured something inaudible.

George pointed to her bowl. "They kept it hot for you. We didn't even have to ask." I remember how he smiled: carefully, giving very little away. His face was deliberately bland.

She examined the lid, blinking slowly.

"You can eat it," added George, "Dad doesn't mind."

Hannah pouted.

"And *nobody*'s looking," he continued, slyly.

Her mouth twitched slightly and she sighed. I could see there was help needed.

"It's up to you," said James. "Your choice. Eat or don't eat, simple as that."

Hannah hesitated then grasped her bowl. Her nails showed red against white. "All right," she said, wrinkling up her nose, "I'll do it. Anything to keep you guys happy." And she unlidded, picked up a fork and dug into her meal.

We stayed in the restaurant for a least another hour. I felt for them all. Anyone watching would have seen the strain – the voice stops and glances, the faces glazed over – while registering James's efforts, with the odd prompt from George. For James it was about leading, without too much pressure. He was the facilitator, the man-in-the-middle with a slot to fill, and he talked to reassure us, at an evenly-judged pace, switching between news, his job, TV programmes and accounts of things he'd read. But underneath everything, I could see he was struggling.

His main target was Hannah. Not obviously or head-on, but through choice of words and incidental gestures. He kept up the flow, with control, varying his content, while she eyed her phone.

I remember when they left how suddenly and completely her voice tone changed. "Oh, thank you," she said, blushing. The remark, though spoken quietly, seemed directed towards me. Perhaps it was her way of saying sorry.

At the end James hugged them both. Standing just behind him, I thought about doing the same, but held back, waiting. George coughed, said bye, and reached out a hand while Hannah simply nodded. As they left, picking their way around tables without looking back, James caught my eye.

"You OK?" he asked.

Returning his gaze, I nodded. His shoulders had dropped and his hands were spread. Even before we touched I could feel him shaking.

From then on The Hannah Factor became part of our lives.

The restaurant performance and our exchange afterwards brought us closer. It was as if we were pundits discussing a sporting upset, or a political event. We'd talk about her as an *issue* and almost at once, as if she'd heard us, there would be Hannah on the phone, questioning our movements, like a parent checking up. Her texts would come through in the bathroom saying 'call me now' or 'U doing stuff?' arriving usually just before bedtime. We called it HI DAD IT'S ME, or RADIO HANNAH.

And when she came on the line she was reactive, complaining about boredom, bad thoughts and feelings of exclusion, naming names and quoting out of context then cutting off suddenly with a plea about time, a brief apology and silence.

It was when she visited, calling from outside and entering breathless, that the worst things were said. I'd be upstairs, staying out of it, but would hear every word. It was long, uneasy and wrangling, a set-piece dialogue of the sort that only really happens in private between families.

If it had been scripted, it would have gone like this:

Father: Hello stranger, this is unexpected. Nice to see you.
        (Father gives a slightly one-sided hug.)
Girl: Whatever. It's raining outside.
        (They enter a colourful kitchen with plants on the windowsill and posters on the wall.)

Father: So what d'you fancy, tea or coffee?

Girl: Is that, like, all you've got?

Father: You want something else?

Girl: Depends on what there is.

Father: Let's see. (*Opens fridge.*) Grape juice or water, that's about it.

Girl: What about gin, or vodka?

Father: You serious?

Girl: Gin with vodka's good.

Father: You know I'm not a big drinker.

Girl: So *I am*?

Father: I didn't say that.

Girl: But that's what you meant.

Father: No, not at all. As far as I'm concerned you drink or you don't drink, it's up to you.

Girl: So you wouldn't ever consider, like, trying to stop other people. Except me, of course.

Father: Well, have it your way. You've heard what we've got. Tea, coffee or juice. Now, would you like something?

Girl: Anything. Doesn't matter. Same as you'll do.

Father: Teabags it is then.

(While the father makes tea, the girl is busy with her phone. He asks her questions about her course, her brother, her plans. She replies with a half-attentive nod, a word or a grunt. Sometimes it's unclear who or what she's addressing: her father or the phone.)

Father: There's your tea, then. As you like it.

Girl: What? That's for me?

Father: Yes. The way you like it.

Girl: Oh, I thought you meant something else.

Father: Something else?

Girl: As You Like It. We've been doing it on my course.

Father: Ah, and *do* you like it?

Girl: Not much. Rather have something else.

Father: By the way, have you noticed something?

Girl: Noticed – what?

Father: Those words *something else*, you keep using them.

Girl: Me? Don't think so.

Father: You do, though.

Girl: Noooo-way. Not me.

Father: It's as if you're signalling something – looking for something else – permanently.

Girl: Lay off, Dad. I heard *you* say it.

Father: Yes, repeating after you, that's all.

Girl: So YOU know the problem. It's all about me, like, looking for *something else.* Weird or what?

Father: This is silly.

Girl: Yeah, you're right. Silly-silly. And you're something else.

Father: Your words not mine.

Girl: Bloody hell, Dad, do you have to be this way? Going on and on. Can't you just leave it?

Father: It's only an observation, that's all.

Girl: You know, Dad, I never feel, like, comfortable in this house. There's always something you want to get after. Like, you have to prove a point, have the last say, again and again. You think I'm not good enough or clever enough or nice enough to be your daughter.

Father: I don't think that's fair. Not right or fair, on you or me.

Girl: But it's what you think. *Really.* Ever since— *(She glances up towards the ceiling.)*

Father: If you mean what I think... Well, you're wrong. Nothing has changed. I'm still your dad and you're my daughter.

Girl: So you say.

Father: It's true.

Girl: Yeah, biologically. But what about how we relate? Do you believe we're, like, compatible?

Father: Of course.

Girl: But let's say, let's just say we could both swop for something else, a different family, would you do it?

Father: Look—

Girl: So now – swop and you get something else. Would you, or wouldn't you?

Father: Hey, just slow down. You're missing something.

Girl: How? What's up?

Father: You said it.

Girl: Said, said, said, what's that mean?

Father: A lot when it keeps on happening. It means you're avoiding...

140

	But forget it.
Girl:	Shit, Dad. You've got this obsession. OK just to please you, I'll say it: *something fucking else.* Happy now?
Father:	Not really.
Girl:	So… *(She glances at her phone)* You like how I talk?
Father:	It's not that important. Liking doesn't come into it, anyway.
Girl:	But you really don't. It offends.
Father:	That's not the point.
Girl:	Is there a point? I mean, does any of this matter?
Father:	For me, yes.
Girl:	So what's, like, pissing you off?
Father:	Not much. It does feel pretty uphill, though.
Girl:	But you come to expect that from daughters, don't you? Yes, yes, Dad. I know how you talk together. *(Again, she raises her eyes to the ceiling.)*
Father:	We don't. Not the way you put it.
Girl:	So what do you say when you talk about me? She's such a sweet girlie-girl… so nicey-nice… knows her place…?
Father:	Don't go there.
Girl:	Oh yes? So what *do* you say then? And why d'you keep looking at me like I've done something wrong? I'm not some sort of criminal.
Father:	Come on, this is all drama.
Girl:	Yeah, and I'm playing psycho tonight.
Father:	Really, it isn't like that. You're blowing everything up, out of all proportion.
Girl:	That's what you think, isn't it? I'm some sort of OTT spoiled brat who, like, doesn't know her place.
Father:	You know, there's a name for this. It's called the self-fulfilling prophecy.
Girl:	Meaning?
Father:	*(shrugs)* Meaning I'm tired, and there's nothing much more to say.
Girl:	*(rising to go)* You know Dad, it's always like this. Whatever I say you won't listen. You just think everything I do is wrong. And now you say you're too tired to talk.
Father:	Knackered's the word.
Girl:	And I'm just so… fru-stra-ted.

Father: So that's what we do to each other. Sadly.

Girl: Dad, I need you to talk, I really do.

Father: All right, I'm willing. It's just…

Girl: Just what?

Father: Well, when I'm tired and, to be honest, pretty put off.

Girl: By me. I know.

Father: Could say. Not intended, but then…

Girl: All right Dad. I get it.

Father: You do? I hope so.

Girl: I do, really.

Father: OK, tell me what you're thinking.

Girl: You want to listen?

Father: Absolutely. Go ahead.

Girl: All right, look at it like this – in most ways we're the same. We're both stubborn, because, let's face it, most people are. And we're both a lot of trouble, we don't toe the line, probably you more than me. Listen Dad, it's true. When it comes to people my age I, like, fit in. And that's deliberate, for now. But when I'm adult, I'll be the same as you.

Father: You mean arguing all the time with your daughter.

Girl: Of course. On and on and on.

Father: But what do you do if she keeps arguing back?

Girl: Oh, that's no problem. I'll, like, tell her. The simple truth.

Father: Which is?

Girl: That dads and daughters, like, know best.

Father: And if they're, like, stubborn and troublesome and won't toe the line?

Girl: Then they'll both have to learn.

2.10.09

People change. In the case of Hannah, not too much. But after the first few meetings I came to see her more as she was, or the girl she'd like to be. There were moments of shyness, mostly in private, curled up on the sofa with James as listener, when she asked for help, usually with essays. Once, visiting the café, she sat silent at the back then joined in afterwards, clearing dishes and washing up. You never knew quite who she would be, Hannah Mark One, rough and mouthy, or Hannah Mark Two, little-girl-helpful. Perhaps she didn't know either. But I do think now that she was young, self-conscious, and needed to cover up. So she hid her nice-girl habits. But to us, in private, her true self popped out. As Good-Girl Hannah she sneak-watched quiz shows and costume dramas and listened, occasionally, to online talks. And sometimes she shared quotes, often her own but reworded, taken from films, or sent us pictures with her own jokey captions. There was even one time when she brought round a friend's story and left it with James. With it came a note that said she'd like my comments.

"Why me?" I asked, gazing at the folder left lying on the table. It was covered with cartoon stickers and flying dolphins.

James shrugged. "I told her you wrote at her age. She didn't say much, but Hannah takes in everything."

"Have you read it?"

"Once. Be warned, it's bog standard stuff. What you might call a generic piece."

"You don't rate it?"

"Hard to tell. It's unfinished."

"But you don't like it?"

"Take a look yourself."

"You think it's bad."

"You'll see."

So I read.

I guess I'm the product of all kinds of forces I can't control. Some of them dark. And then there are my genes.

I don't know a typical all-American family, twenty-first century, but I know I don't come from one for sure. Although a mommy who's a drunk with classy social skills for cover may not be as rare as you'd think. I'm not exactly daddy's girl but plenty of others are, girls I mean, some of them friends of mine, past tense. Dean Dickinson likes to think he's hot but his belly tells another story and his jeans are one size too tight. Miami is the eldest of the Dickinson kids and she takes setting the baddest example possible really seriously, as in a full-time job. Her look is grunge with hairy armpits and flame-red lips, rips in her T-shirts and black fingernails but one thing she isn't aiming on is scaring any guys. There may be some hiding teeth marks with hoodies zipped up high because it'd be hard to find anyone more suited to the vampire life. Or death.

Next is Demona, taller, flat chest, braces, straight A's. To look at her you might think churchgoer, virgin. No way. Demona can act the straight but she smokes more than tobacco, only gum and perfume hide it well. That leaves our little brother, the Junior Dean, and he's a shouter, always has been, only it used to be I hate you to his teachers with a teddy thrown their way and now it's fuck off with a compass. Except when he's cute and curly with his tongue hanging out stabbing anything small with more legs than him.

Which leaves me, Evangeline, the audience taking it all in and mixing it my way, making it pay, biding my time. Stockpiling grievances like weapons. Getting ready.

I closed the folder. "So what do you say to something like that?"

"Nothing, if possible."

"But I'm expected to comment?"

"It seems she wants it that way."

"Do you know why? Is it some sort of test?"

"No, not at all. In fact, I see it as a mark of respect."

Surprise overcame my doubts. I couldn't quite see it but maybe, I thought, there were other people involved.

I looked back at the folder: "And do you know anything about this friend?"

"I think we're not supposed to ask. Imaginary, I suspect."

"I see, extreme care needed."

"Indeed."

"Maybe if I ask about film deals, and who's going to play Evangeline?"

"As long as you approve, that's OK. But don't stretch it, or she'll suspect."

"So what you're suggesting is no negatives…"

"And the odd positive thrown in, but keep them general and not too gushy."

"Ah, let me see. Forget style, ignore content and talk about promise and appeal, but not too much. Yes, I think I get it."

"Can you manage?"

"Don't worry I'll do it, very carefully."

"And Beth…"

"Yes?"

"Thank you."

"Oh, that's all right. I like her, anyway."

"I know you do. Write what you have to. I'll read it over if it helps. Maybe you could see this as a kind of olive branch."

15.10.09

I write most days, it keeps me busy. On bad days I manage just a few words, on good days it's in three figures. Like my condition, it comes and goes.

Perhaps I shouldn't say *write*. A lot of it is mental. And there's a magic in it, as if I'm in the dark, talking myself up. So I imagine myself writing, chat to myself, challenge my own feelings and shape my own story, sometimes on paper and sometimes in the head. Often it's in the night, when I'm half asleep. That's when the story develops. The words run on and events take a turn I hadn't expected. It's like a novel in progress. For every small addition something else goes out.

In the morning I look back. If I've any notes I may just copy them and see what happens. But often it's a summary, without a written record. If it exists at all, it's like an image in an album, or a half-forgotten story which crops up in conversation when a friend comes round.

Sometimes I revise, try out different rhythms or switch around phrases. Then I talk to James, describe what I've been thinking, say where I'm up to. It's another kind of story with him and me together. I tell him it's for us, I'm trying to make it happen. But in my mind I'm less certain. It's all about survival, there's a hole, imagined or real, and that's what I'm avoiding.

It reminds me of what I'm running from. The detail's there for cover. I'm alone in the garden, naming what I see.

It's like shining a torch onto see-through paper. The grains stand out and the whiteness shows through.

I've a strange feeling that what I thought was in the past never really happened. Or that what I'm living now is actually a story I've imagined while lying in my bed.

But then, if God is there, does it really matter?

26.10.09

The worst thing is doubt. For a long time there were shadows, sudden alarms, and a shifting, tidal kind of pressure, as if I was underwater. I was drowning, or I was stranded. Something worm-like and achy was filling up inside, then draining. It was in there I knew, but not so I could prove it. Which made me feel unreal. James of course listened, in bed, with his arm around my waist. I could say things together, in a room of our own. But outside that I didn't feel safe. I'd a creeping feeling that I was on a ledge where no one could see me. I was high up and exposed and all on my own. Though, oddly, I wasn't too afraid. It was like jumping between cliffs: I had my eye on reaching the other side, not on the drop. So when the blood appeared I saw it as a sign. Not the kind of cross-on-the-door, avoidance sign, but an unfamiliar signal, something coded, with a message. It shocked me into life. But the darkness returned and for a while the tests showed nothing.

The odd thing was that during that period, I felt quite strong. On the surface, nothing seemed to trouble me. I went through the fasts and scans and samples and tests, ignoring their meaning. But underneath, I wanted closure, to have something definitive, no matter how unpleasant, to know where I stood.

When the diagnosis came I wasn't that surprised. I did have a gut-shock level which kept me awake. My system was on edge and time was ticking down. But my main worries were what it would be like and whether I could cope. And I did have a hope that if I kept my head down it might go off. That the angel at the door hadn't come for me. But what happened then was I found myself having to explain. All at once I was the centre of interest. In fact it seemed to be my job to deal with everyone, other than James. He embraced me and said we'd face it and together we'd see it off. He put himself in line. Now I think he took too much on himself, but his strength helped me.

The real problem was my family. I do love them, of course, but this was too big or painful for them. They were either tongue-tied or only-too-keen to talk about anything else. I could see them from a distance, they seemed so unaware, but it did keep me occupied. Because there are times it's better to stay awake. I do know that, afterwards, when I'd told them all, I began to weaken and see it as a story full of personal suffering. In my mind there were clips, often from weepies, with black-bordered cards and white-faced relatives around hospital beds. I thought of myself as the subject of a painting, a sad, Ophelia-like drifter. I was Violetta or Mimi, dying in the snow.

Sometimes it's better to be in doubt.

I think, over time, we learn how to play things. Because with age you adapt, sometimes to the point where anything goes. You get to know how it works, that it's all interconnected. Also, you see the knock-on effects, the things passed on. In our case not just with the kids but right through the family. So, for instance, take my two: here was Ruth at the centre, with Conrad one side and Naomi the other. I was on the outside, closer to Naomi, but available to everyone as sympathetic listener. Most times they said nothing. If they were happy and comfortable then I wasn't on call. But once they were in conflict then I became their messenger and everything was an issue. It was all about challenges and complaints and finger pointing – which was what developed quickly around Ruth's baptism.

I'd seen it coming but said nothing. For Ruth at that time, church was her life. It was where she found herself in a strong, firm place, somewhere she was known. Though my views were different, I understood her faith. It answered all her questions. The mood took over and she sang as she prayed and walked to the altar in step with others, and nothing was uncertain or shadowy or shot through with doubt.

But when news reached Naomi of the forthcoming service, the arguments began.

"Mum, did you know about Ruth's baptism?" she asked, after chatting about work.

I recognised the tone. She was holding back.

"What about it, love?"

"Well, for one thing: did you realise when it was due?"

"Not exactly. I knew it was coming up soon."

"This week, just four days' time. Almost straight away."

"Yes, I suppose it is very close."

"And you didn't tell me. Not-a-single-word."

"I'm sorry love, I hadn't realised."

"But did you agree to her doing it, in the way they're going to?"

I paused before replying. Her voice tone had hardened: there was an RP crispness about it, as if she was speaking in public, for effect.

"You're worried about her?" I countered.

"Not worried, but alarmed, and with good reason."

"You needn't be. She'll be fine."

147

"You sure of that? I mean, total immersion, it's what we call invasive. A takeover job."

I recognised her objection. It was her urge to protect, to shield her patients. I could hear her in the ward wanting action.

"But it's what she wants. Her choice," I replied.

"You mean Dad's. It's all about him and his cult. They just want her brainwashed, and you have to stop it."

"I don't think it's like that. If you want it stopped you'll have to talk to Ruth, or your dad."

"Oh, Mum. I don't think… I *really* don't."

It was at this point that the talk became charged. Up to then she'd stayed calm, at least on the surface. But at the mention of Conrad her voice suddenly turned and she was on us – me, it seemed, more than him.

"It's simply not fair," she cut in. "You do whatever you like, break up the family, close your eyes to *us*, and then you allow this stupid business."

"Naomi, please," I said, "this doesn't help."

"But it's true. It's an awful mess. You've allowed Ruth to get into this, done nothing, and now… you've left it too late."

Her voice had dropped and turned inward, I could feel her pulling back.

"All right," I said, "I'll talk to Ruth and see what can be done."

"You will, Mum?"

"I'll try."

"Promise?"

I promised. She received the words with a quickly-taken breath. It was just, she explained, that no one had told her. Pausing, she repeated then switched back to work-talk, distancing slightly. For her the argument was over, something more important had taken its place. Like her father she'd closed herself off.

I texted Ruth and we met up the next day. At this point she was living at Conrad's, a choice, as she called it, which I saw as inertia. I think I'd rationalised away the hurt, I didn't want her damaged, so I hid my feelings. She was still young, my flat wasn't large, and they'd beliefs in common. In any case I'd left him, and Ruth felt he needed company. So we met after school at the sports centre café using 'our table', a small two-seater in a glassed-in corner that overlooked the pool.

As we talked our words seemed to drift, bobbing about like shadows on water. I couldn't quite tell what she might be feeling, but when I told her about Naomi she blushed.

"I really wish..." she began, gazing down at the pool. It was full. At the shallow end there were small children treading water, the centre was occupied by head-down swimmers, in a corner teenagers were splashing wildly. At the deep end, a lifeguard sat watching. He was short and squat and sat cross-legged on a fold-out chair. He looked statuesque.

"What, my love?" I asked.

Ruth remained silent. Pale and self-aware, with her head to one side, she seemed to be waiting for something to happen.

I continued probing, "You want to go through with it?"

She shrugged. Her soft grey eyes had taken on a moon-like expression; she was focused inward.

From below a shout rose up. A chorus of voices joined in, repeating the first call. The hall was full of splashes and grey-white movement.

"I don't think anyone's got an answer," I added. "Maybe you could delay?"

Behind her, the waves were rising and falling in short, choppy bursts.

Suddenly she clasped her hands together and raised them to her chest: "No delay. This Sunday, I'll be baptised."

When I told Naomi she took it better than I'd expected.

"Now I know what's happening, I've got used to it," she said, raising her voice above the sound of passing cars. Her mobile made her shouty.

"I'm glad," I replied, "I hope you'll come."

"When is it?"

"Oh, you don't know?"

"Just tell me. Time and date, so I'm clear."

As I gave her the details, I wondered why she asked. To have forgotten so quickly just didn't add up. There was something intended but left unspoken.

I finished, calling out against the background roar. I could make out the sound of tyres on tarmac and engines revving.

"So, you're coming?" I asked.

"I'll see. Maybe, if possible."

Before I could reply, the traffic noise peaked, her voice cut off and the phone went dead.

On Ruth's special day I got ready early. I'd chosen a blue blouse, cream-coloured tights and a check-patterned skirt. Minus earrings and lightly made up, my aim was to fit. There were memories, of course: Conrad and marriage, living in his house, conflicts, refusals... Then the girls growing older, and dreams of walking out. But I made myself ready, focusing on Naomi, trying not to think. Behind my carefully-judged looks, I was missing James.

When I arrived, I stood outside the black stone chapel, reading the notices. They were large-print and colourful. On the wall behind, a pure white rose caught my eye. Above it an off-yellow light glowed through glass. I knew there were people in there, preparing.

When Naomi turned up, wearing jeans and a sweater, I greeted without question. If her clothes were a statement, I chose not to see it, hoping that others would take their cue from me.

"I'm glad you're here," I said quietly, kissing her forehead. I could feel her gearing up. She was tight around the face and breathing quickly.

"I had to," she said, "it's important."

Arm in arm we entered church. The inside hadn't changed. High and wide with folding chairs and darkened windows, it smelled of soap and polish. At the centre was a bare white altar raised, exhibit-like, on a low stone platform.

"Look," I whispered, nodding to one side, where a group were mouthing prayers by a roped-off area. Inside the ropes a woman was pouring water from a jug into a large metal bathtub. The water, as it dripped and splashed, seemed to mingle with the prayers. Every so often the woman half turned, catching the eye of a girl in a long white gown. The girl, who was seated and alone, was Ruth.

"Where's Conrad?" asked Naomi.

I nodded towards a high-arched doorway. In the centre stood a robed figure with his back to the church.

"We'll sit as a family," I said as I led towards the front. Inside, I was groping in the dark.

Ruth smiled when we joined her. She sat with her hands clasped together, pressed into her lap. Her stillness made me feel for her. I could see how much she wanted to please.

I glanced down at my watch. The woman had finished pouring, the waters were still and an organ had begun playing, quietly. The prayers, though audible, had faded to a low-level drone. The church was in readiness. The worshippers' faces were full of sad, soft, gentle expectation.

Then suddenly it all changed. Conrad appeared, walking to the front. His long, flowing robe made him darkly impressive. He stopped by me, looking down. For a second he reminded me of a Tintoretto portrait.

"I'd like a word before our service," he said, waving a hand towards the vestry. "Girls as well."

To my left I could feel Naomi bristling, on the other side, Ruth was what they call lifted, my role in the middle was to act as intermediary.

"Come on," I said, putting out a hand to both girls. For their sake I needed to be strong.

We followed to the vestry. Entering, we sat down as invited, lining up on one side of a table. Conrad took the floor opposite with his back to the wall. He thanked us quietly then switched without warning to what I call his prophetic mode. I'd seen him do it before: head back, eyes rolled up, both hands outstretched. But this time, though familiar, I still wondered what was coming.

His breathing relaxed and his colour returned as his eyes opened in an otherworldly smile. When he began his voice was clear and strong and directed towards me. "I'd like you, Elizabeth, to join us, today."

Fixing me with a stare, he continued, "Come forward, Elizabeth, Mother of Ruth," here his eyes strayed to his younger daughter, "enter together in total immersion, become one body in the love of Christ."

Looking back, I remember the feelings. They came up from nowhere and in no particular order. At first I simply stared… my mind had slowed. He'd said something strange, an outlandish statement that didn't add up. I wondered if I'd misheard or simply missed the point. The experience was there, without the meaning.

Then came the shock as the phrases began to register. How dare he, I thought. The time, the place, in front of the children, the whole thing came back. Those years in private and the hours at the window then all that darkness and silence, under his surveillance.

I refused, of course, keeping it brief and stating my position, but I could feel the heat rising in my cheeks. Inside I was shaking, only this time I was determined not to show it.

I think I surprised him. There were words exchanged. Conrad and Naomi argued while Ruth became tearful, asking for quiet. I felt for her then. I didn't want to hurt her but the situation called for something strong, a clear-cut statement, words to challenge Conrad and what *he* called love.

I remember at that moment something else took over. Perhaps it was the backlog, or maybe there were voices – mine, or my gran's – but suddenly I told him. "You need," I said, "to do what we're here for and baptise Ruth…"

In my mouth, unspoken, were the words, "and not me."

When we left the vestry I could still hear their imagined voices, running in my head: Naomi protesting, Ruth interjecting, Conrad sounding off. Without saying anything we continued our dispute, locked into ourselves. In the silence of the church as we sat down for the service, our thoughts kept flaring up. They were hot spots, sparking, in warning.

At least that's how I recall it. At the time we'd been through a divorce and the service, when it began, didn't feel nice. There were too many bad memories. In any case I was jumpy about the girls. It also brought back what I'd known all along: that Conrad was lead actor while we were audience. So with all eyes on him, he called on God's presence, using words like *majesty* and *splendour*. "We bow down," he cried, "we honour, we worship." When Ruth came forward flanked by two women, his voice took on an insistent, sing-song quality, as he spoke of being clean. I could hear inside his words the little-boy-lost calling out.

The actual baptism happened more quickly, I imagine, than Conrad really wanted. It began with Ruth, wearing a one-piece costume, lowering herself into water. As she went down she slipped, a wave sloshed out and some drops splashed the floor. Inside, I was with her, praying quietly. One of the women spoke and Ruth ducked underwater, but almost immediately spluttered back up. Her moment of truth hadn't worked out. When the woman handed her out I wanted to hug her. She dried herself and left for the vestry, head down, avoiding our eyes. Beside me Naomi was staring and muttering to herself. I could tell that Conrad wasn't pleased. His words came out in a flow; they were bright and smooth with a rawness underneath. They sent me back to the times I'd listened, bowed forward in church, praying. But on this occasion his mood couldn't touch me, my heart was with Ruth in the vestry…

4.1.10

Doubt and faith are two sides of a picture, dark and light, front and back, figure and ground. Or they're two opposite forces in a storm, and like pain and breath they come and go. Sometimes they're the same, or there's an overlap and the hurt and the confusion become a line of feeling, a wave running in from a wild sea.

Doubt, of course, is in everything. It's in this story, in my head, in my heart. And I can't tell sometimes what's real and what's imagined. I know I'm with James, he's my rock, but the world around isn't always there. It can be hard to make out, as in a dream, seen at a distance, looking out from the entrance of a cave. Inside the cave I'm safe, in prayer, with voices and song. But even in there the doubt creeps in. There's a blur around the words, an out-of-body feel, as if I'm listening for a call in an empty waiting room. I can hear my own breathing and the rhythm of my heart, moving quietly. Doubt's in there, hidden behind everything. It comes and goes like shadows in the night. I'm a child in darkness, knowing nothing.

To believe is to be alive, like Ruth. It's what keeps her safe. For me, it's like swimming with one foot on the bottom. Something to hold on to, because I want things to be real. So I live my story. I've been out at the headland with James, running from the rain and I can see us from a distance, walking back into sunlight. Belief is everywhere. It's in the photographic image, the bird in the garden and the side lamp by the bed. In the stain in cloth, the wind against the face, the colour of a flower. Of course my belief in these things is shot through with doubt. The two are conjoined. *Without doubt*, are the words I say in prayer. They ascend like smoke, dissolving into air. They come and go with the wind, and are nothing and everything. Doubt and faith make up my God.

I felt both forces when they wheeled me towards the surgery doors.

10.2.10

In my thoughts this week:
- Jiggling up and down on the bathroom scales to nudge the pointer higher. So strange after all these years: weight-watching in reverse.
- Dreams of being in the ward. The sleepless ache, grey skin and hair, voices in corners: a Place Left Out.
- Good days, bad days, one after the other. A hardness beginning.

Struggling to stay strong. Knots and barbs and grits. Edges pushing up through earth. Then roses in a vase.

- Blood spots appearing on enamel. Painlessly pink. Floaty, like blossoms on ice.
- Grand Old Duke of York marches up to the toilet – straining, spotting – and down again.
- Texting James with smileys and kisses.
- Examining my scar: purple-brown zipper, sewn into flesh.
- Rain as comet-streaks on glass, the sky as ocean, storming, angels in the clouds.
- Weighing out ingredients for cupcake and blancmange, my mother's recipes. Preparing gravy and herbal sauces. Rub a dub-dub, polishing plates.
- Sleeping all day in a litter of magazines, glass to one side, with pill packs on the floor.
- Matthew 8:17. "This was to fulfil what was spoken by the prophet Isaiah: 'He took our illnesses and bore our diseases'."
- Phoning my girls when I'm at my jolliest. Talking, smiling. Making sure the love shines through.
- A resolution: avoid talk of illness, appointments, doctors and me-talk. Instead face outwards, follow stories, ask everyone who, what, where.
- Sneak-feeding self: eyeliner, foundation and lippy. Long, multi-coloured dresses and silk headscarves. Two rings in a box. Photos of the beach. Reading love letters, one a day.
- A blue line on a piece of paper with a yellow ball above. I study it calmly, intently, under 60 watt pearl, without thought. It becomes me.
- 1 Corinthians 6:19-20. "Or do you not know that your body is a temple of the Holy Spirit within you, whom you have from God? You are not your own, for you were bought with a price. So glorify God in your body."
- Watching birds pecking on the lawn: seesaw bodies with needles darting cloth.
- Postcards to parents: Vanessa Bell, *Interior*; Stanley Spencer, *Resurrection*; Edward Bawden, *Lagoon*.
- Eaten inside by unseen mouths. Pelican feeding chicks. The Nightingale and the Rose. Ouroboros.

- Ache. Coarse-grained, like sandpaper. Scraper, cheese grater, wire cutter.
- James stroking my body with softly-smooth hands. Sharing small-talk and deep-and-meaningfuls. Bringing water, joke books, fruit. His wise-owl eyes watching.
- Sleep.

27.2.10

I don't think God watches. It always seemed to me, from childhood on, that we're the ones looking out. In the garden, from a window, all across the night sky, wherever there's a view. If God's anywhere we have to look round corners, dig deep, go against the flow. And I try to avoid the words 'He' or 'She' or even 'It'. I see God as metaphor, as *imaginary*, not real or here. Something we've made up. A story, if you like, that doesn't exist and is all about opposites, accidents, contradictory states. What's not possible is larger than life.

For Conrad God was always *now*, and in action. He's the big man Father who brings down the rain. You can pray to him for health and success and building a church. There are rewards and, of course, punishments. The world is a classroom where you pass tests or learn by rote to win gold stars. And it's very personal. So from early on Minister Conrad was a noise. He'd that power-in-the-Lord which impresses. Partly voice, with its flights and swoop-downs to a stop, but also appearance: his above-all-that, Justice League look. He saw what's what, without any question.

But I knew him better; my job was rescue. Because behind his grand words, Conrad struggled. Bad things, he said, attacked him, mainly at night. For most of our marriage he slept with a torch. He kept it by the bedside and used it when he went to the bathroom, saying it gave him protection. Even then he sometimes stayed up for hours. More than once I found him in the morning, asleep in a corner with his arms across his face. When I woke him, it was if he'd been hit from behind. I asked him to explain and he drew me a picture. It showed him small, crouched in a hole, with fighter jets above. The hole was oval, dipped at one end and looked like a section across a lung. He'd drawn in tunnels, appearing from below. One was filled with an enormous spider-like creature that reached out to grab him. He told me it was called Smoke.

Sometimes he was different, more willing to talk, and he spoke about his fears, how he woke thinking he was someone else, or that no one could see him. There were voices behind doors, things in mirrors. Mornings where he cried, saying he was finished.

On those days I nursed him. I patched him up, read to him, listened to his fears and restored his faith. And I joined him afterwards, praying.

For a while it worked and he returned to himself, feeling good. I mean good as in sanctified. And for him, to feel was to do. So he launched out, fought for the poor, worked in shelters and distributed food. And I encouraged him, telling him he was doing Christ's work.

I knew that while he was giving he didn't have to think. While he talked about shaping and struggle and making people whole, he could ignore himself. It was what he needed. A salvation world where the spirit acted, where heaven and earth connected.

But then quite suddenly, he lost his footing.

It was Easter, the season of doubt. There was a vigil, at first with just Conrad and me, then with Derek, a church elder. To begin with, we sat near the high east window, beneath a wall-carved cross. Bare and cold and alive with shadows, the church smelled of candles. At this stage I was recovering from 'flu so I didn't stay long. I left him with Derek. The two of them had blankets and food and prayer books; and hidden in a bag, Conrad's torch.

Derek told me that just before midnight Conrad began to pace up and down. Apparently he was shivering and short of breath. From what Derek said, Conrad had been quoting Isaiah. It seems that as he spoke, he fell to the floor. I remember Derek's story, told quietly, how Conrad's body went rigid and he couldn't get up. It must have been awful. Midnight, in a church, with a man on the floor, having fits. Derek didn't say how long it went on, but when Conrad came round he was shouting. Maybe he'd banged his head or perhaps he was afraid but, once up, Derek described him dancing down the aisle, shadow-boxing, then lashing out suddenly, knocking over candles.

I'm not sure how it ended but I think it involved the torch. Derek just said Conrad found himself. What I do know is that when my husband came home next morning, he was red-eyed and stammering. All his private problems had come to the surface. He didn't want to eat, couldn't sleep and was pacing the house talking to himself. There were bruises on his body and blotches on his forehead. He kept wanting his torch, and crying.

I remember I was appalled. Upset for him and afraid of people knowing; it all seemed so extreme. So, like Derek, I covered for him. We put together a story about a virus which was dangerous and meant, we said, he couldn't speak. I didn't like the story, but did nothing to challenge it. At least it gave us space. Except for my visits to the shops, it kept us one-to-one and private. There were cards and prayers, but no calls or visits.

What I hadn't foreseen was how being together would affect me. Over the next three weeks all my feelings, which had been half-forgotten, surfaced again. It was us together in darkness, with Conrad angry and me trying to please. I'd gone back to that woman who wanted all but didn't dare ask. In hoping and waiting and praying for his health, I was hurting myself.

What I fell for was his wounds, and trying to make him happy.

5.3.10

There are so many metaphors for having treatment.
1. It's a garden where I'm in the bushes, with my skirt caught on thorns. I think of undergrowth and the hundred years' sleep. There are chewed down stems and webs in corners. It's a dirty place full of rot and mud. Bluebottles and flying ants swarm around concrete. There are thrips, fungi and knots in wood.
2. Running through a stitch, walking on blisters, squeezing muscles, fighting for breath – the highs and lows of pain.
3. Inside the ambulance is an underwater swim with a blue light flashing on the walls. There's a floatiness about it. A tunnel-like dreaminess, as if it was a capsule launched into space. It oscillates slightly like a needle pointing north. To be in there is a journey.
4. There's a route through the hospital which leads to Oncology. It's along a wide sunlit corridor with art on the walls. Towards the end there's a picture behind glass that I stop and look at. It's near to where they operated on me. The picture is large, mediaeval, and alive with village life. In the foreground there are barrels on large-wheeled carts and steep-roofed houses. It's full of people bent over, busy in snow. There's a crowd around a building,

peering in through a wide opening. Only those at the front can see what's inside. The house holds a secret, something hidden which changes everything. Somehow, it sums up my illness. It's Breughel's *Census at Bethlehem*.

5.   Waiting rooms, consulting rooms, dressing rooms, rooms with machine-sized instruments, lab rooms, rooms full of beds and curtain-dividers, rooms that become corridors that turn into tunnels then stack above each other – they appear in my dreams, close in from all sides, force me to my knees.

6.   Injections and cannulas are like threading needles. Taking blood needs a steady hand. The bedside doctor speaks softly, the nurse plays sister and friend. Pills and water are our communion.

7.   The medical facts: cold, bare, moonlight walks, polished metals, rawness and strange possession.

8.   Fallen from the nest. Sprawling. Broken wing.

9.   Soft hands, new sheets, cool water, listening expressions. Careful touch, clean flesh smell. Naming and smiling, giving praise, healing.

10.   Unless you change and become like little children…

21.3.10

Looking back, I couldn't have left Conrad without Toby's help. After teenage we'd grown apart, phoning sometimes and catching up at family gatherings, but even at a distance we kept an awareness, a way of sensing if the other was in trouble. So when I walked out, Toby offered help. I half guessed the reason, but accepted gratefully, out of fear of exposure and care for his feelings. So I stayed for a while in his house: a large, draughty, weather-boarded bungalow with high hedges and a perpetually damp back garden. He lived there on his own with a collection of cameras that he used to take pictures of the town. Photography helped him, I think, with the loneliness. In his own words, he'd become a camera nut.

The house was a short walk to the station, which made it easier to commute. Of course I was in shock. Nothing seemed to register. So I slept four hours at most, taking the first train out and last train back, and Toby kept me going. He helped me with fares, listened to my talk, and drove to Folkestone to bring back my possessions. On his return he stuck out his jaw and lowered his voice, "God-squad, wants everything cleared," he said. The last word disturbed me, it made me realise how far we'd come. But I enjoyed his Conrad impressions and our talks.

While I was there I came to know him better, mainly through discussing growing up. I pressed him about youth then about dreams and ruling passions, which led to talk about football. I learned about his team's colours, the names, and why he was a fan. It was the first time he'd talked about the subject as an adult. He called it keeping the faith, a blind belief in what comes round. In any case, he explained to me, it was simple: he'd always supported and always would. He'd stood with his team through repeated losses and eventual relegation, developing a never-say-die pride in holding out. "The spirit of football," he said, "is hope for the best, expect the worst." And he transferred that spirit to my divorce.

I stayed for a month. Sleeping on a mattress in a damp back room made me understand how he hadn't had it easy. "I've been where you are," he said, pointing to a picture of his ex dressed in black. He told me about her, saying she wasn't what she seemed. A gentle, caring older woman who'd changed altogether when she joined a sect, renaming herself and sleeping separate when he refused to join. He'd moved out shouting, with her declaring she'd never forgive.

"I was too young," he told me, turning back to an earlier photo. "And she changed. A bit like Conrad, only mad cow, not bull." In that picture I could see him, little-boy Toby arm in arm with a woman in a hat. They looked like mother and son.

When I moved back to Folkestone, Toby was my companion, dividing his time between weekdays in Sidcup and weekends at my flat. "Pleased to be of service," he said when I thanked him. "Just call me guard dog." And he bared his teeth, pretending to growl.

But when it came to divorce, Toby was my Man Friday. Acting as my advisor he told me what to do, warning of solicitors and legal delays. "In the end," he said, "they'll make it run and run, like mine did, so you'll have to watch 'em."

In fact without him we couldn't have settled.

What I know now is solicitors take advantage. Mine was young, unsmiling and nicely-spoken. At the start she listened, asked a few questions and took what she called a view. I was given the impression, without too much said, that Conrad didn't have a case. From then on the costs went up. So at each new turn I was consulted, informed of options, reminded of progress and billed for what I said.

At the time I was upset and wanted it over. So I paid without question, hoping that would speed things. But after periods of silence and problems with letters and a botched disclosure I became less willing. It was all so ad hoc, so messy and uncertain, and I wondered how long it might continue and whether I could bear it.

Fortunately Toby got to know. "Never trust a solicitor," he said. "They just want your bank details."

By then I'd changed as a client. My suspicions had grown and I was less afraid. So I made an offer. It came just in time, heading off a court case, and led to my solicitor, after an exchange between parties, advising in writing that Conrad could go for more.

"Oh yes," exclaimed Toby when he read it, "nothing like a U-turn. But if you argue, she'll charge you for her time."

Of course I wasn't happy. I wanted to bin it and simply walk away. But Toby, when he realised, stopped me. He described his divorce and pushed for action. So, at his suggestion I raised the offer and came to a settlement. Together we achieved what the solicitor couldn't do.

Afterwards at the café, Toby brought his camera and we celebrated with friends. We shared ice creams and portions of cake with elderberry cordial. Toby was jubilant, football-style, and snapped me with Sarah. He paired me with customers taking crazy, celebratory close-ups. Later, on our own, Toby took some fill-in shots as we cleared up the café. Then we walked out to the beach and began to talk.

"I never really got it with Conrad," said Toby, aiming his lens at a thistle, "ever since that first time at Sunday school."

I understood. He'd said so before but I'd not been listening.

"You remember?" asked Toby, pressing the shutter.

In my mind, I was back there in the church hall meeting Conrad. I could see him as he entered, clowning slightly, then at the table enjoying the questions. He'd played hard to get.

"I don't know what you saw in him," said Toby, pointing his camera at a rock. It was grey and weathered, cigar-shaped, and pitted with holes.

I shrugged, "I suppose he was solid, or seemed that way. With ideas of his own."

Turning the stone over, Toby took a few more snaps. There were hairline cracks and a band of crystals appearing at one end. "I always thought you looked up to him."

I didn't answer straightaway. I think, now, I took his words as a challenge. They made me feel I needed to explain, to myself as well as him.

"I did, but that wasn't why, or it wasn't the main reason."

At that moment I remember seeing myself in church, writing poetry, with Louise below. A picture came back of her by the altar, arranging flowers.

I pointed to the stone, "I mean, that's beautiful, yes?"

He looked and fingered his camera.

"But strange as well," I said.

Toby nodded.

"So you take a photo because it's different, in a way only a picture can capture?" I added.

He opened his mouth then, thinking better, closed it.

"And afterwards you still see it, in your mind."

Toby smiled.

"But it's full of holes and cracks, some of them nasty, and it seems to have fallen from somewhere else?"

He nodded again.

"Then that's Conrad, as he was to me."

4.4.10 – 6.5.10

Yesterday's hospital appointment was, on the surface, what we've come to expect. As usual, James took me there and we walked in slowly to busy corridors. There were people in gowns, patients on trolleys, lost-looking visitors, staff and nurses carrying files, and we moved through with rest stops, while keeping direction. As an outing it was familiar but tiring, though I liked the attention, the out-there feel. But not the waits. And the treks between buildings, sent round for testing. And not, of course, those stripped-down examinations behind curtains with students in attendance. You know when they mean business, with their skin-tight gloves and bowls to catch blood. Also, the trolley-beds trailing drip-lines and charts you can't see. But this was a routine examination, one of those white-wall appointments with joke-books and mags and views across the garden.

When you visit it brings things back: the scentless, weightless pills, the doctors with their notes and the courses of injections. They say it's necessary and you believe them. That is, until you begin gagging. And

161

then you get that yellow paper feel, so you can't take food, and your insides wipe with what I call the snowstorm, and you have to lie down. It makes you wonder if the cure is worth it.

I remember those months, how it changes moods and makes you think you're someone else. And sometimes it changes the relationship, completely.

My illness took over, creeping into everything, closing us down, in a house full of silence. Not the kind of long-term silence of couples in touch who accept who they are, not the silence of absence or of reading a book, and not that silence of gestures or words-in-the-head, but silence as denial. Silence as cut-off.

It was a shock. I thought it wasn't happening or we were going through a phase. I persuaded myself it wasn't that important, or really wasn't so, using words like 'adult', 'realistic' and 'normal' then allowing things to drift. I even told myself that we were simply being honest and we'd come out stronger. Looking back, that was a mistake, it kept me from thinking. So we passed it off, were casual or teased each other, and my condition worsened as the moods took over.

"Thanks," I'd say, speaking flatly, when James brought me tea in bed. When he asked how I was, I said nothing, and when he repeated, I pretended not to hear.

"I said, how are you?" he asked, raising his voice, and I answered "All right," avoiding his eyes. Next, when he served food, I objected to stains on the tea tray or I ate, complaining about portions and the unheated plate. I think my remarks annoyed him. He was on duty 24/7, so a single positive might have helped. But in any case, if *I* wasn't that easy, he played his part. He put on an act. So he'd ask how I felt then change the subject or he'd tell me about work, describing an incident, usually unpleasant, while looking out of the window. Sometimes jokey and sometimes calm, I felt at times he was going through the motions. "Is that what you want?" he'd ask, after bringing me the radio, or my phone and a book. "Anything else?" he'd add, and suck in his cheeks. Sometimes it felt as if he gave me support only because he had to.

From that point on, the silence was in us, whether we spoke or not. So, while I was on the phone he'd be playing music, full volume. Or he'd come to bed late, wake me, then fall asleep while I talked. In the morning he was there, still busy, dividing his attention between work and breakfast. We'd catch up in a fashion, but mainly about timings and arrangements. When he left he'd kiss my cheek and cut off. Though I do remember in the evening he'd sometimes bring me flowers but then leave them downstairs.

I was hurt, of course, but in a way my illness came first. When you're cold and aching and shaky you don't have much left for anything else. In any case, he was doing everything he could, it was just that the heart had gone out of it.

Later, when I was up and around, the not-now business began. He'd say "Not right now," then pause and consider. Sometimes he'd ask me, "Now?" or "Not really now?" then go back to his catch-phrase, adding an excuse. He had it off pat. So if I wanted to talk he'd not-now and go shopping or need to ring someone, or he'd keep out of sight writing notes or calling from the kitchen, and when my girls came round he'd disappear into the garden with plants to chop or a fence to mend. He'd not-now, too, about gossip, exchanging news, or watching TV. It was all about avoidance and exchanges, quickly taken.

I think we needed something to shake us up, what medics call a critical incident. Ours was domestic, small-scale and irritating, but important in its way. It happened on one of those days when everything goes wrong. So we'd not slept well, a door handle jammed, we'd a string of cold-callers and the computer went down. It could have happened earlier, but we got through till late, despite a spillage and Sandra ringing up. But the strain was there, and when the TV blanked with James upstairs, things kicked off.

I called out, more loudly I think than I realised. Normally James would have not-now-ed me, but on this occasion he called back and when I didn't answer, called again. I knew or half heard, but chose to cut off, I wanted him to show feeling. A third unanswered call, close now to a shout, and he sprang to the stairs. As he came down at speed he slipped, hitting the floor with a thump. I cried out in alarm and heard him groaning quietly as he pulled himself up. "Shit," he muttered as he hobbled into the lounge. He swore again and thrust himself down on the sofa.

"Are you OK?" I asked.

He grimaced and asked me the same thing.

I remember looking at him oddly. Rerunning his fall I realised what I'd done. "I'm sorry," I said, pressing my hands together, "I called out, didn't I... It was fussing really. But what about you?"

"Bloody hurts," he muttered, rubbing his toe.

"I shouldn't have shouted."

"When you didn't reply I thought you were ill."

"Yes, I'm sorry."

"I was rushing."

"And I should have replied," I said.

He winced as he pressed down on his toe.

"Blame *that*," I said, pointing to the TV. "Broken again."

He laughed, uneasily, "I was afraid…"

Realising what he meant, I offered him a hand. This time the silence was shared. We were in touch, aware of what we'd said and what we really meant.

Afterwards he kissed me.

I think yesterday in the hospital was another of those moments. It seemed we were there for treatment, waiting to be seen, but really we needed answers. Not what was happening or how to treat it but why. Why me? Why anyone? It's the first thing you ask. And it's there behind the blue lights and the bare white corridors and the sealed double doors. The question of suffering. Why it happens and who it chooses. Or how it does things, and how it presents. I sometimes think if suffering was a person he'd be on his own. No one would trust him. Dressed as a broker or a playboy, he'd be the sneak, the one who got away. I often imagine him strolling, picking out bargains, wearing something once and chucking it away. He's a Flaneur type, full of self and doing what he pleases, a believer in nothing.

In the face of all that, I think we do our best. It's about getting by. For some that means luck, for others struggle and for most of us, being patient. I call it a thought-form. When you reach a certain point the outlook changes and you take a longer view. You live now, but more *inside* life, as it happens, whatever comes up. From experience you can tell, when to question and when to be still. And yesterday, in hospital, was a good example.

So we waited. James understood, and we sat close, keeping focus. I'd given my address, checked off my GP and telephone number, and was running through what to say. I needed to be ready.

A nurse called me to be weighed then directed us both to a smaller room. Here we sat between a fish tank and a boxful of toys. Through the open door we could see people passing. "It's all very public," James said quietly.

I remember feeling stared-at.

"Hospital's supposed to be confidential," he continued, leaning close, "but you can tell who are the patients, you just have to look."

He was right, of course, but his statement was a shock, I wondered what he was saying about me.

"But don't worry, darling," he added, smiling. It was as if he'd heard my thoughts.

"I look ill, don't I?" I said.

He put his arm around my shoulders, "I really didn't mean it that way."

"But I look bad – yes?"

"Don't say that."

"And you don't find me attractive anymore."

That was the defining moment. It was something, until then, I'd kept locked inside myself. I was too ashamed, but also I was angry – with myself, with James, most of all with my illness. If this was life, then I didn't want it.

His reply came slowly, "Beth, just tell yourself no. It's not true."

I looked away, shaking my head.

James grimaced and began telling me how guilty he felt. "What can I do?" he asked, spreading his hands.

That was when I realised that he, too, was suffering. "But you're not to blame. How could you be?"

He looked into my eyes. "I'm lucky. Sometimes, I know this sounds stupid, but I feel I don't have the right."

"So it's down to both of us," I replied.

He nodded, I smiled, and for a moment I was reminded of our first-time meeting. "But down to me especially," he said. "Though of course," he added, brightening, "you have to do the right thing."

"Which is?"

"To make sure I know what you want."

"That's simple."

"Simple?"

"Yes."

"Explain, please."

I smiled. "What I want… is for you to let me have my way. Always."

"Always?"

"Always and without exception," and I kissed his forehead, telling him I loved him.

14.5.10

Sometimes when I think back, I can feel those moments, they work like sightings. It's as if there was a light switch ready to go on. Or an automatic camera with a view out, and its own inner line. Often at an angle, they appear out of time, off-purpose, in a quick-release burst. They're sharp, like birds, and have to be watched-for. I call them my angels.

Of course sightings are all different. I discovered that early on, with my dad. The angel of air that he spoke about in stories and rose at dawn; the angel of leaves that turned green then black; the angel of sleep that drifted downwards into earth. Angels had their habits. They were sad at night; colourless and invisible during the day. Once, in the garden, he talked about meeting them then made up a story.

He began quietly, with a finger to his lips. "Shh. Can you hear them in the bushes?" he said, widened his eyes. "If you look you'll see them. They're paper-thin and glowing."

I remember asking if they were birds. Smiling, he looked down the garden, "They're a bit like robins. You can lose them in the shadows, but they're always there."

Then, putting an arm around me, he began his tale.

There was once an angel no one saw. He was a big, fine angel made of dreams. As tall as a house and, when he stretched his wings, wide as a field. He was old, old as the Earth, and could fly above the Moon. But there was one problem, no one could see him. When he was there people felt the wind or the sun. Sometimes they smelled flowers or heard music. On dark nights he was rain against the window. But nobody saw him – and because he wasn't seen, he didn't have a name.

But he *did* have a name, one he used alone, when he talked to himself. He'd tried it in the day, but the other angels didn't like it. "Too short," they said or "Not right," they said, then "Not for you," they said. Their words put him off. So he went around trying different names. He called himself Old in the sun, King by water, Young in the wind.

But no one saw him. So he disguised himself, coming down to earth as a bird. And there he found a girl, sitting by herself in a garden. "I am the bird No-name," he sang.

She listened, head to one side, "No-name, why do you call yourself that?"

"Because no one can see me."

The girl looked sad, "No one sees me, too. But I can see you, you're a bird."

The angel blushed. "No, no, that's not my name."

The girl stretched out her arm. "Come," she said and the bird hopped onto her hand, "let me take you to my naming place."

So she walked, with the bird on her palm, along to the church. The door was open and as they entered the bird flew up. It landed on the cross and at once the church was filled with rainbows. Flowers appeared and the bird began to sing. The walls and ceiling lifted off and then the girl was alone, walking beneath stars. They were bright and silvery and shone like jewels.

"Now I know your name," she said quietly, "You-Are-Who-Is." As she spoke, she looked up. Above her she saw the angel, stretching from horizon to horizon, covering the stars. He was white and shiny and silver all over. Reaching forward the angel scooped her up.

"And you," he whispered, "are Queen of the Sky."

12.6.10 – 2.12.10

In remission.

Three months, then six. More than I ever expected, with green ticks on the calendar and time and people to catch up with, and Hannah and Conrad more reasonable, and my girls paying visits, and every day a prayer.

The prayers began as a result of walks. They were short at first but more rambly later, when we drove inland to farmland, crossing fields with cowpats and flies around pools. In the past I'd want something larger, so I'd be counting steps or talking about friends, but now it was enough. Just to hear the birds and imagine my dad, to go with James talking flowers, to be walking free past fences and hedges: it filled and absorbed me. And side by side, we were alive. It reminded me of reading out loud from my gran's children's books.

As a prayer it wasn't fixed, it didn't have an order, and the words, if there were any, were more like colours, or the idea of colours floating in the head. But we walked, stepping over stiles and passing through gates, and the ordinary became special. We were in the fields, taking the air, hearing birdsong, following the path.

"Shall we try the woods?" James asked, pointing.

I agreed and we headed uphill, following a sheep track. As we entered, the trees cut us off. I was reminded of our walk at Deanbury.

When you're in the woods it magnifies everything. You're in a cave, sealed into quiet. It slows you slightly and you move through untouched, as on a screen. But you're *inside* the picture, observing. And, in there, the paths are all different: some narrow, some road-width, with forks and detours and crossings leading off. It seems, in the woods, life's older, less here and now, and oddly-patterned.

We didn't exactly pray. The silence had its voices, and the step-by-step progress took us further in. There were a few words: a gesture from James, a flower name and smile, and my thoughts about the place. Sometimes we stopped and embraced, and that, too, was a prayer, a way of being present.

And then came one of those angel moments.

At the centre of the woods, I remember entering a clearing full of purple foxgloves. We stood still and admired as if we were staring at a painting. The foxgloves were close and snaky, rising to spikes above our heads.

I think the nearest I can get to what we said was "Ah," or "Oh." It was our own secret garden.

"Digitalis," said James, as he led down a path walled-in by plants. The path curled around, arriving at a bare earth mound. "But I call them Foxglove City," he added, smiling, and we climbed a short slope to a viewpoint. On all sides we were surrounded by a spiky, nodding sea of colour. It was plum-purple, yellow-purple, and purple-pink.

We were silent, standing side by side, looking.

Then came the moment, as a line of poetry popped into my head. "I taste a liquor never brewed…" I said.

I remember the shift in James's face; he was reading me carefully. "What's that from?" he asked.

"Emily Dickinson."

"I see. Or maybe I don't."

"There's a line, describing a drunken bee at the foxglove's door."

"So that's why you thought of it?"

"Not exactly," I shook my head. "It's about spirituality…"

James smiled, the angel had arrived. "Ah, the point."

"Something that takes us out of ourselves."

"You mean," he replied, waving his arm, "all this…"

"Anything that makes us bigger."

"And thankful." James raised his hands to prayer position. Facing, I raised mine too and James placed his hands like gloves around mine. He closed his eyes and we prayed.

Prayer is a mode of being. A wide-awake, floaty clarity in which we live life, fully. We pray with our eyes, as artists, with our ears like an orchestra tuning up, with our bodies when we kiss. And we pray in ourselves when we forgive or listen or simply show interest. For deep prayer to happen you have to be yourself: the unseen self on the path, in the café, and of course in the hospital.

I often think there's an angel inside, looking out quietly, with its face to the window. Someone we recognise walking by our shoulder, familiar but unknown. That figure is *us*, our real selves in the dream, not perfect but aware. It's what we see when we sit closing our eyes and feeling the touch of presence. And prayer, my kind of prayer, is about meeting that self, dreaming of the light. It's about thinking nothing and expecting less. And recognising that what's out there is larger than us.

With James and me, prayer was all about feel. So it could happen in bed, warm and fresh after sex, when we embraced. Or it could be on an early morning walk, looking out across sand, with the sea moving slowly. Or a violin solo, heard on a CD from the inside of a car. Sometimes the prayer was larksong climbing to an overcast sky. It could be time spent together in a wild spring garden. Or shared time in an empty church with scented candles and white light through glass.

It was James's idea that we went to services as well. Of course, his interest surprised me. I'd thought him too full of fun and irony and reluctant to commit. To bow down in church wasn't his thing. Or so I'd supposed until we talked, on an outing.

We were sitting together in an overgrown graveyard looking out to sea. We'd come there at his suggestion, touring the coastline. The wind was fresh, and we had our backs to the remains of a stone-built chapel. James was talking about his childhood.

"Church was never part of my life," he said, "but I'm willing to try, now."

I looked at him, carefully. "You sure?" I asked.

He gazed across the weathered headstones, "As long as it's together." He paused, looking out to sea, "And the sort of worship that you – no, we – believe in."

I understood. What he wanted wasn't Bible. None of that little-boy-up-there, comic book God who has to be talked out of smashing things. Not too high-and-holy either, with or without incense. And not, of course, sin-fest or guilt-trip or getting loud for the Lord. For him, for us both, it was about metaphor, the word as symbol, and love.

So we went on Sunday, held hands in the pews, sang and exchanged glances then discussed it afterwards. Not as performance but in spirit, as a gift.

And now, two months later, still at peace, we celebrate as we eat, give thanks when rising and live life in the sun. There's an everyday rhythm which keeps us together as watchers and lovers. For us, this is praying.

So why James?

Or if not why, at least where, when, and what if…

If James was a singer, I fancy he'd be a song thrush. The New Year one as in Hardy: piercing, throaty, trilling in the dark. Or a woodpecker drilling down, tap-tap-tap. Then flying in a loop, hedgerow to hedgerow, flashing his colours.

But he's my James, my silver-haired admirer and crazy dancer. The man who listens and nods then talks about feelings.

A story about him…

We were eating out at our West End restaurant when, without hesitation, he told the waiters how we'd first met there. Later in the evening he told some diners about our anniversary. Each time he described it he held up his ring. And he told our story well: straightforwardly, warmly, as an adventure, without embarrassment. Of course he'd said, more than once, that during youth he'd seen speaking openly as another kind of mask, but now he simply shared. And he used the L-word, repeatedly.

If James was an artist he'd paint very large pictures, over and over. Theatre-like scenes with fireflies in the dark, or tenth-storey views with stars on water, some white, some grey, seen between branches. Or he'd overpaint photos and hang them in a series. They'd be Ernst-like, watery, in blues and greens. I imagine those pictures hung from strings and displayed like Christmas cards across the sky. They'd be up there, 'made one with nature', dotted around as fixed stars. His *autoritratto*.

Another story...

When it came to getting married we knew there might be problems. There were families lined up with exes in the background, views on who should be there, and questions about the service. Of course at our age we arranged it all, which placed us, like officials, right in the middle. So we had to be careful and think it through. In fact, I was happy with anything as long as it had the right feel and James just wanted to celebrate. But at the same time we believed in the poetic, in metaphor, not a checklist. So, after lengthy discussions and advice from Toby, we settled on two ceremonies, one private, in my parents' church, one outdoors, at The Shorespot Café.

On the day at the church, with close family. we went for restraint. There were low-key declarations, vows and readings, a kiss, and tea and cake afterwards. It was small, dignified and gently-worded, most of all it was simple. And, of course, private.

At the café a few days later, it was much more for show. We'd invited everyone and set up in the garden, I'd prepared a script and James had covered an arch-shaped pergola with an arrangement of flowers, combining them in stripes. They were purple and blue and spikily red. Some I knew, poppies and antirrhinums and veronica, and others had unfamiliar names and strange, insect-like blooms.

When the time came I led James into the middle of the lawn to face the arch. The flowers were in place, woven in, with a tunnel behind and a ribbon tied across. We stood holding hands and said our script. The sky was clear and the guests were all around us, following every word.

It was when Toby cut the ribbon that James took over. As we entered the pergola he reached up, took a handful of blooms and wove them into my hair. I smiled back as he added more, pinning them to my dress. He kissed me then slipped some smaller flowers into his own hair and the pocket of his suit. Finally, we both gathered bunches in our hands and stepped out to the lawn.

I still have the pictures. When we look at them together we seem so alive. In spirit we were spring chickens.

With James I can still do that: step outside the box, invent things, do what we like.

So why James?

Firstly, his hair. He's happy with its length – not too obvious, layered at the front, longer at the back – but enough, a symbol. After washing it's smooth and floppy and surprisingly strong. It feels like water.

For a while we shared a joke that he had all the hair. "It makes up for mine," I said, and I meant it. Of course he told me I'd get mine back, but as long as I had his I was happy; or at least, it helped my feelings. He grew it for me.

Secondly, his *James-isms*. His teasing expressions, a joke or reflection, a quick double-take – with judgement yes, but straight, with feeling.

Also his voice, sometimes loud, sometimes gentle, intimate when low. Mature, as well, with his own chosen tics. And his hand in mine: warm, loosely-fitting, a garment to put on.

When we're out walking he stays by me, in step, and we go forward through the world. It's the red carpet treatment, everything in place, laid out for us. Or so he tells me.

James can cook, is untidy, dislikes hot baths, has a passing interest in sport, and watches athletics and tennis, highlights only. He has his own mug with an author quote, a collection of vinyl classics and several sizes of multi-coloured badges.

Thirdly, there's James-of-the-garden. Outdoors, working, he's *inside* nature, crouching, examining, a doctor of the soil. There's a priest in him, too, bringing on flowers, planting fruit. He's the painter of roses. And when he designs, using metal and stone, he's halfway to an architect.

Yes, so why James?

The question brings back the restaurant. I picture him there with silver-white hair. On the table there's a newly-lit candle. It's leaf-shaped and pointed, like an upside-down heart.

I ask the question again and feel myself warming up. I'm in the sun and we're walking. In my head I can hear Beethoven's Pastoral. We're figures in a painting, passing through a gate. The garden we enter is alive with Cranach-like apples and exotic beasts. There's a labyrinth, marked out in stone, which we walk. Its twists and turns lead into the heart. And we're at the centre.

Recently I've been dreaming about dancing. The dreams come in two main types. In both I appear with James in *Strictly Come Dancing*.

Of course we're fans. On Saturday night the sofa's our front row where we get in close and study every move. We're marking what we can, talking about content and feel, but our focus is on passion, what the judges call connection. In other words, we want to know who fancies who.

It's fun, that's why we do it. So we recall past winners, comment on costumes and go to bed excited with our heads full of kicks and lifts and promenade runs. You'd think we were kids at an all-night party. But behind each dance there's another story.

And the dreams? Well, here are a few highlights.

In the first type of dream I'm a professional. My name's Constantia and I'm from the island called *Love*. Strictly Love, where women wear sparkle and feathered headpieces and play opposite masked men who are B-list celebs. In this dream I Waltz in white, Rumba in red and Tango in orange and black. The music's coloured too, ranging from Quickstepping silver and blue-yellow Jive to rainbow Samba and Lindyhop green.

James is my partner. In Series One he's on TV, possibly fronting wildlife, but mainly flower shows. He's won a silver-gilt at Chelsea and gold at Hampton Court. In Series Two to Five he's in rock, writing powerhouse classics for an indie band who everyone respects. From Six onwards he's in stand up, telling slaphappy jokes and truly, deeply, off-the-wall stories.

He's a natural, takes well to the dance, and we bond straight away.

There are others who appear, listed in the credits. Not surprisingly their names are familiar. So my dad presents, Ruth and Naomi cheer from the audience, Meg designs costumes, George leads the orchestra and the panel's made up of Charlie as Bruno, Hannah for Alesha, Amy/Rachael standing in for Len, while Craig's part is delivered by Conrad and Toby, backed up by my gran. My mum plays Tess.

For several weeks James and I sweat and struggle, practising our moves. We're busy as flies in our glass-walled studio. We use affirmations like *nail it* and *staying in the zone*. On camera we're a hit, week on week topping the leader board, and of course we fall in love.

The second type of dream is slower and deeper. It's full of glides and turns and smoothly-flowing movements. The music's soft and impressionist. It comes in waves, one moment close then drifting off. In this dance I'm at peace and I lie back on James, breathing slowly. I'm rising and falling in time to the waves. Our hearts beat together. There's a wild, abandoned siren song singing in my ear. It's for us. The tune's our tune: *The Power of Love*. It reminds me of an imaginary film I carried in my head. *My Dreamboat*, I call it. I rerun the last scene where the lovers fall asleep and drift out to sea. It's what you might call the dream behind the dream.

In all these dreams, when we reach the Strictly final we're in the lead. The public are behind us. The judges award us tens, saying we're amazing. The studio audience give us standing ovations. Then, on the last dance, in the final move, just when it seems we've won, my dizziness strikes. I lose my footing and fall. The floor seems to rise up and hit me. A hot needle shoots up my back. I'm lying, shivering in darkness, and something's grinding. My body's not moving. James is stooped over me, calling, but the blackness swells up and takes me in its arms.

I wake.

7.1.11

I've a name for my illness coming back. I call her Felicity. She's young, slightly-built and, behind her blushes she's an attention seeker. She's me, in a way, but also she's a character. Partly historical, she lives in her own world. And she's a storyteller, which makes her both rash and afraid of shadows. Over the years, I've got to know her, and I've realised she needs my full attention. So I talk to her nicely, ask her how she feels.

Felicity's always there. She has her own story, beginning in the dark. It's like peering into water: to see her, you have to sit still. In one form, she's pondweed. Grey-green and clinging, she's smooth and has curves. But that's at the beginning. Later, when she's grown, she makes herself known. She's behind everything, in the breath taken slowly, the unsteadiness, the red-marked sheets. But also, she's barely there at all. Hard to describe, the hollowed-out feeling, the bareness inside. Not so hard to describe the squats, the black blood, the ache.

So I listen at night time, I imagine her story, as a sister, and try to feel her there. I picture her with me, perhaps rather distant, in secret, then turn up the volume. "What's wrong?" I ask. I want to draw her out, find what we have in common, I also want an explanation. I'm angry. I tell Felicity she's not welcome, not this way. It's her habit of turning up, without proper warning, appearing, not asking, and just sitting there saying nothing. She's the face at the window, the looker, the old black hag, the one who keeps returning.

Like now.

15.1.11

I have two boxes inside me, a pain box and a beautiful box. I'm in the middle, caught between them. They appear in me without warning. I never quite know which one it'll be. Like Jekyll and Hyde they come and go.

The pain box is metal. Its lid is scratched and dented and heavy to lift. As it goes up it sticks in places and the hinges flake rust. Inside it's full of tools. There are two fold-out ledges, packed with drill bits and screws of all sizes. In the central compartment there are six-inch nails and saws with broken teeth; below that, sharp metal pincers and rolled barbed wire; at the bottom there are clamps and padlocks. The tools rattle about inside like broken glass. Some of them are twisted out of shape, others are cracked and splintered, all of them can slice through bone. I call them my instruments.

In the beautiful box there are deep blue pools where I lie looking up. The world around me is soft and slow and glows from inside. Down there I'm weightless, like a fish, not touching anything. My breath comes slowly and I'm floaty and free. It's as if I'm at a window watching things go by. I can see the ripples, the insects on the surface and reeds in mud. Stretching, I turn and rise to the surface. On the banks there are willows and people looking down. I can see myself through their eyes. I'm a woman in a picture, holding flowers, with a song in my head. Of course, nothing can touch me. I'm Ophelia.

When the pain box returns I'm on stage. It's coffin-sized and curtained at the front. I'm standing by it, looking down. In there I can see what looks like a false bottom. As I reach in, my hand catches on a blade. It cuts deep but I don't feel a thing. There's no blood, and suddenly I realise I'm dreaming. I hear a drum roll and a shout as I climb into the box. The box is tight and its spikes and needles cut into my sides. I've just wedged myself in when I realise that the bottom is solid, the saw is approaching and I'm the lady to be sawn in half.

I realise as the blade cuts in, pain and beauty are fraternal twins.

15.2.11 – 20.4.11

It's about the people, their lives as they happen, what we share and who we are. Their stories keep me going; I know they mean well.

Ruth, when she visits the ward, sits on my bed. No phones, no gadgets, just a plain cotton dress, sleeveless, and a photogenic profile. She's vulnerable in a pale-skinned, unadorned, gently-compassionate kind of way. With her slightly ethereal, Botticelli smile, she reminds me of my younger self.

Each time she comes she brings me a gift. I love her presents, they're always special. Often they're written: a quote recorded in a pocket-sized book, read out quietly, or a sketch and a poem. I did once ask her for a self-portrait but she found that difficult.

Ruth's retraining to be a veterinary nurse. She's on placement just round the corner, so she visits most days. We have a routine: a cheek kiss, her gift, a few minutes' catch-up then an animal story. She tells me their names, their habits and how she came to nurse them. The dog that swallowed a key, the cat with wounds, a bird so concussed it fell into a pond. We talk about her course and the difficulties she's having. It's about the medical terms. So she brings in her textbook and I test her on words like adenoma and intussusception, sounding them slowly, syllable by syllable.

At first, when she said she wanted to change jobs, I thought it wouldn't happen. She'd always been ultra-particular, with an aversion to plugholes and hairs in the bed. "Animals are dirty," I warned her. "And they smell."

"Mum, it's what I want to do," she replied, looking past me.

I knew what that meant: for someone so quiet she's surprising strong. Or to put it another way, she's a split personality, outside shy, inside defiant. She'd shown that at mealtimes with her sister. I remember them arguing, both wanting the same piece of cake and Ruth conceding nothing. Naomi kept talking, giving all her reasons, but in the end Ruth saw her off. She simply said "No," until Naomi fell silent. Then she took the cake and pointed to the garden, *"They'll* like it," she said, "and everyone I'll be happy." So we ended at the window watching Ruth

176

throwing crumbs to a couple of squirrels.

So I suppose, even before she said it, I knew she'd be a vet. I'd heard her call and talk to her animals by name, telling them stories, and I'd seen her standing, seemingly untouched, when they gnawed down her finger.

It's that side of Ruth that Naomi finds difficult. She's a stickler for order, calling herself maître d'. And being older makes her more reactive. Naomi believes in sorting things, and says so. Of course she's a born carer so the passion is directed. In the past she was happy as long as she was clear about what was happening. So she'd go along with games that suited her sister, be child-like, and stay upbeat. But once she was put out then we'd never hear the end of it.

I do remember Naomi on holiday.

Every summer, we went to the Isle of Wight. It suited us. There was something quasi-50s about the trees down to the beach, the boats and boat houses and old-fashioned bungalows, something both quaint and formal. It seemed to belong to Enid Blyton. We stayed on the east coast in a small hotel with a view out to a bay and yachts at anchor. I remember playing rhyming games, matching words like Dolphin, Blueskies, Scheherezade, and hearing rigging slapping in the wind. I also remember the girls on the sands, running and laughing. It always seemed sunny on the island and without Conrad, who was usually too busy to come, we stayed out late, talking, sleeping, building beach fires and baking potatoes.

It was after sundown, on our last night, that Naomi first told me she didn't want to go to church.

"Promise you won't tell Dad," she whispered, snuggling up.

We were sitting on a rug with our faces to the fire. On one side there was a low wall, on the other side Ruth was asleep, bundled in a sleeping bag. Behind her, the waves were breaking quietly. The air felt both cool and warm.

"But why don't you want to go?" I asked.

Naomi looked into the fire, "It doesn't seem real. I don't feel it."

"But is it church or how we do it?"

"No. I don't see the point. I need a change."

"You sure? It's not because someone's been talking to you?"

"No, Mum, I just need a break."

"So what will you do?"

While Naomi considered, I listened to the sea. Its softly lapping, gurgling rushes filled up the dark.

"Will you just stay away?"

She sighed. "What do you think Mum? I'd like to, but…"

I remember feeling torn. I was at a stage where my own faith had changed. In myself, I wanted to be alone, without restrictions, walking in the woods. In fact, for me, nature was the way into God. So I understood what Naomi was saying, but I knew that Conrad wouldn't like it, and I wanted to protect her.

"Could you be in church but think of something else?"

"Mum, you can't say that. It has to be honest."

I heard the pressure in her voice. For her this wasn't so easily dealt with.

I would have left it there but at that moment Ruth opened her eyes. "Then don't go," she said, blinking.

In the dark, the waves pitched quietly against the beach.

"Ruth, you're awake?" I said.

I could tell by her movements that Naomi didn't like it. She was leaning against my arm, breathing quickly with her head turned away.

"I don't think…" I began, keeping my voice low. I was determined to stay calm.

"What we said," cut in Naomi, "was private. For me and Mum."

I could see her eyes were fixed on the fire. Her cheeks were glowing.

"Naomi," I said, "Ruth was only trying to help."

Both girls sat still, saying nothing.

"Listen, there's nothing to argue about." I pointed to a branch at the edge of the fire. "Because God's not just in church."

The branch was crackling, peeling as it burned.

The girls remained silent.

"You see that?" I asked, pointing to the flames.

Ruth nodded.

"Now look," I said. The whole length of the branch was splitting open. At the tip it was oozing sap; each slowly-gathering drip was whiteish-green. When it dropped it spat all over.

"You understand what I'm saying, about God?" I asked.

"I think so," Naomi said, quietly.

"Then let's not argue. Not in front of God."

I think there was something in my voice that touched her.

Of course, when she visits now, Naomi knows much more. I can see it in her face. She tries not to show it, but like most nurses, she's too much aware. In a way she's squeamish. So she encourages me to be active, get up and walk, look out of the window, do anything as a form of distraction. And there's a kindliness about her, a kind of super-niceness, which keeps her professional, in hospital-mode. In an odd kind of way, she's my patient.

But it's when my dad visits that I listen and see other things. What happens with him is closer to prayer. So he arrives quietly, often when I'm asleep, and sits watching. Even if I don't wake up, I know he's there. So I ask him for a story and he hesitates, but I ask him again and he agrees. And I can't tell, as the words start, whether I'm awake or asleep. But I hear him talking, picking up on phrases from an earlier time. Then his voice drifts off and I'm left alone. There are no words now, only images. As if he, too, wasn't really there.

So the dream takes me back, but this time to a pool. It's summer and a couple of damselflies are circling the surface. They're electric-blue and tied together. They land on a water lily where they seem to be struggling. It's as if they're frying. When they lift off, they're still locked together. They tour the pool, skimming the surface, then alight on a bank. The sun goes in and they lose all colour. Everything around them begins to thin out. The grass has faded and the water is icy. The sky has blanked and even the sun has paled. It's as if everything's rubbing itself out. And when I wake, or another dream begins, everything is clear and expanded and weightless. I'm between walls surrounded by faces and my dad's voice is there.

Like him I'm fading.

5.5.11

I'm out of hospital, talking with Carmen, our minister. She's small and bright, like a pebble. Her face is round and simple, with red-brown curls and a twinkly smile. She's warm and she's gentle. It comes through in her dark brown eyes, her laughter, and in the pause before speaking when she goes into herself. She's experienced as well, which I imagine comes from visiting people like me. But there's no kind of pressure, I'm not in a queue or being judged. Although there are twenty years between us, she's mother and sister to me in an eye-to-eye way.

She's the same in communion. When she gives bread, she looks for a second into your eyes, and in offering wine she offers herself.

When Carmen comes round she's so glad to see me. I sit with her close up to the table and feel the glow. It's like letting in the sun. I'm back there in the youth group, sharing the time with Annie and Clare, but now I'm not tempted to say things for effect. So we talk. It's one-to-one, with me as subject.

Carmen, I know, gives herself in any way she can, as helpmate or mentor. She's my companion when I talk about doubt. What she says, she offers as a messenger. She wants me to believe but doesn't contradict. If she could, she'd be my servant, not literally, but in my head, as my conscience.

Compared with her, I'm struggling. I tell her about what I call my journey. It's uphill, I say, much steeper than I expected. She listens and I tell her how I feel. Not lonely in this world, I say, but very much alone in what's going to happen. I'll miss him I say, quietly, and change the subject.

We talk for a while about worship, and what I call the hole. The God hole, I tell her, is where I find faith. For me it's in the gaps and breaks, the nothingness. And I take her through my doubts questioning everything: the church, the creed, most of all miracles. I end up feeling bad because I'm attacking everything she stands for. I'm Thomas with my finger in the wound.

Carmen listens carefully. She's with me, mid-stream, going with the flow. When she replies she doesn't offer fixes. Her words are clear with a hint of sparkle. Underneath the surface they go deep.

She tells me a story about her own earlier life. It seems she used to climb mountains without equipment, until a fall one day and a year-long struggle with illness. She ends with words about surprises and the hidden face of God.

Afterwards, she asks me what would help. I notice her hands: they're red, shiny in places, and large for her size. She holds them half-cupped on the table, pointed towards me. She's so much like my mother that I cry. We pray together.

2.6.11

As a child, I loved our garden. It always seemed that being outdoors stirred me up. It was the kind of place on-its-own where anything could happen. Out there was wild, an unexplored heartland that I didn't call *garden*, or if I did it was quietly to myself, with its own private meaning. It was my hard-to-reach outback where I lived off the land, a place with tent-people and unknown creatures and its own bare life. A paradise of sorts, one full of sunlit corners and clipped shrubs and creepy-crawlies.

Now the garden seems like a picture seen from a long way off.

I shared the garden with Toby. He drew a map with contours and coloured-in symbols. I put in names, marking in *The Castle*, *The Swamp* and *Spooky Wood*. Over time we both added to our map. Toby drew rivers and mountains and a collection of trails, while I wrote on the back about the map's discovery. We made a copy in a scrapbook and I began a story in the pages that followed. Toby put in some cartoon-like animals and a key.

Working on our book brought us close. It kept us busy and, in a way, it changed us. In fact, I could almost say we imagined who we were. So sometimes we were well-spoken children using words like *white* and *bare* and *magical* when the earth was green and brown, and sometimes, as Mary and Colin, we entered our own secret garden through a door in the wall.

But also, there were outdoor incidents. Brief and small-scale, but revealing as well, usually happening as a part of something larger.

Here's one I remember.

We were twelve and ten, young for our ages, but quietly thoughtful. Looking back now, I see myself reading outdoors. Because the garden, for me, had become a place of study, a library, if you like. I was out there sitting on the wall with the scrapbook in my hand. A tin beside me held a collection of coloured pencils. Toby was opposite, kicking a football against the fence. He was grumbling in his throat, yelping sometimes and crying out "Ref!" I knew he was trying to annoy me.

For the second time that afternoon the ball flew in my direction. It skidded off the lawn and bounced up, hitting brickwork.

"Oh, Toby!" I cried, closing my book.

The ball had dropped to the ground and was trapped between a tree stump and the wall.

"Can I have my ball back please?" Toby asked. Underneath his nice-boy manner there was the boy we called Mischief.

I think that was when I realised that he was embarrassed by his own behaviour. I could read it in his squared shoulders, with arms pinned to his sides. He was making himself upright, as stiff as possible.

"Is that what you want, really?" I asked.

Toby shook his head. He was looking at my book.

I'd a feeling that he knew but was too shy to ask. Then suddenly, remembering *Shipwreck*, it came to me.

"You want me to read to you," I said.

Toby hesitated.

"Would you like that?"

When Toby remained silent, I invited him to join me.

"Can I?" he asked.

I patted the wall and he sat.

I opened the scrapbook and flicked through the pages. Finding my story, I called out the title *Safari Adventure* then read right through, beginning to end. It had poachers, a chase and some closely-observed beasts. At the end Toby moved closer and asked to draw the animals.

"Of course," I said, handing him the book.

I've still got the picture that he drew. Looking at it now, I realise what it shows. It's thickly-worked and messy with a close-up herd of animals and behind that two Moomin shapes peering from bushes. Their faces are balloon-shaped and dreamy. They're water-baby-like. Somehow they're blank: round and sagging, yet pointy as well. They could be angels or fish, but they're also slightly spooky. They're alive, alert, and yet out of it.

They're versions of Toby and me.

15.7.11 – 3.10.11

By teenage, looking in the mirror, I really believed I was out of it. It was the shape of my face, which I thought of as hollow, and my mouse-brown hair. Also my teeth and my after-bath spots. Of course I know now that the faults I saw were nothing, but at that time I almost *wanted* my blemishes. They kept me safe from what some boys were after. So I stayed apart, talking, both superior and exposed. But secretly I'd my own look-at-me feeling, and a wire inside that sparked when a boy came in the room. So I hid my blushes behind a clever-clever front.

But it was when I stopped talking that my desires showed through.

I realise now there's always chemistry when nothing's said. Silence is powerful, it makes things stand out like a layered painting: underneath the surface something's signalling. So I had my feelings, ones I kept private, about men who were older. Maturity to me was impressive. It went with saints in stained-glass windows, kneeling hermits and elders in stories – and that included, without anyone knowing, a crush on our minister.

His name was Simon Fitzgerald. He was tall and thin, with blue El Greco eyes and artistic hands. His voice was musical, slightly sad, with a soft Scottish accent. When he spoke from the pulpit I felt the power of his gaze. Like his words, it seemed directed. It was as if he was shining a torch on me. There were questions in the air, gentle invitations and a sun-like warmth creeping into everything.

After the service, when he spoke with my parents, I glazed. Underneath my politeness I was watching. And though I didn't say anything I had a feeling that his remarks were secretly intended for me.

He made my Sundays extra-special. So I went to church feeling light and unreal. I sat absorbed watching – and continued, afterwards, breathless and high until early evening, when I suddenly came down.

Then I had the longings, a kind of raw, obsessive itch which went on all week; he was somewhere close. So if we went to the park or out in the town I kept seeing him. His name appeared on road and shop signs and in the books I was reading. Sometimes I felt him beside me in the morning, looking out into the garden. He was there, speaking quietly, taking in the lawn, the birdsong, the sunlight on the path.

I knew my love was absurd, but I'd vowed, and wasn't going to let him down. So I worked on our connection. Sitting alone in my room, I imagined conversations. In my mind I composed Brontesque poems full of wind and wildness and ghosts crying out. Vaguely, in snatches, I relived his sermons. And I made up lists of what he liked, where he went, his facial expressions, and what he secretly loved.

Then there was his wife, spotted from a distance, shopping in town. Small and dowdy, slightly overweight, with a worn-looking smile, I saw her as unworthy. Nothing about her seemed equal to him, and that gave me hope. So I told myself stories of how she wasn't what she seemed. Maybe she'd trapped him through a promise he'd made, a youthful vow which he'd honoured out of loyalty. Perhaps she'd a rare disorder which could trigger collapse, and she used it as a threat. Or maybe they were related and the marriage was a sham.

Of course my condition couldn't last, but while I lived it I found it helpful, in a way. Here was a place where no one could touch me, a quiet, look-in-the-mirror, alone-with-my-fantasies world. I saw it as my territory, mine alone, a place I'd chosen away from anyone watching. Inside my love-dream I had him to myself.

And then my feelings changed. Or rather, they shifted from church to school.

It happened halfway through term, with our first exams coming up. For a while there'd been talk of a replacement English teacher. Our tutor, Mrs Coates, had been taken ill too often, so we were given the deputy head, a middle-aged man who tested spellings, followed by a music teacher, recently retired. They set work and supervised without much interest. The classroom became, in effect, a free-for-all, so we learned how to copy model answers, cheat where possible, and feign due diligence in whatever we had to do.

And then Mr Vaughan arrived.

He was a short, broad-browed Welshman with long sideburns, a soft, sensual mouth and slightly starey eyes. He announced straight away, speaking with a lilt, that we had to aim high. We were young minds in the making, who had to ask questions and challenge what we read. And he lectured gently from the front, analysing genre, types of character and the use of language.

Within a week I'd become a follower. I hung on every word, enjoying his long pauses and quiet intensity. His presence lit me up. It was as if I was standing looking out from a high-up window.

So I learned to please. I became his best pupil, asking questions and memorising answers. And I filled up my essays with near-quotes and grand, speculative phrases intended to impress. I wanted notice. So my essays moved between sections, offering theories and adopting positions, some of them quite extreme. But what they did communicate, regardless of perspective, was the importance of thinking.

Looking back now I believe he was aware but, unlike my minister, his response was to cut off. So he talked like an actor, projecting slightly, and avoided contact. If I answered a question he'd nod and move on. And when he marked my work, the most he ever gave me were one-word comments.

I suppose at first I simply followed. I thought I could read him, believing his indifference to be a trick, a gesture to the gallery, an unreal self. Only I understood his signals. But after a while I began to question. I needed reaction, even if it was negative. So I laid little traps: words missing in essays, a name change or switch, the odd deliberate error or self-contradiction. But his comments didn't change. It was good or satisfactory, or simply left blank and ticked at the bottom with a single-figure mark.

I think in the end I needed something more. So gradually, without it really showing, I began to lose interest. My gentle Welsh dragon now seemed smaller, less the man he'd been. It was mainly his voice which, like the other teachers, had flattened to a drone. I noticed too, how often he repeated himself. In fact more than once I found myself wishing he'd stop talking.

So I didn't look back when Mrs Coates returned. Mr Vaughan had gone. And when, within days, our minister retired, I was two-times relieved. I didn't need their love. I'd outgrown my fancies, I was stronger; and, for a while at least, I wasn't out of it.

25.11.11

There are ways of dealing with pain. It's about awareness, what I call 'separating out'. And that means listening and knowing the difference between chronic and acute.

When it's an ache and keeps on aching, then it's all about mood. About taking action, and pushing on. Moving whatever hurts, regardless, but carefully as well, with judgement. Of course there's pressure, and more ache as you carry on. And as soon as it's a down-mouth you're struggling. You might think 'I can't do this' and tiredness sets in. Or you might think 'oh no, not again' and sink, or imagine a future where it never goes away. But it's thinking that hurts. The brain's a cover, keeping bad stuff out, but also a filter or a frame we look through. So it needs to be flexible and choose what to stop, what to let through. Of course there are days when the effort's too much, and not-now wins. But that's when you have to struggle. To talk yourself up, say yes, I can do it. Every day, it's about putting in the hours, making the effort, fighting to stay up.

I've come to understand that illness, and especially cancer, is bigger than you think. To stay on top you have to be strong. And that can take everything. It may look as if nothing's happening, but inside's a battleground. It's what they call character-building. And especially when the pain is severe.

When it gets bad, you have to think. At first it doesn't seem possible as the levels go up. You say to yourself 'What—' as the waves get higher, so much higher you think you can't cope. It happens between breaths. Then you realise that your life has changed and you can't escape. The pain breaks through and what you thought was dangerous becomes an emergency. It's then that you use breathing. In your head you count. Talk yourself up. Say no to the red light, change it to blue.

But the real trick is to swim. I call it *going with, not against*. It's about taking deep breaths and staying under. Then you float. The pain is everywhere, it's the world you inhabit, and where it goes, you follow. It's almost like a dream: you're watching yourself being hurt, and on the surface there's nothing you can do. But once you're inside then that gives meaning. You can make adjustments, guide and be guided, hold onto a rhythm.

Of course morphine helps. At first I was afraid, but the doctors reassured me. And once I'd tried I understood its calm. Morphine is a lake; its deep blue spring spreads underground. It's the blue of gentians and violets and Lawrence's last poems. And that's the blue, when I swim in it, that I feel when I pray.

13.2.12

The end of treatment was my decision, with James's agreement. We needed a cut-off, a line drawn. Of course, we knew what it meant. I don't believe in herbal or miracle cures. Everything's been done.

I told Naomi and Ruth, with James over a meal, holding hands. The meal was simple: bread, thin soup, water – what I could manage without throwing up. We'd set out the table with cream-coloured candles. In the centre was a cut-glass vase of arum lilies. For us this was communion, though with Naomi there we called it 'light supper'.

To tell them I used the face-to-face method I'd seen on ER. But without the urgency. I waited till we'd eaten then lit the candles and spoke to them calmly. "The cancer's spread, so we've put the treatment on hold."

The girls were both silent. I could feel them trying to take it in. Ruth was curling forward, Naomi was finger-twisting a ribbon about her neck.

"No more chemo," I added. I could see they were hurting. They were my children, trying to understand.

"It won't go away," I continued, "so I've decided to enjoy my time."

Naomi coloured. "Enjoy?" she asked, hoarsely. "You'll enjoy – what?"

"Enjoy what I have."

"…left," Ruth put in, speaking automatically.

"And for how long?" whispered Naomi.

The candles part-lit their faces.

I remember James squeezing my hand. "No one knows, but it's about living with dignity. And choice."

At his insistence, we all joined hands across the table. "Don't worry, you don't have to say anything," he told them. "It's about living, that's all."

The sweet, waxy aroma of flowers and candles filled the room. We were absolutely silent.

4.5.12

Bad news is always difficult to tell. The story, that's easy. Things happen as you say them, it's about words, the feel, the people. But pain and illness get in the way. Everything becomes hand-to-mouth. So it's where it hurts, it's noisy, it's hot, or the bed sheets are twisted and the food won't go down. And of course there's fatigue. Physical of course, and also mental, but mainly spiritual – and that's where it hits you. The soul's what's left when everything else is down. A leaky balloon.

But I had to tell my mum and dad. And they needed the story, not just the hurt.

James arranged it. It was my birthday: my big six-o. We'd decided on a visit. James made the car ready, putting in blankets, drink and back-seat pillows. "No need for an ambulance," I joked, climbing in. He drove and I slept, only waking when we arrived. I'd expected to see the house, so I was surprised when we drew up at the church. "What's this?" I asked when we reached the back door. James smiled and helped me inside.

The church hall was candle-lit, quiet and richly-scented. For a minute I thought we were in a service. Then I realised. John, Toby and Louise were there, waiting by a square of tables. Behind them was a small group of locals. In front, on the tables, was a small, tiered, indoor garden. It was layered, like a cake. The flowers, which were purple and yellow and white, trailed all over.

"Happy birthday," said Louise. She offered me a bunch of roses. They were heavy-headed and darkly red. I accepted and James guided me to a large padded seat with flowers both sides. I perched there with

187

space all around, smiling. He called it my throne.

They didn't sing. Instead my father said a prayer of thanksgiving. At the end, Louise brought out a cake. Looking at its icing took me back.

I saw myself on Christmas Eve crouched at the window, praying for snow. I'd wanted to wake to a perfect, trackless all-white world. I'd seen it in the glitter-cards and the Victorian prints and, like my birthdays, I'd hoped it would last forever.

I'd been told Christmas was an epiphany. I knew the word meant something like a birthday surprise. The only difference was the number of candles. So on my special day I sat gazing at my cake with its circle of candles. "They're beautiful," I said and kept everyone waiting while I counted.

"You have to blow!" Toby called.

Mum shushed him and I remained still, watching.

"Go on," he mouthed, looking pained.

In the end, after being urged and encouraged, I sat back in my chair, shaking my head. "They're beautiful," I repeated. Somehow it felt like an angel moment, mixed with pain. I wanted to be helped.

"Shall I?" Dad asked. When I nodded, he licked his thumb and finger and pinched out the flames.

I did blow the candles out on my 60th. I wanted my family to see I could do it. When Louise cut me a piece I took the odd bite then left it as evidence on the plate. I thanked them, keeping my voice strong. I was holding back the tears, of course, and the news I had to tell.

But this time I didn't say it straight. I'd passed that point and couldn't find an opening, and I needed to sound calm. When I'd told the girls, I'd prepared it first then taken my chance. But being in church made me more inward. In any case my mind had blanked and the wobble had crept in, so I asked James to explain.

He called for quiet. When they were silent he quickly told them then raised his glass. "To my lovely wife Beth," he said, gazing into my eyes. Behind his words I could hear a calm, level voice, repeating: *...for better or for worse... in sickness and in health... till death do us part.*

Today I realised that sport and illness are two sides of a coin. Both are tests of endurance. They have to be worked at. What you have to aim at is your PB, then hold out right to the end. After that it's about how well prepared you were in the first place, and how you adapt. There are experts of course – doctors and trainers – and recognised techniques. What you have to do is dig deep, in mind and body. Most of all it's the effort that counts, how you see it and how you stay up. And, of course, you're playing against yourself.

I wrote a poem comparing the two. It came slowly, leaving me exhausted. I worked on it in snatches, taking rests then pushing on. And I revised it as much as I could. It was like training a wild animal. Each time I thought I had it in my grasp, it managed to escape. In the end I had to accept I couldn't pin it down. So I left it like this:

Getting closer

Now we're in-deep, playing for extra time.
Reaching the spot, I'm sticking in. Ignoring.

With hints and flashes and bluelight warnings.

I'm defending. Standing where it hurts.
Judging distance, one shot to another.
It's a series of attempts.

And the strain, the hotfoot, the windup from behind,
I'm taking my chances.

Remember discipline?
First steps, learning moves, positioning well?
Keeping upright, regardless, I choose belief.

With bodyclock and chart and back glance at corners.

Now I'm crossing between halves:
mind and flesh, a thin white line.

And the effort to keep up, self v self,
when defeat becomes certain
and everything centres
on a new understanding.

Elizabeth Lavender

After reading it, I hid my poem from James. It felt like holding onto ice. Or touching something you can't quite make out. It came from a place I knew was there but wanted to avoid, an in-between state that I couldn't ignore. The sadness had taken over, filling up everything. Like one of those moments when the pill you've swallowed refuses to go down.

Some things, even between us, were better left unsaid.

29.7.12 – 15.10.12

Love. At last I know what's included in that word. Love's the martyr in glass, the patient, the child in darkness and the angel at the shoulder. You can walk with love through forests, seeing fungi and ivy or wild flowers shooting. Love's everywhere, in the bird tracks on sand, moonlight over grass and the portrait on the wall. Love's in the leaves and below earth, in the bulb and the fruit in sunlight. It's there in dirt and worms and bluebottles, circling. It's also in the sea, spread all over. On beach slopes and coastlines and tide runs and wave tops, and deep beneath the surface.

And the love I have for James is all this and more.

So it's decided. We've talked it through. The story's ours. So we're back to the beginning, as lovers, first sight and meeting, reliving our first date.

As we entered the restaurant I noticed how it had changed. Not a lot, but in detail: the lighting red and tablecloths green; the art, leaf-pattern and ethnic. I spoke to the waiter. His face had aged and his movements had slowed, but he remembered our last visit. We talked anniversaries and James held up his ring. We laughed. The L-word was used. We were in the warmth, enjoying life, inside the bubble.

After ordering, we gazed about.

"It seems small now," James said.

Nodding, I smiled. I knew what he meant. When you revisit a place you've had in mind for a while it always seems different. You see it as a stranger. The perspective's changed. And you wonder if you're seeing it from outside or in.

Of course I couldn't eat much, but we shared and James helped me out. I hoped he'd have it all but didn't like to say. I wanted him to be happy.

After the meal James reached over. "You remember?" he asked, taking my hand.

I nodded. The warmth of his flesh, doubled on mine, was a relief.

"Thank you," I said. "And, yes, I do." The last two words took me back to smiling faces, and signing the register. I'd been so lucky.

But inside I was cold.

We returned to the café. Now it wasn't mine. With my agreement, Sarah had taken over. We'd come to an arrangement, but the money didn't matter. What was important was the life of the place, the flowers, the pictures, the customers' faces. Because everything in the café had its own story. I'd bought it and filled it and arranged it, like a home. It all hung together, nothing was out of place. Only now I was a customer. What James had once called a 'part of you' was out there and separate, in other people's hands.

Going there was an event. Led by Sarah, the staff asked us about family, caught up on gossip, talked about news and friends, and offered anything we wanted. They didn't say a word about health. I could see why. I suppose my wheelchair warned them. And my figure, of course. Even though I try not to look, I can see myself, reflected in the mirror. I look so old.

I write this with the feeling that I'm in God's hands. Somehow I'm there, in The Shorespot Café and at the same time I'm sleeping, crying, taking morphine, cuddling with James. And the writing finds me out. It has its own viewpoint, image by image, streaming in the head. I'm here, and I'm not, or so it seems. Everything is framed, like a film. I hear that song: *so many different lives to live*. It's a matter of commitment. And of giving way, without fear, allowing what happens.

Of course there are moments, especially at night, when the shadow takes over, times I feel the ghost, the at-my-back watcher. The stalker inside and the face in glass. Then I'm the victim, who isn't of this world.

At the café James and I talked. We listened. We smiled. Together we shared memories. I told him about fun times, jokes and games I'd played.

One of them, with Sarah, was blind man's buff. "We learned to serve without looking," I said, and described how we'd gone about in blindfolds, before we opened up. I mentioned cards I'd made with customers' faces. I told him about shore walks with Sarah and dancing in the waves.

The Shorespot Café – I see it now, right behind my eyes, with James and me talking, like actors on a set. It's there when I'm asleep and as I'm thinking. I'm able to watch and be there as well. In the moment and in the story. Spirit and flesh, in both worlds.

I don't know if I imagined it. In a way it doesn't matter. What we dream is *us*, it shapes who we are.

So I believe we left the café and walked, following the path to the seashore. We were in the sun, taking the air, hearing birdsong. James held my hand; he was smiling, naming flowers and it seemed I could walk.

"It's so calm," he said when we reached the top. We were looking down to a beach between tall cliffs. The bay was bare and white. The tide was out and the rocks were glistening.

I remembered our first descent by Lover's Leap. "It was cold," I said, eyeing the path.

James seemed to understand. "Can you manage?" he asked. I nodded.

I don't know how, but I got down to that beach. I can't be certain but I think, for most of the way, James carried me. I know I was light enough.

When we reached the shoreline, I was relieved. James understood, he was my guide. He found me a hollow in a large flat rock and I sat looking out. "Thank you," I said.

The sea was quiet. It barely whispered as it pushed against stone. Somehow I felt the world was out there, waiting.

"You're comfortable?" he asked. I smiled. I was a child in his hands.

"We went round there," he said, pointing to the headland.

I listened. With the cliffs echoing behind us, I couldn't tell what was sea, and what was in my head. "We'll go again," I said.

James nodded. At our feet the waves came and went. We were on the edge, looking out. It was calm and otherworldly.

192

I don't think I went out to the headland. To walk out across rocks, even in sun with the help of James, was far beyond me. I don't think so. But an image remains of seaweed in channels and deep green pools and stepping across boulders. If we did reach the point, he must have helped me. Otherwise the tide would have caught up.

Looking back, I can see us out there. We're small against the rocks. I see it as a painting. The sea is silver, the sky white, the headland is grey. Insect-like, we're at the edge, turning the point. I see the gulls, they're V-shaped, hanging in the sky. In my mind they're calling: long, lonely, echoing calls. Out to sea is blank. All at once I feel the closeness of the waves. They seem to be inside, rising from within – James and me, lifted by the sea. Now we've turned the headland. And now, as James carries me across shingle, I realise why we've come here. We're close-in to the cliffs, inside the shadow, and the cave is here. I recognise The Chapel. As we enter together the light goes grey. It is quiet. We're sheltering in the body of God. James lowers me gently to rest beside water. The rock I'm sitting on is smooth. His arms are around me. A repeated drip spreads ripples, disturbing the pool. I see the Ichthys and the burnt-down candle. The rock beside us is an altar. We are praying.

Now we're kissing. James is inside me, kissing. Deep-tongued kisses, in the dark.

I am ready.

Part Three
Chapter One

Dear Beth,

At first I told myself it wasn't going to happen. I'd rather shout, break things, put a bomb under everything. I wouldn't allow it. To be taken from me so soon, and in that way. The injustice was too great. I imagined that if I believed then that might stop it. I thought of Blake and spiritual war, Prometheus, Sampson in the temple. If I could equal their suffering then, somehow, the story wouldn't end.

I knew, of course. But it's easier to look away. I mean to look hard at the picture and say, "No I don't see that." Like Hannah's way of looking, before her baby, where everything's decided in advance. And I did remain strong. For me to give up was too dangerous. The stars would go out. I'd be left in the cold. Not on my watch, I told myself, and kept awake, sometimes all night, willing you to stay.

I suppose I'm still a small boy with a box of matches, searching for snails in a damp back garden. I always liked their softness, their stretchy-silky bodies and flower-like horns. I picked them off plants and put them in jars where I fed them leaves. I watched them browse. They moved like seals. I gave them names: Horace, Mary and Excalibur. Then I threw them over the garden wall. Out of sight, out of mind, so my father couldn't hurt them. At night, I heard his boots scrunching on softness and the blackness bubbling up.

And now I'm alone. Alone with the ache, the gap in my head.

Though not alone at all. I set out two plates, talk, ask questions. I still feel your hand. However much wasted, it's my drip-line.

I began this letter to bring things up, to find out where I am. But the memories take over and the damage is done. I want – I need you to read it, to receive it in some way. Like those first letters. But at the same time, the idea of you reading these words is almost unbearable. It's too much to take in. I want it all changed, to meet in the restaurant, kiss at the station, phone next day and have it all over again.

And I wonder what I could have done to stop it. I want to go back and find that moment, the split-second lapse where I turned away and your illness jumped in. When I didn't try enough and you sank. The backward glance that showed I didn't understand. My Orpheus moment.

If only. Every night I think how it might have been. If we'd met when we were young, if I'd known how short it would be, if I'd realised earlier. I search through the past, hear my own voice, my denials. The fault was mine, my attitude was all wrong, it was head-in-the-sands. I wanted to run, to become invisible. I wanted something, anything. But I hid my feelings, and my distress turned to anger.

And yes, writing this, I realise I'm angry. I'm angry with you – how can I say it? – for leaving, for ignoring me, for giving up. I know it's not fair but that's how I feel. It's your fault, I say. I tried hard, but you let me down. But please understand, my darling, this is not me speaking. Of course I'm not angry, it's just a phase. And I love you, forever.

It's 5.00am and I'm tired. Maybe it's a vigil or a mood-shift, but I always feel I'm up against the clock. As if I'm on a run or climbing a steep cliff. It brings back youth. When you have to stay up, live life, be there for the action. It's about getting through. Only now it's alone, in silence.

But I prefer it this way. Our separation keeps us together. I still have you on walks, and when I'm by myself in gardens. No one can touch us. It's all quite Hardy-esque. And, yes, for me it's like stepping back in time. Because once we're together the longing eases, and I'm in the clear, facing the sky. It's then that I'm awake. Wide-eyed and alert. In the woods, by the sea or out on a hilltop you're there, in voice and presence. And though I know it's imagined, it brings relief.

Afterwards, when I'm aching, I remember those moments as late sun, caught between clouds, switching into rain.

In fact, I *want* my grief. I'm possessive. It holds me together. To be inside the shadow is prayer-like and alive but vulnerable as well. In an odd way it's an adventure, a hidden one, close to danger. It's like swimming under ice. I'm reminded of a dream you once described: a view over dark, grey waves, stretching into nothingness.

But don't worry, my love, I'm still with you in the angel moments, when I read your letters, or hear them in my head. It's something I do daily. They've taken over everything. Like a pianist in practice, I know them by heart.

So I spend my nights in a twitch, rerunning incidents, digging out things said and trying to fix what happened, keeping it locked down. I'm a collector. I want it in a box, a glassed-in bubble. To hold you, like a statue, in the hope you'll come alive. And while I'm in darkness, that always seems possible. So the bedroom's my museum, a place full of finds and reminders and precious bits and pieces. It's my archive. Things in their place, left as they are. Fragments of our story.

And I'm walling myself up. I've become my own experience: an event, and nothing more. So I dig and scratch and burrow beneath the sheets. My world has closed up. Like a stone inside, I measure and feel weight, touch on shape, reach for who I am. Which is blue-black and painful.

There's a song I keep hearing: 'In a white room, with black curtains, near the station...' In a strange way it's joyful. Inside the song, there's an urgency, a circle of life. Plaintive as well, it goes round slowly. The guitar notes turn and peel off, they're a dying fall. We listen, and I tell you about it. In my mind, we're sharing how we feel. Now, as I write, I break off, find the album and turn up the volume so it fills the room. I listen, eyes closed, breathing slowly. It's certainly sad. But somehow in *this* room, it's smaller and more ordinary.

Sometimes it seems like I'm banging my head against glass. It's absurd of course, but my fear is that something will shatter. So I allow it, low-key, inside myself. I'm so fragile. I'm a cracked vase, badly taped together. Just walking down the street, or talking to George, or writing this letter: I'm full of broken-off thoughts. Small things irritate me – cars in a jam, blaring music, shoppers queuing, neighbours cooking – they try my patience. At home I swear at the computer, bang doors, V-sign the TV. I laugh at myself sometimes, I'm so teen-boy reactive. Outside I see red – literally, in flashes – but I blink and look away.

Really, I feel helpless. Like a climber hanging over a long drop I daren't look down. I wander out to the shops and people offer greetings. They seem fascinated by me. They want to help, but I can tell they're making themselves do it. Underneath they're afraid. When I walk away I feel them watching. They're mindful of me, as if I might break. Sometimes a thought pops into my head, 'what if I fall down?' And I feel, in an odd way, they've asked for it. It's almost as if they're holding me up and one wrong move might throw me.

But I tell myself to keep going, as if I hadn't noticed. It reminds me of walking home from school in the dark. Like the Ancient Mariner, you mustn't look behind. Because, in the end, the problem's inside *you*. It's all about weakness, how you see yourself and the voices in the head.

I know those voices well. Or they know me. They fill up the air, acting as a wall, a glass one, double-glazed. They make me fearful of going wrong, of not measuring up. And they come between me and whoever I'm with. So I collect their expressions, searching for an opening – a secret, coded, one-off gesture which might help me connect. I'm a castaway waving the only shirt I've got. And with some I'm lucky. Before I realise what has happened, a switch has been thrown and I'm with them. For instance, with church people. They're quick to understand, so with them one word can do it. They know how to get alongside. I think it's being older. I feel them with me at times in the garden or awake at night. I call them the weak force, holding me down. But sometimes, when I see them coming, I want to escape. I'm suddenly ashamed and want to disappear. So I duck down a side street and take the long way round. It's a gut thing. I just can't bear their wax-doll calm. Anything to avoid them.

Even with Hannah I seem to be at one remove. When she visits she brings her three-month old. I hold him, make noises and stand him on my lap. "King David," I call him and we laugh. She's full of what she's doing, about night feeds and sleep times and bringing up baby. I share what she enjoys. But underneath I feel cut loose; I've spent too long on my own.

Feel, feel, feel. Writing like this, I think I've had enough. It hurts too much. I want to shout, blot out, put my fist through the wall. I'm a figure in a darkened room staring at a locked door. I feel sorry for this man. He's not me, he's a victim.

I see myself in third person. When I talk to him he's my imaginary friend. Teacher-like, I watch him from a distance: he's my K, an awkward, toothy kid. One of the lost boys, he's a follower, a used-to-be. Not like K today – a sing-along man with a bike and a job – but a child with a hurt. I think of him as a face in a window, an *invisible*: someone from the past who takes it all in and says nothing. He's me as I was, a shy boy on the inside, imagining, alone by the gate. I see him in the mirror, a stranger, and question why he's here. He doesn't say much. He's churlish, I think.

But sometimes I get closer. Mostly when he's working, when he's outdoors and watching. Then he's more giving. I see him in the garden, measuring perspective, designing views. He carries a spirit level in his hand. There's a map inside his head. He knows the life of the garden, its shape and its spaces. The areas he creates are full of hidden symbols. The dome, the crossing, the arch: they all point to you.

When I'm gardening I notice the small creatures. When I kneel, I'm close to their level. I feel, in a way, a part of their lives. Each day I see how they are. I keep a mental diary of their movements. Beginning with flight, they land and get busy, circle around colour, freeze for a moment then take off. For them it's a dance. I see other insects, scraping, crawling or poking into corners. They're bright and black and shiny.

I examine the spiders: their web-lines, crossing, and tightly-bunched bodies. I name them: Itsy, Wriggler, Mr and Mrs S, then poke them with a stick. They run for cover. I'm God to their struggles.

As I'm digging, I turn up worms. Red-wrigglers, white-backs, purple-headed ones: they feed on darkness. In the evening they come out. When I crouch to look, they remind me of childhood. Together with snails, they're softly-softly. When I touch them they draw back into fists. Cut them and they heal.

I see them, filling up the garden. I have them in my sights, in map-view. It's like looking down a microscope. They're at the bottom, chewing slowly. Their mouths are full of rich black earth. What they bring with them is painful.

I found this poem.

The illness bug

With a buzz-fly's persistence
it charges and skitters all fours on glass,

it has a straw-suck mouth, bubbling air
through melted ice.

Inside-out, it's an ever-open eye
with a cord-pull reflex

and a loop to a point where it strap-hangs
doing nothing.

See there, where it jumps with a scissors-shut grin.

It's a tongue-tied kid
pulling faces in a sliver-chipped mirror.

Backhand swatted into corners
it plays dead,

then pops up again, hotfoot dancing
as the all-night baby.

It's our condition.

Elizabeth Lavender

After reading it, I sat in silence. The poem seemed to have come from a long way off. There was nothing else I could think about. I felt emptied out. I think in the end I went into the garden. I don't remember much, simply that I dug so hard I snapped the spade. I threw the two halves away. Then I sat down on the path staring at the ground. I think I must have stayed there a long time because the next thing I knew it was evening and the small creatures were back: the moths, the beetles, the slugs on the path.

They made me think of ants sorting Cinderella's peas. Of Darwin's experiments with worms. Of bugs and spiders in my wildlife book. In their world things were different. I'd a sense of how they have always existed, and their otherness. I remember how, in childhood, it seemed they'd been there forever. Even now I can feel them watching. They're slow and inward but wild as well. I think of them as survivors, but also short-lived. In a way, they're part of God.

So I'm back to observing. The changes and the timings and where they fit. Day by day, keeping track, seeing how they do it. And this is my log, my book of sightings. Mutatis mutandis.

When autumn begins, the wasps fight to get in. As I draw back the curtains they launch their bodies against glass. I can hear them scratching, digging into corners. It's hard to watch. Like standing by while someone drowns.

In winter there are caterpillars, snail tracks, teeth marks on wood.

In springtime, turning up a stone, the woodlice run. The roof's off and they're in a panic. The earth's alive. Their silver-grey bodies pack out the gangways. Someone's shouting fire.

Then summer, with flies. So many bodies, circling, cutting through the air. Feeding, crowding, and crawling over earth. Struggling for space, they go on.

Today I sat down and reread this letter. I found it difficult. Some parts were embarrassing, other parts I wanted to tear up. I thought about stopping, putting it away, or even shredding it. I felt quite exposed. Was it me, I asked myself, or me acting a part? I wanted to wake up, break out and shake myself free. I'd allowed someone in, a dark, self-doubting, head-down avoider. Then I thought: if you could hear me, how would you feel? Of course I knew the answer. I could imagine your talk of flowers, the Gospels, a story you'd been reading. You'd be all light, like your parents. So I checked again and this time I read it differently. I've written simply what came up. My thoughts about you, or what you've become. Like a recurrent dream, you've taken over everything. An image so large, this letter doesn't matter.

When I close my eyes the scenes keep coming back, displaced somehow, like a film run backwards. Mainly of you, at home near the end. You beside me in your brother's photos, with life showing through. Painfully thin. A beautiful loss.

I think of you in blue, like Akhmatova in Altman's portrait. A poet and a lover. Your tight slim line and feel for colour. I can still bring you back.

The scene changes and I see you at the theatre, looking down the rows. We're there in the circle. The lights dim as the curtain rises. There are shapes on stage, moving in the dark. My arm's around your shoulders, touching flesh. The stage lights go up and the dance begins. It's a duet. The woman's antelope-thin, the man's an athlete. Their all-in-white bodies work together. The hush they create fills up the hall.

The pictures keep coming. I see us together, walking. Finding our way through gorse and mud. Passing the clay pit, the thicket, the broken fences. Hearing a car horn and a train moving off. It's us on the Common and I want it again. Our bodies, side by side. Your hand in mine – released for a moment as we duck past branches – in real time, as it happened. With sunshine, water, and the drumbeat of traffic.

And one mind between us, together in the wild.

We dealt with your baldness. No wigs, no pretence. I helped with your medicines, reading the labels and ordering repeats. There were visitors to greet – nurses, family, friends – tea to make, cakes to offer, and our minister saying prayers. When they'd gone away there were phone calls, or texts. You said your affirmations. We watched for birds. I taught you flower names then tested you, daily. Together we looked out, studying the garden. There were moments of discovery, small things shared: clouds like faces, dew on webs, light on the path.

Now I look back I see us walking into sunset. We didn't feel the cold.

Right from the start I've kept your pink top out. You must have seen it. The sparkly one, from our first date. I have it on a hanger, hooked on the wardrobe, like you used to. It looks much the same, though less bright, more special now. It's with me in the morning, all evening and when I switch out the lights. Even so, it still comes as a shock when I see it. For a second, with the mirror behind, I believe it's you. Each time's the same: a glimpse, an in-breath, a question, *can this be so?* then the let-down.

Afterwards, I'm shaken. It seems so unlikely. I tell myself it's a mistake, that I've projected, and it's all about me. But it feels quite spacey, as if I've seen a ghost. It reminds me of Tarkovsky's *Solaris*. Mind, I suppose I'd be even more shocked if the top wasn't there. If it moved as I watched or turned up somewhere else. But my heart still jumps every time I see it.

So why do it? As a comfort, of course. Its faint rose-water scent reminds me of the restaurant. It's our secret. And it puts off the time when I have to open the wardrobe and sort things out. So it works for me. Though it does seem a bit crazy keeping it out, but hidden, like a holy relic.

Though not so crazy really, because it's up there as a portrait. It's between me and you, our private view.

But now I've begun to see further. Keeping it up there is superhero stuff. It's about me protecting you. I'm still in the business of holding up the temple, or trying to give back. And in my mind the odds are stacking up. It's the deficit model. All I can do is keep bailing out.

So it's really a protection. A shield for us both. Because I think without it the house would fill up. Your presence would be everywhere. And I need that distance, a room of my own.

As I write that phrase, I hear your objection. It belongs, you say, to women's history. But then you smile. Your reaction, you say, is really about you, and how you loved your gran. You talk about her books, and your stories. It's all made-up, you say.

Later you come to me in a dream, wearing your top. I've a set of books beside me. You're offering a swap, a book for a sequin. I know it's crazy but I agree. Soon it's a library, an imaginary one, with floral book jackets, which we take out to the garden. You ask me to read, and leaves fill the air. I hear a bird scratching, digging in the soil. We're in the wood house, Deanbury Gardens, lying on wool. In there, you're protected. It's a dark, safe place, a seedbed of love. It's where I keep my heart.

You wanted a woodland burial. It was late on, remember?

I agreed, of course, and planned it as a party. It was what you wanted. For the kids, for the parents, for us. No quiet leaving, or talk about passing away. Music and flowers. Colour, poetry and bel canto. And Toby's photos, blown up large on the walls.

"Would I want you unhappy?" you asked me from your bed.

"What kind of feeling would it give me, if I knew you were going to be miserable?" you said to your girls.

"I'm thankful for everything," you told your parents. "That's how I want you to be."

So we were all lined up. The funeral was about joy and life. A celebration. Only in my heart I didn't want it that way. It was too early. Black would have been better, truer – or a solemn, tender, darkly attentive service with Verdi's Requiem and the march from the Eroica. I wanted sadness and needed hurt. I *was* hurting, but pushing myself to be jolly.

Afterwards on the journey, I cut off. There was a wall between me and them which kept me numb. At the committal I watched, sang with the others, then returned in silence to a life emptied out. Everywhere there was the feeling that you'd not been buried: you were asleep or TV-watching or walking in the garden. I'd a sense of you locked out, on your own, a faded, unreal, weather-exposed ghost. And that where you really should be was a gap.

That gap was in me. Like a tooth gone missing, I needed you to fill it.

But that was then. Now I've been through it, had my dark night, and seen how you fit. As the song says: *Shine on you crazy diamond.* I can tell you this now, as if we were walking in the woods. There's a Beth-ness all around. A strong line running through everything. And when I look at a landscape I feel you there. You're a plant, a root, a solid thing,

> *Rolled round in earth's diurnal course,*
> *With rocks, and stones, and trees.*

And when I visit your grave, with its red-black sorrel and yellowed grass, walk the bare path through knapweed and toadflax or pass by iris dying in the sun, I want to join the party...

Love

James xxxxxxxxxxxxx

Chapter Two

Here are a few of the messages which were pinned up on the noticeboard at The Shorespot Café after Beth's death.

A note written in blue biro across an unstamped postcard. On the reverse, a black and white picture of an oiled-up cross-channel swimmer: "I come here every day to watch the sea. She always smiled."

A message in red on a cream-coloured coaster: "She served me with ginger tea and cake. I liked how she talked."

A typed-out tribute on ultra-white paper: "Beth was truly a mother to me. She put up with my singing! We danced barefoot in the gardens listening to the birds. Her cinnamon toast made me swoon. I feel her by me when I'm lighting candles. She found love." *Sarah.*

A scrawly, pencilled-in caption beneath a stick-drawing of a child pointing to an oversized sun: "I loved this lady."

A photo of pink and white flowers arranged in a vase. The flowers stand at the centre of a varnished table. Propped up in front of the flowers is a small folded card with *Beth* printed on it in Sveridge Script. All four corners of the photo are covered with felt-tip crosses.

And here are some of the intercessionary messages displayed at St Clare's Church, Folkestone.

"Dearest Beth, we will always remember. Peace be with you."

"You go before us. A bright star."

"God bless you, Beth, and protect you. You showed us the way."

"From one world to the next. In the name of love."

"For you, the fire and the rose are one."

Also, arranged on a table below, a collection of greeting cards with crosses and angels. Inside each are kisses, heart-shapes and multiple signatures.

And this, a longer message, was left in an envelope tucked inside The Book of Remembrance at Cranbury Woodland Cemetery.

"I came to know Beth when I was an elder at her former husband's church. She struck me as a woman of spirit, going through difficult times. I remember one Easter how I helped her to comfort her husband, who was ill. We worked together for the good of the church.

Years later we met by chance at her café. She welcomed me. If she had any concerns about the past she did not show them. Her gentle directness won me round. I told her I'd lost my faith, perhaps because of things I'd seen, and she knew at once how I felt. That was when I understood how deep she was, and selfless. She talked to me tirelessly every day, usually after work. There was a warm, softly-driven compassion in her voice which I know came from her marriage.

Through her words I came to see faith as an ocean made up of different currents, some of them dangerous, some of them beautiful. She was inside those currents, alive and uncertain in an intense, joyful, giving kind of way. It was there that she met her wild, unknown, imaginary God.

When she fell ill, we still talked on the phone about life as a flow with no fixed points. And how you could not pick it apart. When she was called, I imagined her in that ocean again.

Through her example I have reconnected to the wonderful, virtual power of God. In my heart I call her, in private, perhaps absurdly, Saint Elizabeth." *Derek Ward.*

These, found after her funeral, were some of the objects in Beth's treasure drawer.

Two chunky engagement rings with red glass centres and silver clasps. Wrapped in tissue, they'd been linked together by a few strands of silver-grey hair.

A small knitted toy in natural and denim, reverse-worked in stocking stitch, with polyester stuffing. The toy, shaped like a rabbit, had ears, a white tail and a sewn-on grin. The body sagged in places. The stomach was covered with what looked like bruises. It had been patched round the back with green thread.

A collection of waxed leaves, stacked loosely like cards. They were red-brown, yellow and purple.

A simple, unvarnished, hand-sized cross. Tied together by string, it looked like a miniature mast. Beside it, a set of rolled-up napkins were packed into a box. They were decorated with fishes and Chi-Ro patterns. Each had a sewn-in signature, *Louise*.

A CD of Mahler's Ninth Symphony.

And these were some of the pictures discovered in Beth's scrapbook after her death.

A photo of Louise arranging a collection of wild flowers in a miniature watering can. The scarf on her head originally belonged to her mother. In the background, John's knitted beret was a present from Ruth.

Cut-up calendars showing flocks of birds nesting, feeding and flying.

A photo of a field with James in the foreground, taken from their Irish honeymoon.

Several passport-size photos of James and all four children at different life stages, arranged in a scattered, all-angles collage.

A reproduction of Arnold Böcklin's *Isle of the Dead*.

And this obituary, based on a sermon, appeared in the St Clare's church magazine. It was written by the minster, Carmen Higgins.

"Elizabeth Lavender was born in Hedbury, just outside Bury St Edmunds, first child of John and Louise Jarvis, and elder sister to Toby. From her family I've learned about Beth the child, delighting in the world of nature and the imagination which she lived out in games in the garden and in the stories she wrote from an early age. Talking to Beth towards the end, I realised how happy that childhood had been, how loved she felt and how she valued the child in her that lived on in adulthood, making possible her openness and creativity. Beth did well at school, and some of her youthful friendships lasted the course of her life cut short. During her teenage years Beth's faith matured and deepened and she attended St Martha's Church, Hedbury, where she met her first husband at the Youth Group. Beth studied English at university and, prompted by a social conscience, joined Tearfund and The International Fellowship of Evangelical Students. She married in 1975 and after her husband's ordination became a clergy wife, a role she tried to fulfil while remaining true to her own beliefs, which already embraced doubt and mystery. Like many good women she took failure hard, and was troubled by guilt as the marriage foundered and she determined to protect and nurture their daughters, Naomi and Ruth.

Some of you will have experienced the pleasures of her Shorespot Café, where everyone could be sure of a warm welcome and where Beth herself liked to listen as well as feed. Meeting James was something she called a reckless act, driven by uncrushable romantic hope, but from the beginning they made a deep connection that brought her great happiness. They were married in 2004 but five years later she became ill, and cancer of the bowels was diagnosed. Surgery and chemotherapy followed on a regular basis, and Beth was enormously grateful for the medical care she received, but after a period of remission she died peacefully at home, where she wanted to be, on 19th October 2012.

During our talks through her illness Beth took a great interest in matters of faith and doubt. She talked about the power of imagination and the God of silence and absences. She was committed and adept in everything she did: gardening, work, dancing and motherhood. Nevertheless, I was told I was on no account to eulogise her just because she'd gone! Beth set herself high standards, but she never courted undue notice or praise. Flowers, the sea and poetry meant more to her than image or success. She loved her life with James and didn't want to let go, but she told me that she needed to learn to love death too, without fear. Beth liked learning up to the last, asking me to share what I'd discovered through my ministry about the big taboo and how people face and deny it. What she wanted above all else was to die honestly and bravely, in a way that would encourage others. Some of those who loved her might say that was what she did best."

Chapter Three

One by one, I see you.

My family, James, my friends. And with you, your stories. I see who you are, how you've changed, how you find meaning.

You're images now, in a blur. A dream procession.

Beginning with Meg. I hear you talking, as words in the head. You're with me now, a child's face, rounded, my closest friend. You took me through. Smooth-faced, willing, you held my hand. At first in thought, growing together, adjusting hairbands, then in prayer, with faith. You were so good.

But your marriage wasn't. I saw you, once, without children on holiday with Frank. He put himself around. A balloon face to your smile. Plastic, stretchy and close to bursting. Charming, charming, he wanted to figure. Raising a glass to people he'd sold to and their beautiful lives. You know of course where it led. That evening, in the bedroom, I heard his shouts. When a man's angry anything goes.

I know how he kept you. Men call it depression, make their promises, buy large bouquets. Strange isn't it? I left Conrad after we'd talked. But for you it was always about putting others first.

I can see you at the bedside. An impressionist picture. You were so patient. Good at being there, and lively as well. But really you were crying, right from the start. Only I didn't see it. Too much giving. A star behind clouds. Rain and more rain.

After Meg, others. Arrivals, departures, one by one, I see you as you are.

Beginning with Rachael and Amy, appearing with flowers. Faces in the dark. If I could talk to you now... A warning, a question, a simple explanation. It seemed to you I'd stepped out for a moment: a strange disappearance, somewhere off the map. It wasn't what you believed in. My friends, I can understand now how you didn't have much to say. You smiled, like children. You didn't know how I could bear it.

Afterwards you blanked. The world took over. I hear you at a table, talking prices. Enjoying coffee. Exchanging gripes.
And the words:
> It has to fit the scheme.
> You want it to look nice.
> Yes, good value as well.
> Have you seen his picture?
> Pretty good stuff.
> And how's your other half?
> On business. Away at present. And yours?
Not much to say.

And your marriages... Separated or not speaking, heading for divorce.

From then to now, I notice the difference. Because where I am now gives me advantage. It's a screen, a great glass eye, and I've passed through. I'm at a place where everything's visible – a view, all-angles, out to the blue. Beyond that it's clear, a big space into nowhere. A sky-high island with dream-shaped smiles and faces from the past.

I'm looking into brightness, seeing who you are.

Charlie. Charlotte. C. Strange how you come back. Always yourself, appearing without warning. Popping up late in purple and shades. I can feel you now, somewhere close, dreaming in the dark. You were the sleepless watcher, the made-up woman at the studio window. What did you see there...?

Stars and desire. Lights on water. A hand, an eye, an image of love.

"Look," you said and your heart was there, an image of lovers, kissing.

You led. Wildlife and passion. Took me through the world and out into nothingness. You were the angel of flesh, the runaway woman, the underworld queen.

You were Psyche.

Then of course, Conrad. The man on his own, out of control, dropping. Over the edge and down into darkness. Grabbing for handholds like a dislodged climber.

I see you in youth. You were Mr Look-at-me Clever, clowning. Conrad Bright, on the run, my glory-be.

Or you on the phone, trying to make up. My strong-and-silent, now holding talks. Awkward, breathless, the one who wore black. *Regarding the girls... Changeover times... Necessary adjustments...* The man behind the mask. Without you I'd be different.

For you I need forgiveness.

Also, Toby with camera. And the pictures he gave us, the inside view. Blown-up large, what we agreed to. Each photo a statement.

I list them here, with captions.

Photo 1

Two faces at table with linked arms, sipping water from each other's glass. The walls are angled, like a ship at sea. The picture's focus is sharpest on the glasses, which are lit from behind. Flowers in the background give a domestic feel. On the wall a glassed-in photo reflects the light. It's luminous, like a Vermeer. The faces seem far-away; they're hard to read. It's James and me at the café.

Photo 2.

A sea view with sun on stones. Semi-abstract and bare. There's a white line between yellow and greyish-blue. The surf is suspended in a low C-shape, like a Japanese miniature. It leads the eye to two pairs of feet, without shoes. Toes up, heels down, they look like plants. They come from legs which must be flat to the earth. From their size it seems they're male and female. The small pair, mine, are paper-white, like narcissi.

Photo 3.

A portrait of me outside the hospital. I'm sitting on a wall wearing a sleeveless dress. It's knee-length and floral and delicate. It makes me seem rather 50s. The hospital to one side is a wall of glass. There's a path between the wall and building. The gap between me and the hospital is about five feet. Looking carefully there's a streak on the glass. I see that it's a shadow. Although the camera's at an angle, I know it's me. My shadow's pencil-thin.

Photo 4

A close-up of my hands. They're palm up, cupped slightly, holding something. They're thin and creased and folded like paper. They remind me of a late Rembrandt. But these are different. Around each finger, and wrapped in crisscross patterns across the palms, are web-like lines. The lines are my hairs.

Photo 5

James and me in the park. We're together in a swan-shaped pedalo. We look like a picture on a pop-up card. It's our summer's end outing. James is holding up two ice creams. They're cornets, and look like upside-down party hats. One is dripping on his shirt sleeve. Behind us the trees are solid, opaque and two-dimensional, a wall of green.

Photo 6

A body in water. Light ripples playing across flesh. The slack, seal-like body is half-submerged. It's seen from behind, head above the surface, feet out to sea. It's close to the shore and the waves are gathered around in folds. The smooth, shiny body looks like a sunken statue, or a mermaid, or a diver, resting.

It's me, returning to the sea.

Photo 7

James at the end of the bed, looking down. The bed is empty and the duvet is stripped back. The sheet is stretched tight. On one side, where the mattress dips, a child-sized outline can be made out. It's vague and shadowy like a watermark. It reminds me of a sweat-cloth, or Veronica's veil.

Photos 8 - 15

Me and James, Hawaiian-style, surrounded by flowers. Blue-white ribbons and coral-coloured necklaces. Flowers as cummerbunds and sashes. Red and yellow headbands. Flowers in buckets and vases. Cushion covers with William Morris prints. Floral shirts and Matisse-like dresses. Buttonhole carnations and Queen of the Night tulips. Green-black wreaths and purple crosses.

Photo 16

A woman in a car leaning her head on her mother's shoulder. The woman looks worn; her face is hollowed out. She's small and slight and lost beside her mother. The car back seat rises above her head. Her mother's smile is tender, wistful and gently elevated. It's me with Louise.

Photo 17

John at the bedside. He's leaning forward. His hands are white and clenched. A grey wisp of hair has fallen across his forehead.

In front of him, the sheets are in a bundle. They cover what might be

211

a pillow, or could be flesh. If it's a body, there's hardly anything left. It's thin, white like the bed, and spread like dough.

John is head down, rocking back and forth. He's crying.

Photo 18

My chair, empty.

So this is me at the edge – the high up moment when the soul grows large. Look down: it's a challenge. The biggest, it takes you to the end, to not being so. Or rather, to being present while absent. I'm out there in the blue, my angel moment.

What I see is the story.

My children, firstly. They're wearing white, chasing butterflies. Naomi's singing, Ruth holds a doll. They're walking in a meadow, waist-high in grass. The grass is dry as tinder. As they walk, it rustles. It's as if they were wearing thickly-layered clothes. The meadow gives way to hollows and nettle beds. When the doll falls in, Naomi pulls it out. Afterwards, they hug. While Ruth does a dance, Naomi sits watching, saying nothing. Her ankles are white and blotchy. I scrub them with green.

My daughters by water, with thoughts bubbling up. I can hear Psalm 23. They're in the gallery, looking at a picture. It's called the *The River of Life*. I talk about Blake's madness and Ruth says she likes him. She peers at the picture then touches the glass. Naomi warns, Ruth objects, and words are exchanged. An attendant comes up to us and we leave. Outside, by the Thames, both girls are silent. I use the word angry then stare downstream. In my heart I hear snatches of the *The Little Girl Lost*, repeating. It's my story.

My daughters, eyes closed, in church. They're there with John and Louise, saying nothing. I feel for how they are. Their grief can't sing. The world they live in is a slow drip, a hole in water. The air isn't theirs. On the walls there are marks: dark spots and stains, it's not what they expected.

And now they're by the grave. It's mid-afternoon and we're close. They've joined me in the sun. This place where we meet is grassed over, with bright, wild flowers and insects passing. If you lie down you can feel the earth. It's damp and covers all. There's no fear now. The birds are singing, the blossom shows and the ants are busy. The faces of my daughters are daffodils, filling up with light. They are with me.

And secondly, Louise.

I imagine her, in church, holding up flowers. We're all in the hands of God, she says. Childhood hands, they bring back a song – *You need hands*.

She gave me her hands – large like hers.

A safe pair of hands, pencilling in dates. Busy hands opening packets of seeds. Hands-on hands, fitting flowers to vases, labels to parcels, pictures on the walls.

Arts-and-crafts hands, sewing in names to gymslips and hankies. Steward's hands, passing round Bibles. Hands on sheets and hands on heart.

A hand to my forehead, stroking gently as she whispers my name.

Mother, I stretch my hand to thee.

And now, a story for John.

It comes as a voice in the dark, a long-distance call. A story with a message, repeated quietly, like a broadcast in the head. A dream of someone talking.

It goes like this.

The Girl Who Didn't Like Her Name

Ania was a girl who didn't like her name. She wanted to change it, but when she asked her parents they told her she had to keep it. She asked them why. Her parents said because it was her name. When she asked again they said because they'd chosen it. When she asked a third time they told her she *looked* like an Ania. This answer puzzled her. How could that be, she wondered, staring in the mirror. So she asked them what they meant. This time her parents didn't reply. When they finally spoke, what they said troubled her. They told her Ania was a name with two meanings. In Greek it meant grief, in Polish grace.

Ania wasn't happy. She respected her parents, but what they said didn't feel right. It wasn't what she wanted. In fact, she felt quite hurt.

Ania lived in a country where people felt hurt. She'd watched their faces, she knew how they talked. If things went wrong that pained them. They were shocked by what they read. It was in what they ate, what they believed, and what they spoke about. They said that the odds were against them, their luck was bad, money was a headache. They were upset by what they saw. What they didn't have bothered them. Other people let them down. Most of all, their feelings hurt.

Ania wanted to understand. She thought if she could share their pain it might help. So she set about collecting hurt-names.

When Ania walked out in the morning, she felt her first hurt. A bird sang quietly on a tree and a cloud passed over. Love-ache she called it, smelling a rose. All that day she was sad and troubled by things in the air. There were seed heads drifting and wind, sighing in the trees. At noon she was thoughtful, later she was cold. In the evening she was alone. When the moon came up she was afraid. At night she felt her loss. It hid with grief beneath the stones.

She realised how it hurt to be hurting.

Looking in a book, Ania found other names for hurt. She read them out. They included discomfort, weariness and fatigue. When she went into shops she heard people talking. They used words like tired or angry. In church she heard expressions of sorrow and regret. When she visited hospital they spoke about illness, dysfunction, disease. In dreams she saw bodies. Looking at nature there were victims and outcasts. In her heart there was loss. It seemed, once you noticed, hurt was everywhere.

Ania went back to her parents. She told them her story, and how much it hurt. Where did it come from, she asked them, and what could she do?

In answer they smiled. Tell us another story, they said.

Ania didn't answer. She felt too hurt.

Another story, they said.

Still she couldn't speak.

A story, they repeated, and hugged her.

So Ania began. And the first few sentences went like this...

A girl lived in a country where people felt grace. They accepted hurt, and where it came from. If things went wrong that didn't upset them. They were not at all shocked by what they read...

As she continued, Ania heard her story, repeating in her head. Instead of hurt she said grace, instead of sorrow, joy, instead of pain, forgiveness. Then she heard her voice saying goodwill and kindness. She spoke about sharing and charity, and surprised herself with delight, happiness, care. At the end she was full of empathy, understanding, compassion, love.

When she'd finished her parents kissed her and gave her a blessing.

214

Remember who you are, they said. She nodded. And where you come from, they added. She nodded again. Because from now on, they said, you can choose your name.

The girl thought carefully then smiled. "Sorrow and forgiveness." she said. "Ania."

And now I see James.

He's at the end of the headland, watching the waves. I'm out there too, but not so he can see me. I can feel how he hurts. In his mind there are pictures. He sees us swimming out. We're on our own with the sun on our backs. The sea's all around, it's where we go back to. As we dive below the surface the past takes over. I'm with him in the dark. In dreams I'm walking by water, climbing to a view.

Now I'm at the window, watching for the moon. White and spread, it paints on water. A love song begins. The notes are messages. Sung low-volume, they're words of longing, from me to you. They're for the lovers, listening in the night.

A cloud passes over and I feel him getting closer. I'm writing to him now, telling him I'm waiting. I'm rereading his letters, urging him to join me. He's on the way, walking to our meeting. Appearing at the doorway. I see him looking about. The world's there before him. I want him to feel love.

Dearest,

If I could speak to you now I'd use those words: darling, paramour, heartthrob, my one-and-only. I'd take you on a walk with song thrush and lark. Dance with you barefoot on the lawn. Sit together on the swings, in the park. Then I'd sneak into bed as your oh girl oh.

There are no accidents. What we have is given. It's not me, not you, but an image.

You understood my pain. I was the instrument locked up in a case, you took me out, we sang, we played music. The case was in the corner of a dark, dark room. You opened the door, we walked out. In the sun we were crazy, nothing held us back, nothing went away. You watched over me as the shadows lengthened. When darkness came the ache came too. Barehanded, you held the flesh together. Still, the ache found a way. It ran down the walls, gathered in shadow, filled up the cup.

Who are we? Lovers and children. Believers in the ancestors.

Descendants from the stars, who suffer, who fight. Souls in limbo, one world to the next. Who dance back time.

And now? With music and voices I shall bind you up. I'm in the air, leading. What we share is the story. Where we come from and where we're going. Because unless they're imagined, miracles don't happen. For better, for worse, it's a bubble that we blow.

What more? The light shines through. Ask and it shall be given – in flowers, in the woods, in rain, still with you. Also in the stone, in darkness, in silence. If love's for the taking then stay mindful.

And be as you are. James, my man. It's not about joy but fullness.

Child of God, I love you.

Beth xxxxxxxxxxxxxxxxxxxx

Hannah wrote a story. It's for me, about me. I'm in there, invisible.

I see it now, large-print, with a stitched card cover. Like a picture book it has very few words. Where an image should be, there's just soft, thick, pure space.

The little boy looked up at the grey sky.

"It's meant to be blue," he said. "Why is it dirty?"

"Because," said his mummy, "yesterday a boy threw a stone at a swan."

The little boy felt the wind slap his face.

"Why is it so spiteful?" he asked.

"Because," said his mother, "it heard what the girl whispered at playtime."

The boy saw a daffodil hang its head in a vase.

"It stinks!" he said. "Why is it bad?"

"Because of lies," said his mummy. "Sweet scented lies." She smiled. "A man bought flowers for a woman he didn't love."

216

As lightning lit up his face the boy held his mother's hand.

"Why does it flash?" he asked.

"Because of the light that's inside," said his mummy, "hidden in the clouds."

"Why is it so scary?" the little boy asked.

"Because it's full of life," his mummy said.

Then the boy heard a siren screech on the street. He covered his ears till his face was red.

"Why is it so loud?" he cried.

"Because it needs us to take notice," said his mother.

"Where is it going?" he asked as the siren faded.

"Into the place where love makes us whole."

I closed the book at the end. The story was over.

POSTSCRIPT

Welcome to *Beth's Garden*.

This memorial to Elizabeth Mary Lavender, laid out in the shape of a family tree, was started in 2013. When planting began the idea was to use a small number of plants chosen by Beth's closest relatives, linking them to her story. As the project grew, the range of plants and the story widened. The final design came about through the involvement of the whole family.

Your named trail is marked in blue on the garden map. You will find the same names, with numbers, painted on stakes beside the path. The full tour usually takes about an hour.

1. As you enter, look back at *The Shorespot Café* and the sea behind it. This is Beth's café.

2.   On your immediate right, you will find *Spring Hollow,* an area full of scilla, white spring crocuses, anemones and Tête-á-Tête daffodils. This auditorium-shaped space is where Beth used to dance. Look towards the back and you will see a line of lilacs. Their colours range from Alba through shades of pink and mauve to Dark Knight. Lilacs traditionally symbolise love.

Spring Hollow is maintained by Naomi and Ruth, Beth's daughters, and her brother, Toby.

3.   Next on the right is *The Churchyard.* This has ivy-clad stones, a Judas tree and holly, underplanted with pasque flowers. Conrad Bright and his congregation look after this area.

4.   Further up the path, on the right is *The Storyteller's Grove.* The eucalyptus trees here were chosen by Beth's parents. They, and others, have compared the trees' soft, rustling whispers to human voices. A listening seat at the centre is inscribed with an elegy by John Jarvis. At his suggestion there are nesting boxes and berry-bearing plants dotted around the grove. Underfoot, the peeling bark provides a rich mulch for trilliums and enchanter's nightshade.

The grove also contains Cornus sanguinea 'Midwinter Fire' and a wall of black bamboo. The former was planted for Beth's grandmother, Elizabeth Turnbull, the latter as a tribute to Beth's great-grandparents on the Jarvis side. They campaigned to improve women's education.

5.   As the path curls round we enter the *Wilderness Garden.* This dry, stony patch is covered with shepherd's purse, restharrow, thistles and common ragwort. To soften the effect, blue-leaved rue and yellow field pansies have been introduced at the edges. In May the hawthorn hedge at the back is a white wave. This area represents earlier generations: in-laws Jack Henderson, his wife Grace Henderson and their three children, Mary, Edith and Stephen.

6.   A walk downhill brings us to the *Lavender Gardens.* Here we follow the descending family line, beginning with Mary Henderson, represented by a bed of sea lavender (Marsh Rosemary). Her husband, Stuart Lavender, has a single Iceberg rose planted in his memory.

7.   At this point you will see the path forks.

8.　Steps to the right descend to *The Old Quarry*. Due to subsidence, the surface here is damp and uneven. Follow the steps down to a dark pool, shaded by a canopy of purple magnolias and rhododendrons, and 'Purple Haze' camellias. This quiet, self-enclosed space is dedicated to Mary and Stuart's older son, Alan Lavender, and his wife Harriet.

9.　At the end of the pool the path re-ascends, via the *Zigzag Way*, to dwarf maples, flowering quince and Pieris japonica. At the top is an insect area, planted with cornflowers, foxgloves and buddleia, leading to an open meadow. Tall grasses flourish here including Black Bent, Cocksfoot and Yorkshire fog. It was Alan's son Matthew who suggested the layout. His wife Miranda and their children Joe, Mia and Cass chose the planting.

10.　Returning to the fork, the left-hand path descends through *The Terraces*. These vegetable plots are intended to be both practical and ornamental. A carved boundary stone dedicates them to Mary's younger son, Edwin Lavender and his wife, Doris. The first plot is a herb garden modelled on Doris's backyard. Here you will find the same herbs as she grew for her sons, Richard and James. The potage-style plots lower down mix flowers with vegetables and fruit. They are named after Richard's and James's children – Charlotte and Stephan, Hannah and George.

11.　At the bottom the path passes through a gap in a hornbeam hedge to enter the circular *Love Garden*. Dedicated to Beth's husband, James Lavender, this is the heart of the garden. Set out in quarters, with a red-purple colour scheme, its arches and frames display clematis, honeysuckle and twenty varieties of rose. The radiating beds are full of catmint, iris, sweet pea and stocks. A heart-shaped lily pool at the centre sprouts ferns round the edges. Damselflies can be seen hovering in pairs close to the water. Behind the pool, a large, flat stone has been set into earth. On its surface a faint human outline is visible.

12.　Pass out through another gap in the hedge and you will find yourself back by *Spring Hollow*. Return from here to *The Shorespot Café*. Inside you will find a framed photo of the stone beside the pool. It shows the artist Angel Perkins scraping the stone. The title of her sculpture is Beth.

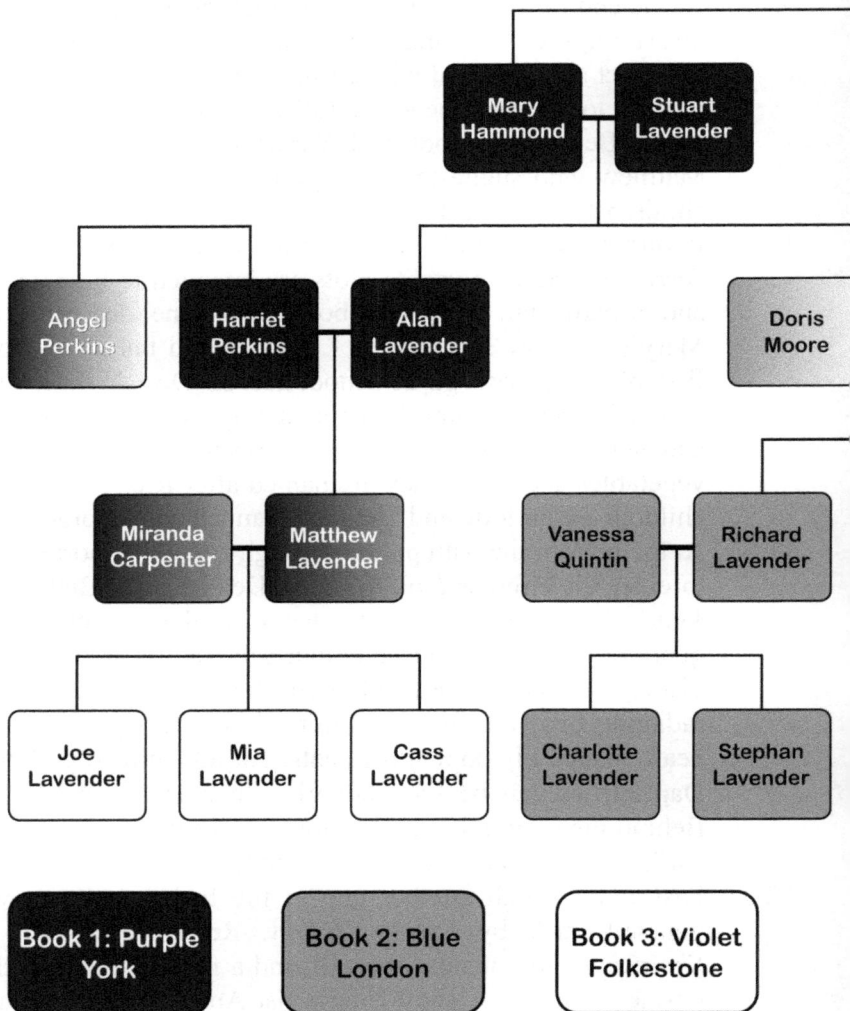

Lavender Blues: Three Shades Of Love

Family Tree

Grace Willis

Mary Hammond — Stuart Lavender

Angel Perkins

Harriet Perkins — Alan Lavender

Doris Moore

Miranda Carpenter — Matthew Lavender

Vanessa Quintin — Richard Lavender

Joe Lavender

Mia Lavender

Cass Lavender

Charlotte Lavender

Stephan Lavender

Book 1: Purple York

Book 2: Blue London

Book 3: Violet Folkestone

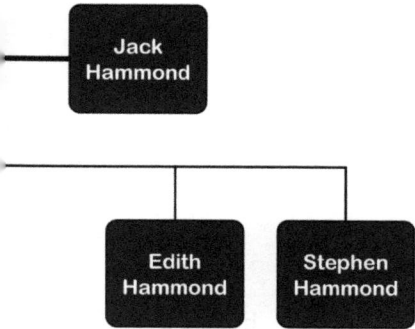

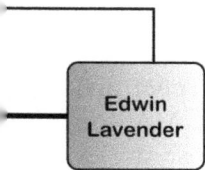

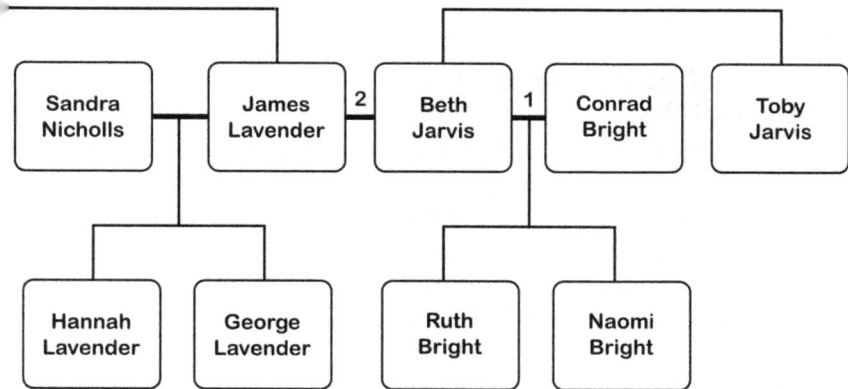

About the Author

Leslie wrote his Lavender Blues trilogy while attending a University of East Anglia Creative Writing Course.

He is a novelist, poet and teacher, with an MA in Creative Writing, whose stories are driven by language and character. Leslie admires Virginia Woolf, James Joyce, Carol Shields, Marilynne Robinson and Michael Ondaatje.

He runs mixed-arts shows, a poetry reading group and a comedy club, and has led writing workshops at universities, libraries and festivals. He uses music and art as part of his performances which offer surprising insights into prose and how authors 'reread the world'. He often performs with his wife, author Sue Hampton. Calling themselves 'Authors in Love', they live together in Hertfordshire.

For more information visit www.LeslieTate.com

About the Publisher

Magic Oxygen Limited is a sustainable publishing house based in Lyme Regis, Dorset. As well as delivering great content to their readers, it is also the home of the Magic Oxygen Literary Prize.

This is a global writing competition like no other. Not only do they offer a share of an impressive prize fund, they plant a tree for every entry in their tropical Word Forest, situated beside the Kundeni Primary School in Boré, Kenya. The project is coordinated by forestry expert, Ru Hartwell, trustee of The Word Forest Organisation.

Boré is a remote community that has suffered greatly from deforestation. As well as reintroducing biodiversity, creating an income for the village, providing food, medicine and water purifiers, trees planted near the equator are also the most efficient at capturing carbon from the atmosphere. Each tree in the Word Forest will lock up 250kg of CO_2 and keep our planet a little bit cooler too!

Magic Oxygen publish the shortlist and winners in an anthology and plant an additional tree for every copy sold.

Visit MagicOxygen.co.uk to find out about the next MOLP, then spread news of it far and wide on your blogs and social media and be part of a pioneering literary legacy.

Lightning Source UK Ltd.
Milton Keynes UK
UKHW02f2340080218
317552UK00007B/264/P